# Fateful Lies: A Paranormal Shifter Romance

**Fated Moments, Volume 3**

Kristyn DeMaster

Published by Kristyn DeMaster, 2023.

# Also by Kristyn DeMaster

**Brothers Pub**
All of Me
Believe in Me
Count on Me
Trust in Me
Stay with Me

**Fated Moments**
Fateful Choice: A Paranormal Shifter Romance
Fateful Path: A Paranormal Shifter Romance
Fateful Lies: A Paranormal Shifter Romance

Watch for more at https://linktr.ee/kristyndemaster.

**Fated Moments...**

Imagine one day struck out of your life, and think how different its course would have been. Pause you who read this, and think for a moment of the long chain of iron or gold, of thorns and flowers, that would never have bound you, but for the formation of the first link on one memorable day...

*Charles Dickens*

# Copyright



• • • •

COVER DESIGN BY KELLY Pennington

Proofreading and editing by Laura Walsh of Peace, Love & Commas Editing Services

# Chapter 1

Bethany

I was staring. I knew it – knew I was being rude – but I couldn't make myself stop.

I'd drag my eyes away and two seconds later, they'd be right back where they'd been. The sight in front of me was just too irresistible.

Trying not to be too obvious, I watched the big, well-built man from across the café. It was early afternoon, well after the lunch rush, and the café wasn't busy, giving me a clear view. He was stunningly handsome, dressed casually in a t-shirt that stretched snugly across his muscular torso and arms, his blondish hair catching the sunlight streaming through the large windows. No question, he was well worth looking at in his own right.

But what sealed the deal was the baby girl he held comfortably in his arms. She looked tiny cradled against his broad chest. Completely at ease, he talked to her quietly as she gazed up at him. My heart nearly melted as he kissed her on her little head, then set her in the carrier on the table in front of him. He tickled her tummy, and I found myself grinning along with him as she waved her little arms and kicked her feet.

Then he looked up, locked eyes with me, and my heart stuttered in my chest.

His eyes were an unusual greenish-blue, nearly turquoise, and they fixed on me like a laser beam locks on to its target. The smile slipped from his face as our eyes connected across the space and I watched his slowly heat with interest. He watched me intently and I swore I could almost hear him ask me who I was and where I'd come from. That alone should have been alarming enough for me to break the connection, but still, I didn't look away. Everything around us seemed to pause, the rest of the world fading away, a tenuous thread of something that felt strangely like recognition stretching between us...

Only to snap as two women walked up to the table where he sat, severing our line of sight.

I sat back in my seat, not even realizing until then that I'd leaned forward in the man's direction and drew in a shaky breath. I'd never experienced anything so visceral, so intense, from just a look. If he'd watched me much longer, I wouldn't have been surprised to find myself out of my chair and crossing the café toward him, his eyes drawing me toward him like a homing beacon.

And wouldn't that have been a disaster? Considering that I'd just arrived in town and was trying to keep a low profile while I did some discreet digging, the last thing I should be doing was "making eyes" as my mom would have said, at a man across a restaurant.

Let alone one who was obviously already in a relationship.

I watched out of the corner of my eye as the two women – one tall and slim, her blond hair pulled back in a tie; the other shorter and curvier, her red curls tumbling down her back – fussed a little over the baby as the man stood. Forcing myself to stop watching them, I focused intently on the remains of the salad in front of me, pushing a crouton back and forth with my fork, fighting back a surge of envy as I thought about the fact that one of the women was likely the man's wife or, at the very least, his girlfriend. Call her whatever you wanted to, one of those women had had a baby with him.

I frowned hard at the crouton, envy morphing into indignation as I thought about the look he'd given me just moments before. Why had he been looking at me – *staring* at me – like that, like I was the best thing he'd seen in a long while if he was already in a relationship? To be fair, I'd looked first, but I hadn't known, had I? The presence of the baby probably should have been a clue, but he could be a single dad, right? I mean, it was possible.

But he'd known. And he'd looked anyway.

And my, what a look it had been. My skin tingled even now at the memory.

In my peripheral vision, I saw the little group move toward the door. I stayed focused on the crouton like my life depended on it, even as I felt the man's eyes move over me again like a touch.

When they were gone, I breathed a sigh of relief, shaking my head slightly to clear it like I was coming out of a daze.

With a tinge of regret, I realized I'd probably never see the man again. Not that it mattered. Not only was he was obviously taken, he had no qualms about flirting with women other than his wife or girlfriend *while* holding their baby daughter. Ick. No, thank you. A man like that was the last thing I needed in my life.

More importantly, I wasn't here to hook up and I wasn't here for the long term. I was here to find someone from my past and, once and for all, after all these years, separate the lies from the truth.

After that, hopefully I could leave this place behind again as I'd done so long ago and, this time, finally be free.

# Chapter 2

Brody

"You should be the alpha."

I took a sip of my water as I glanced over at my date, setting the glass down on the bar top before responding to her comment.

"What makes you say that?"

"It's sexy." Melody moved a little closer, laying her hand on my thigh. "It means you're the strongest and most important, right? Like you're in charge and everyone in your pack has to do what you say."

Where had all this come from all of a sudden?

"Clan, not pack," I reminded her, having mentioned the distinction before. "Different shifter groups are called by different names." Melody shrugged as if it was all the same to her as I went on. "Becoming the alpha, being the alpha...it's more complicated than that."

"It doesn't seem complicated to me. You should challenge whoever the alpha is in your pack. I bet you'd win."

I laughed as I thought about challenging my alpha, Rhyne. This woman had no clue what that would entail and how very badly it would likely end for me. Rhyne was the long-time, well-liked and respected alpha of my large mountain lion clan. He was strong, fair, and effective, having been destined for the position from a young age. He'd recently taken a pure human mate, Kyra, the eldest daughter of one of our region's legacy families, which had further solidified his position as one of the most prominent alphas in our region. I didn't bother to explain any of that to Melody, though. She couldn't even make the effort to remember that we were a clan, she certainly wouldn't spend the mental energy to understand how clan and shifter hierarchy worked and didn't.

"I appreciate the vote of confidence, but that's not something I have any interest in doing."

Melody pressed closer, leaning into me and giving me an admittedly fantastic view of her cleavage.

"Think about it, though. If you were the alpha, we could get married, and I'd be your...what's the alpha's wife called?"

Married? Not a chance. Not to her. Still, I wanted to see how far she'd take this.

"His mate," I answered honestly. "In our clan, the alpha's wife is simply his mate."

Melody wrinkled her nose, unimpressed at a distinction my clan considered a high honor.

"I thought it would be a better name than that. But still" – her expression brightened, a less than exciting title in her estimation apparently not enough to dissuade her from her plan – "his wife has a lot of power, too, right? Kind of like she's the queen of the pack?"

I laughed again as I pictured Kyra, who was not only my alpha's mate, but one of my best friends. I'd have to remember to ask her later how she felt about her place as the clan's "queen".

"It's different from group to group, and yes, she's shown a lot of respect, but again, it's more complicated than that."

Melody sat back a little, clearly miffed that I wasn't showing an appropriate level of enthusiasm for her ridiculous plan.

"It doesn't have to be. We could run things however we wanted. If we were in charge, it would be our pack and we could make the rules."

I nearly corrected her again – clan, not pack – but I didn't bother. Instead, I just shook my head, done with this conversation, this date, and this relationship, if that's what you wanted to call it. I wasn't trying to be a jerk. Any pure human like Melody dating a demi-shifter like myself, let alone a full shifter, as rare as they were, was sure to have questions. Though we all coexisted peacefully for the most part, shifters were different than humans in a lot of ways and each shifter group had their own way of doing things. I would have explained to Melody how my clan worked if she had sincerely wanted to know, but she didn't. I'd seen enough over the past few weeks dating her to be confident of that.

This was my fourth date with Melody. I should have ended it after the second one – maybe the first one if I was being honest – but she was beautiful and fun, with a sense of humor that had seemed like a good match to mine. It didn't hurt that she was up for just about anything in the bedroom, either. In the bedroom, my truck, the elevator of her apartment building, and damn near in the middle of the dance floor on our last date – you name the place, she was down for it. As a single male in his early thirties, it was damn enticing having a woman ready and willing to go at it whenever and wherever the mood struck. Despite that, though, it was obvious she wasn't the one for me. I cringed internally as I realized I couldn't avoid it anymore – it was time for "the talk".

I waited until I pulled into the lot at her apartment building later that evening. I knew she was expecting me to come up, so I did my best not to be an asshole while I let her know that wouldn't be happening.

"I was thinking..." I pushed my hand through my hair, wishing this conversation was over. I no longer had any interest in spending time with Melody, but breaking things off always sucked.

*Just spit it out, Klein.*

"This has been fun and you're an amazing woman, but I think this has run its course."

Okay, "amazing" was maybe overselling it a little, although if the frown Melody shot my direction was any indication, she didn't think so.

"'Run its course'? Are you saying you don't want to see me anymore?"

I draped my wrists over the top of my steering wheel, hoping to get through this without a scene.

"I think it's time we went our separate ways, yeah."

Melody's face flushed with anger as she glared at me.

"You're dumping me? Are you being serious right now? No man has ever dumped me!"

Well, there was a first time for everything, so...

"I'm not dumping you." Not exactly. Okay, yeah, I was. "It's been great." That sounded lame even to me. "I just don't think I can give you what you want."

Especially if her future plan was to be the "queen" of a shifter group.

"Whatever. Your loss." Melody bent and snatched her purse up off the floorboard before turning to glare at me again. "It's not like you're the only man I'm seeing. The others are all more than happy to spend time with me. In a week, I won't even remember your name."

That stung the ego a little. I hadn't asked to be exclusive, but I also wasn't the kind of man who dated more than one woman at a time. When I was with any woman, my sole focus was on her.

Out of nowhere, the face of the woman I'd seen at the café the day before filled my mind. Her rich brown hair framing her heart-shaped face, mesmerizing brown eyes fixed on mine...I could feel the instant jolt of our connection even now.

Whoever she was, she was fully human like Melody – that was as clear to me as the fact that I wasn't would have been to her. Humans and shifters just felt different. There was never any question of who was who.

I hadn't approached her, hadn't spoken to her, but if I was being honest, that brief moment would have spelled the end of me and Melody even without Melody's crazy plans. I was attracted to Melody, sure – or had been – but it didn't come anywhere close to the shock wave that had hit me when I'd locked eyes with my mystery woman.

Not that Melody needed to know any of that. I kept my expression neutral as I responded to her.

"I hope you find what you're looking for."

Melody tossed her hair and yanked on the door handle, popping her door open. She still had more to say, though.

"Well, it sure isn't you. You never even bought me any gifts! For future reference – not that I care if you ever find another woman dumb enough to give you the time of day – but real men, *human* men, buy their women presents! Your kind may not care about that, but human women do!"

*My kind*? Funny how up 'til now the same shifter blood she was being so disparaging of had seemed to be a draw for her – a little walk on the wild side for her maybe. Either way, I was done with this conversation and done with her. My mother had taught me to treat women with respect, but Melody was skirting dangerously close to my limits. I ignored her last barb, just wanting her out of my truck and out of my life.

"Do you want me to walk you up?" Like I said, Mom taught me well.

Melody scoffed at my offer.

"The only thing I want from you is for you to stay away from me!"

No problem there. I winced a little as she stepped out of the truck and slammed the door. Seeing her bitchy underlayer killed any lingering attraction I might have had for her. Still, I stayed where I was, watching as she stalked the short distance to the front door of her apartment building and safely let herself in, turning to give me the one-finger salute before stomping away. With that classy last image of her in my mind, I pulled out of the lot and headed toward home.

# Chapter 3

Brody

"How are things with Melody?"

I grinned at my best friend, Lacey, as we stood at the counter of our favorite donut shop, waiting for our order.

"Couldn't even wait until we sat down, huh?"

Lacey glared at me in mock irritation as the store employee, Pam, set our order on the counter with a friendly smile and a "here you go".

Lacey gave up glaring at me to return Pam's smile.

"Thanks, Pam. Have a good week."

Carrying the tray with our drinks and donuts, I followed Lacey to our usual table. We met here one morning a week to get our donut fix and check in on each other's lives. Now that Lacey was married to Jackson, a bear demi-shifter I'd known for years, and I was taking on additional responsibilities for my clan, we didn't see each other as much as we had. Our weekly "donut date" was our way of making sure we didn't miss out on too much.

Lacey waited until we were seated and I'd taken my first sip of coffee before pouncing again.

"There, we're sitting down, and you've had some coffee. *Now* can I ask how things are with Melody?"

I couldn't resist needling her a little.

"Nosy, much?"

"Curious," Lacey corrected. "I know how you struggle with women, and I want to help any way I can."

My grin turned into a full-out laugh.

It wasn't true – not the part about me struggling with women, anyway. By most measures, I was highly successful.

The parts about Lacey being curious and wanting to help? Yeah, those were accurate.

"I appreciate it, but in this case there's nothing to help with. Melody and I are done."

I knew Lacey wouldn't be shocked to hear it – she'd known I wasn't all in on Melody – and she confirmed that with an understanding nod.

"I have to be honest that I don't hate that for you."

"I don't hate it for me, either. She wasn't the one."

"It didn't seem like it. Not that I ever met her, but you obviously weren't over the moon about her."

"No, I wasn't." If I had been, I'd have introduced her to Lacey, no question. I was closer to Lacey than anyone else, shifter or human, even my mother. Whoever I ended up with – assuming I was someday lucky enough to find my mate – she and Lacey would have to get along. Just like Jackson and I did.

"When she started telling me the other night about her grand plan for me to challenge Rhyne, become the alpha of my 'pack', and marry her so she could be the pack's 'queen', I knew it was time to end things."

Lacey nearly choked on the bite of sticky bun she'd just taken. She washed it down with a sip of her latte and looked at me, her eyes wide.

"I'm sorry, she what?"

"Exactly," I confirmed, knowing Lacey recognized every ridiculous aspect of what I'd just said.

"Well, she's got a good imagination if nothing else, I guess." Lacey shook her head and her vibrant red curls, tied back in a ponytail, bounced. "I know both Kyra and I had a lot to learn about the shifter world, but I don't think either of us was nearly that off-base."

"Not even close."

As members of the most exclusive circle of our society's purebred human class, neither Lacey, nor her best female friend, Kyra, had known much about the shifter world. Of everyone, the world they'd been born into was the part of our society that interacted the least with shifters. Unlike other shifters and humans, who co-mingled on a regular basis, families like Lacey and Kyra's avoided it unless absolutely necessary. Both Lacey and Kyra had had a lot to learn when they'd gotten involved with Jackson and Rhyne, respectively. There had been some missteps and miscommunication along the way, but now it seemed that they navigated both worlds seamlessly.

Knowing Kyra and Lacey had given me hope that maybe my mate was a human woman. So far it hadn't worked out that way, but I knew fate worked in strange ways sometimes.

Lacey and I talked for a while longer, then I checked the time and reluctantly pushed back from the table.

"I've gotta get going. I have a meet-and-greet with the woman we hired to ramp up our social media presence. She's starting with our new hiking venture, so Rhyne asked me to show her around and get her acclimated."

"Oh, your new person is a 'she', huh?" Lacey wiggled her eyebrows at me suggestively as we left the donut shop, making me grin.

"Down, girl. One, she'll be my co-worker; two, from her application, she sounds young; and three, even on the off-chance I'm interested in her, she may already be involved with someone, or just not interested in me, demi-shifters, men, or a relationship in general. Altogether that adds up to nothing close to promising."

"I'm just saying, you never know." Lacey stood on her tippy toes to receive my hug, eyeing me as she stepped back.

"And I'm just saying that bear shifter of yours has your head so full of endorphins that you see little hearts floating around everywhere you look."

Lacey sighed happily.

"He does. He really does. Not that you mountain lion shifters aren't pretty, but my big, grumpy man-bear just ticks all my boxes, if you know what I mean."

I shook my head at Lacey as I backed away.

"And that's my cue to get out of here before you decide to elaborate."

Lacey's laugh followed me to my truck a few feet away.

"Drive safe. Love you, Lace."

Lacey climbed into her car with a wave.

"Love you, Brody. Be good!"

I got to the office with a few minutes to spare. As much as I didn't love meetings, I was looking forward to this one. When Rhyne had asked me to head up our new hiking venture, I'd jumped at the chance. Our clan already operated two successful businesses – a mountain search and rescue and a sustainable lumber company – and I was ready and eager to help us build a third. The fact that Rhyne had tapped me to lead it was a huge vote of confidence and I didn't intend to let him down.

Ready to get going, I headed across the lobby of the big two-story building that housed our clan's offices on the first level and Rhyne and Kyra's residence on the second. I'd nearly reached the smaller of our two conference rooms when a strange buzz, almost like electricity, ran through my body, just under the surface of my skin.

A second later I saw Ingrid, Rhyne's assistant, coming toward me with a woman by her side.

When I saw the woman's face I came to a dead stop.

Walking towards me was my mystery woman from the café.

She fared a little better than I did. Her jaw dropped and her eyes grew wide, but she at least stayed in motion, faltering only momentarily before continuing at Ingrid's side.

Whether it was her expression that caught Ingrid's attention or me, frozen in place, I didn't know. Ingrid slowed to a stop several feet from me, looking silently at me, then the woman at her side, and back at me.

"Have you two met? It seems that perhaps you may know each other." Ingrid's tone was smooth and calm. As a 70+ year old demi-shifter – the strongest shifter in our clan, by far – who had been the alpha's assistant for years, very little ruffled Ingrid.

My mystery woman recovered first.

"I..." she tore her eyes away from mine to look at Ingrid. "No, we, uh..."

She paused again and I wondered what words were running through her head. *We shared a moment in time a few days ago that was unlike anything either of us has ever experienced?* Was it too much to hope that it had been a first for her, too?

Ingrid shot a look my way, questioning, and I did my best to pull myself together.

"My apologies. You took me by surprise." Nothing like stating the obvious. I stepped forward, hand out, polite smile firmly in place. "I'm Brody Klein."

The woman shook my hand, her skin soft, but her grip firm. She pulled away more quickly than I would have liked, then stepped back, reestablishing more space between us.

"Bethany McKay."

"Bethany is our new social media manager."

My pulse jumped at Ingrid's words, and I fought to keep my expression from showing it.

My mystery woman was our new employee? The one I'd be working side-by-side with for who knew how many months to come?

"It's nice to officially meet you, Bethany." I waited as Bethany returned the sentiment with a brisk, "Likewise", then answered Ingrid's earlier question.

"Bethany and I crossed paths briefly a few days ago but didn't have a chance to speak and so didn't realize the connection. Small world," I said with a more genuine smile.

Which my mystery woman – *Bethany*, I corrected – returned with a barely-there, just warm enough to be polite, curve of her lips.

Had I offended her somehow? It couldn't have been anything I'd said. I'd barely spoken fifty words in her presence. Maybe it was just nerves from starting a new job?

"Yes, isn't it," Ingrid agreed, still eyeing me a bit. "Well," she stepped back, aiming another friendly smile Bethany's way, "I was just showing Bethany the way to the conference room for your meeting. I'll leave you to it. Welcome again, Bethany."

"Thank you, Ingrid. I appreciate all the time you spent with me this morning."

That answered that. Bethany's words to Ingrid were infused with far more warmth than her response to me. Whatever was causing the chill between us – be it nerves, instant dislike, or something else – it was directed solely at me. The heat that had flashed between us a few days before was long gone, at least for Bethany. As for me, I could still feel the hum.

Just as Ingrid walked away, Kyra appeared at the top of the main staircase looking, as usual, like she'd just stepped out of the pages of a magazine in a simple, slim blue dress and matching sandals, her blond hair up in some kind of twist. She started down the steps, bag over her shoulder, carrying Lexi in her baby seat.

Happy for a distraction to help break the ice with Bethany, I headed in Kyra's direction.

"Perfect timing, Kyra." I crossed to meet her at the bottom of the stairs, relieving her of the baby seat for the moment. "Come meet the newest member of our team."

"You must be Bethany." Kyra's years of training as a social hostess shone through in her graceful and gracious greeting. "Please excuse me for not being here to welcome you earlier. Lexi picked this morning to be extra fussy. She's scheduled for a doctor's visit today and I swear she knows."

Lexi gazed at us all, her turquoise eyes – the dominant characteristic of our mountain lion clan – bright and curious, well aware that she was the center of attention.

Bethany shook her head at Kyra's words.

"No apology needed. It's good to meet you. She's adorable."

"Thank you." Kyra looked down at Lexi with a smile. "Though I'm pretty sure she knows that, too, and uses it to her advantage." She shot me a look as she continued, "No thanks to certain people who spoil her every chance they get."

I could feel Bethany's scrutiny as I made a funny face at Lexi, my grin matching Lexi's as she gurgled with laughter. "Guilty as charged. I'm no match for that smile."

"Heaven help us when she gets old enough to start asking for things." Kyra reached for the handle of the baby seat and I reluctantly handed it over. "Between you and her father she'll own every toy on the planet."

At Bethany's look of confusion, I realized that I hadn't fully introduced Kyra. As if I needed something else to remind me that Bethany's presence had knocked me completely off my game.

"Kyra is the wife and mate of our alpha, Rhyne. I believe you met him already?" Bethany nodded slowly, like she was processing my words. "Lexi is their daughter."

Bethany looked at me, then back at Lexi, and after a moment, nodded again, her expression clearing a little.

"I see."

Her response felt loaded, like there was more to it than the simple words she'd said.

If there was, it didn't seem to register with Kyra.

"Speaking of Rhyne, I need to go find him before we're late." Kyra stepped back, turning her smile on Bethany again. "We're glad you're here, Bethany. I'll leave you in Brody's very capable hands. Brody..." she leaned in for a quick one-armed hug, "I'll see you soon."

Then she headed off in search of her mate and it was just me and Bethany.

# Chapter 4

Bethany

She wasn't his.

Not the baby, and not the beautiful blonde. Both of them belonged to Alexander Rhynehart – introduced to me as Rhyne – Brody's boss and more importantly, the undisputable alpha of the Smoke Range mountain lion clan, of which Brody was a member.

I'd met Rhyne earlier that morning and had been nothing but impressed. He was a formidable man, tall, handsome, and fit, with alpha power simply rolling off him in waves. From what I could tell from Ingrid; Rhyne's second-in-command, Athena; and the others I'd met and talked with, Rhyne was held in extremely high regard by his clan and the community. I'd lived surrounded by demi-shifters my whole life and knew enough to know that wasn't true of all alphas.

The fact that, as a prominent alpha, Rhyne's mate was fully human like me was surprising. I was sure there was more to the story, just as I was sure that it was none of my business. I was an employee, and an outsider, at that. Everyone had been welcoming, but I didn't need to be digging into their personal business any more than I needed or wanted them digging into mine.

Which brought me back to Brody, the man now sitting across the conference table from me, no doubt wondering what on earth I was thinking about.

This was the man I had to work with. The man I'd been nearly mesmerized by from the moment I'd seen him across the café, those beautiful, unusual eyes of his drawing me in and his energy – just his mere presence – reaching out and wrapping itself around me like nothing I'd ever known. The same man I'd made some not-so-nice assumptions about and treated somewhat less than graciously earlier because of it. He wasn't the cheater I'd made him out to be in my head.

I'd misjudged him. I felt like I needed to apologize, but how could I do that without also reminding him of the look we'd shared? The one that now felt completely inappropriate given that we were going to be working together?

I couldn't. That was my answer. There was no way I could bring it up without making both of us incredibly uncomfortable. I needed to file it away, forget about it, and move on like it had never happened.

Fine, then. Here went nothing.

I folded my hands together on the conference table and launched in.

"Rhyne told me earlier that you'll be heading up the new hiking business line. Do I have that right?"

Brody looked at me, his eyes fixed on mine, and for a moment I thought he was going to call my bluff, bring up what had happened at the café and force us both to acknowledge it.

If I felt a twinge of disappointment when he didn't, well, so be it.

# Chapter 5

Brody

So, that's how we were playing this? Now that it was just the two of us, we were still going to act like that moment in the café hadn't happened?

I didn't like it. I wanted to talk about it, get it out in the open, at least between us, and figure out what happened next.

I guess I had my answer on that, though. If Bethany wanted to pretend our connection hadn't even happened, then the obvious answer to what happened next was nothing, at least in her mind.

I shook off the instant denial that filled me at that thought and reminded myself that this was still the first morning of the first day of Bethany's new job. No doubt she had a lot on her mind. She hadn't expected to run into me today – or any day – any more than I'd expected to run into her.

I also held a distinct advantage over her in our current situation. This was my clan, my turf, and my business line we were discussing. If I were in her place, I'd probably be uncomfortable, too.

*Later,* I promised myself. Some other time and some other place, I'd let her know I hadn't forgotten – wouldn't forget – and see what she had to say.

For now, I'd stick to business.

"You have it right," I confirmed while I refocused my brain where it needed to be and away from where I wanted it to be. "I'm wrapping up my responsibilities with the security team and search & rescue team in the next week or so, then I'll be fully focused on our new guided hiking service. Have you seen any of the promo materials for it?"

"No, not yet."

"I have them in my office. Let's go take a look." I pushed back from the table and stood. I stepped back to let Bethany go ahead of me into the hallway and couldn't help but notice the amber highlights that shot through her dark hair like strands of gold, even in the office lighting.

*Focus, Brody.*

"Do you do any hiking, Bethany?"

Bethany shook her head in response as she walked next to me, back across the lobby and down the short hallway to my office.

"Only casually, mostly just glorified walks in the woods. Nothing close to what it sounds like you're planning."

I laughed at Bethany's description.

"A glorified walk in the woods is sometimes exactly what you need and want. Remind me to show you a couple of our best one and two-hour trails in case you decide to explore."

I reached inside my office door to flip on the lights, then stepped back, again letting Bethany precede me. Once inside I waved her over to the small table set off to one side of my desk. The surface of the table was covered with mock-ups of print ad campaigns, brochures, and sample logo wear, water bottles, hats, and other swag.

I grabbed a brochure off the pile and handed it to Bethany.

"That will give you an idea of the scope of what we're planning. Have a seat."

While Bethany seated herself in one of the chairs in front of my desk, I crossed to the small fridge near my desk. I held up a bottle of water to her in question and at her nod, grabbed another for myself. I managed to ignore the zing of energy that streaked up my arm when I handed Bethany her water and her fingers brushed mine.

I took the chair next to her rather than the one behind my desk and we both studied the cover of the brochure as I continued to talk.

"As I mentioned, we have a set of trails on our land that are open for use by the public. We don't require permits for day hikes, only for overnight camping. We have some of that, but the vast majority of the hikers we have are self-guided and only on our land for a few hours. We offer a handful of guided hikes now, mostly for groups looking to hike together and wanting an experienced guide with them, but those are day hikes only, no overnights. That's where the new business line comes in."

I reached over and flipped the brochure open in Bethany's hands, tempted but careful this time not to brush against her skin.

"With the new venture we'll be focusing on both of the things we haven't up until this point – overnight, even multi-night, campers and guided hikes. Both open up a lot of opportunities to attract a whole new population of hikers and significantly increase revenue."

I went on to explain the hut-to-hut hiking service we'd decided to pursue, building several small cabins or "huts" at strategic points across the parts of our clan's lands that were accessible on foot. I talked about the pros and cons and the different sizes of huts and the possible hiking packages and routes and a thousand other details.

I finally noticed Bethany looking at me, faint amusement shining in her eyes, and realized I'd been talking for...I glanced at the clock on my desk...I had no idea how long.

My face flushed and I felt the tips of my ears sting with embarrassment.

"Well, it's really too bad you have to be in charge of all this since you're clearly not excited about it."

"Yeah, I...uh..." I laughed self-consciously, even though Bethany's teasing seemed good-natured. "I guess I can get a little into the weeds on the details."

I rubbed a hand across the back of my neck, off-balance and wondering how to get us back on track when Bethany saved me.

"Details are good, though. An hour ago, I had no idea hut-to-hut hiking was even a thing and now I know enough to have some ideas where to start with a strategy."

An hour ago? I'd been talking for an *hour*?

"Just remember this when I'm trying to get you to focus on social media impressions and engagements and clicks and hundred other things that I promise you are far more interesting and important than they sound."

"Done," I agreed, appreciating the out she was giving me. "You listened to my details; I'll listen to yours."

Ready to get the focus off my unplanned monologue, I pushed a hand through my hair and thought about what to do next.

"Have you had a tour yet? Seen your office?"

"Office, yes; tour, no."

Grateful for an excuse to move, I stood.

"Let's get the tour knocked out, then I'll introduce you to a few more people."

Bethany stood to join me, holding out the brochure.

"Go ahead and hang on to that. I've got a whole stack."

Bethany looked up at me, her brown eyes on mine, and I almost physically felt myself get caught in them, as if she'd reached out and grabbed me. Then, like she was shaking herself out of a fog, Bethany stepped back, looking everywhere but at me as she said thanks.

It took me a second to remember that she was thanking me for the brochure.

"Yeah, no problem. Let's...uh..." what the hell was I supposed to be doing?

Tour. Right.

"Let me show you around."

The awkwardness between us that had dissolved for a few short minutes was back as we left my office. I rubbed the back of my neck again as we walked, trying not to show my frustration. I usually had no trouble talking to women – young, old, co-worker, friend, date, potential hook-up, actual hook-up, no problem. But this woman had me so far off-balance I had no idea which way was up.

Now that I'd had a few minutes with her that had felt easy – good – I wanted more. The only question now was how to get back there.

# Chapter 6

Bethany

I left the coffee shop, looking left and right as casually as I could, all the while half expecting someone to jump out from behind one of the decorative potted trees by the entrance or chase me down from inside, demanding to know what I was up to.

I shook my head at myself as I did my best to discreetly shove the nondescript tan envelope I'd just received deeper into my shoulder bag. I'd make a terrible spy or double agent. There was no reason for anyone to be watching or following me. I was no one special – just one of the thousands of people on their way to work at that very moment, caffeinated concoction of their choice clasped in their hand like a lifeline.

The fact that I was also potentially carrying the information I'd waited years for had me checking my surroundings again and tucking my bag closer. It was times like this when I realized with pristine clarity that the constant vigilance and paranoia of my upbringing may have diminished, but they were still far from gone.

As much as I'd wanted to rip the envelope open right in the middle of the bustle of the coffee shop and as much as it was killing me to wait, I knew that I had to. Just until tonight, until I got home to the small apartment I'd rented and moved into a few days earlier. I wouldn't even chance opening it at work.

I crammed my bag next to me in the driver's seat, not wanting to take the chance of setting in on the passenger seat out of reach and headed to work. As I drove, I let myself check the rearview and side mirrors more than I needed to, knowing it would help keep the worst of my nerves in check.

I walked into work and of course immediately ran into the one person I'd been hoping to avoid. Brody Klein shook me to my core on a good day. Today, with my nerves already jangling like a manic tambourine? The best I could do was keep our interaction brief and try to avoid him the rest of the day.

I nodded at him politely as we drew closer to each other.

"Good morning, Bethany." That smile of his should be illegal. Not to mention the way he filled out the cadet blue button-down and black dress pants he wore.

He stopped, ready to chat, but I continued on by without breaking my stride.

"Morning, Brody. Sorry to run. I have a call."

Lies, all of it. I wasn't the least bit sorry to keep moving and my schedule was wide open. Not that those were things he needed to know.

Though he didn't respond, I felt his eyes on me as crossed the lobby briskly and turned down the short hallway. I breathed a sigh of relief as I reached my office and shut the door behind me. In the three days I'd worked here, I'd noticed that people kept their office doors open most of the time. It made things feel more welcoming and I'd followed suit, but today my fictional call gave me an excuse to close it, at least for a while.

I checked my bag, reassuring myself that the envelope was still there, then set it inside my lower desk drawer, pushed it all the way to the back, and closed and locked the drawer. Who I thought I was hiding it from, I had no idea, but it made me feel better to have it as far out of sight as possible.

I busied myself sending and responding to a few emails, then dove into past ads and social media campaigns used by the clan, both for their self-guided hiking trails and for their other businesses, trying to get a feel for their overall look and feel. I made notes as I went along, and time passed without me realizing it. It wasn't until a knock at my door made me look up that I realized nearly three hours had slipped by.

"Come in."

I stretched a little in my chair, working out a kink or two as Ingrid open my door and stuck her head in.

"Sorry to disturb you, Bethany, but do you have a few minutes to go over something with Rhyne and Brody?"

So much for avoiding Brody for the rest of the day. I couldn't exactly refuse to meet with him and Rhyne, though, so I checked my desk drawer, reassured myself that it hadn't somehow unlocked itself in the past few hours, then stood.

I followed Ingrid to the large conference room where Rhyne and Brody, along with Athena and Cason, who headed up the clan's security and search & rescue service, stood looking at materials spread across the table's surface. I ignored the zap of awareness that seemed to hit me whenever I was near Brody and focused my attention on Rhyne.

"Thanks for joining us, Bethany." Rhyne extended his hand toward the table, indicating the items. "We're considering whether to change the branding for all our businesses when we launch the new hiking service. We know creating a new brand isn't part of your responsibilities as social media manager, but given your past marketing experience, we thought we'd ask your input into which direction we should go."

I looked at the table, studiously avoiding Brody's gaze, and breathed carefully through the sudden twist of nerves in my stomach.

I'd known that exaggerating my knowledge and experience on my application for my current job could come back to bite me in the butt at some point; I'd just hoped it wouldn't happen this quickly or in front of this many people.

It was true enough that I'd once worked in a marketing department. It was even true that – as I'd said on my application – my title had included the words "senior associate." Unfortunately for my current situation I'd been a senior *administrative* associate, aka an executive secretary, not a senior *marketing* associate.

Another thing that was true? I'd needed this job and I'd lied to get it. From listening in and taking notes for my past boss during numerous meetings on branding and marketing and media strategy, I'd picked up enough of the language and best practices to bluff my way through the interview for this job, and – I'd hoped – through as many months of this job as I needed it to.

Now, as I looked at the materials in front of me and listened to everyone's silence as they waited to hear what I had to say, I wondered if this charade of mine might be over long before then.

"I...well...hm."

*Brilliant, Bethany. Great start.*

"Take your time. We realize we're springing this on you."

Brody's voice came from much closer than I expected. I glanced up at him quickly, then back at the materials, moving away from him smoothly, as if I wanted a closer look at something farther down the table.

Grasping for something, anything, remotely intelligent to say, I focused on something I'd noticed as I'd researched other hut-to-hut and adventure hiking and camping services over the past few days.

"The colors..." I paused and looked up, blinking in surprise at all the eyes focused intently on me, then cleared my throat and went on. "The pairing of the sort of smoky blue and smoky green" – I was 100% confident those weren't the correct terms to describe the colors, but I pushed on as if they were – "along with the gold accents" – I pointed to two sets of the materials on the table – "that seems to be a very common color palette."

I was relatively sure that was the first time I'd ever used the word "palette" in a sentence.

"A lot of outdoorsy businesses and services use those same colors, and for good reason, but it makes it hard to stand out from the crowd."

I risked another glance up at Rhyne, encouraged as he nodded thoughtfully.

"This palette" – I gestured toward a set with bright sky blue and black – "catches the eye but may be too different from what's expected to be effective. But that one" – a pairing of the same familiar smoky green, but this time with smoky purple and a touch of bright burgundy – "stands out a little, but not too much."

I paused, continuing to focus on the materials, realizing belatedly that I should have asked if they were leaning towards one set of colors over another. What if I'd just dismissed the one they liked best as "too common" or "too different"?

I stepped back from the table and looked at Rhyne again.

"Just my quick opinion," I hedged. "There could be good reasons for choosing any of them."

"The one you liked was my top choice, too," Brody interjected. "Both mine and Cason's."

Athena frowned at Brody from where she stood, arms crossed, near Rhyne.

"It will mean re-doing all the materials we just had done for the hiking service, along with everything we'd need for the other businesses. That will be a significant expense. I'm not sure it's justified just so the colors are prettier."

My cheeks flushed a little at the implied criticism, but I kept my chin up, refusing to show in any other way that Athen's words had been a hit to my confidence.

"It's not about being 'prettier,'" Brody argued. "It's about getting noticed. People can't choose us to do business with if they can't find us in all the noise."

"People have been finding us just fine for years," Athena responded, not giving an inch.

"They have," Rhyne agreed. "But that doesn't mean they'll continue to do so. It makes sense to update everything while we're adding the new business line. The expense isn't an issue."

There was a little more discussion, but I could tell the decision had been made. As soon as I felt I could, I slipped out of the conference room and hurried back to my office. A few minutes later, I heard footsteps in the hall. They could have belonged to Cason, or Athena, or one of the half dozen other people who had offices in this wing of the building, but somehow, I knew they belonged to Brody.

I held my breath as the footsteps paused. I stared at my open doorway, waiting.

Would he stop at my door and look at me with those captivating eyes of his? Or continue right past with a casual wave?

The answer was neither. I was just about to pass out from lack of oxygen when the footsteps started up again – in the opposite direction.

Disappointment and relief swamped me in equal measure. Relief because I needed to keep my wits about me and my head on straight – both of which I was severely challenged to do in Brody's distracting, compelling presence – and disappointment because...well...because I'd missed out on everything that made Brody so distracting and compelling.

I worked through the rest of the day with no distractions, my anticipation and nerves building as I got closer to the moment I could open the envelope I'd received that morning.

I made myself wait until I'd closed my apartment door behind me and locked it. Then I pulled the envelope out of my bag, sat on the hard couch that had come with the apartment, held the envelope in my hands, and stared at it.

I swallowed hard as nerves swamped me. I'd wondered for so long, waited a lifetime for answers.

What if I didn't want them once I had them?

I turned the envelope over slowly, gearing myself up to pull open the flap. He'd cautioned me that this information wasn't conclusive – the man I'd hired to help me find it, that was. He'd said that he'd keep looking, keep digging. This was just the start.

Might as well get started then.

I took a deep breath and opened the envelope cautiously, careful not to damage the contents. A single paper spilled out onto my lap.

It was an old car rental agreement, dated when I would have been about three and half years old. I recognized my mom's signature at the bottom, but what caught my attention were the images of two drivers' licenses that obscured the lines of the rental form along one side, as if someone had paperclipped the licenses to the form, then made a photocopy.

One driver's license was my mom's. The other one...

My breath rushed out of me as I studied the name and photo on the second license. The photo was dark and grainy, the image quality poor, but the name was clear.

Rafe Logan.

Rafe. The name I'd remembered all these years.

Tears sprung to my eyes as I realized that I'd been right.

For almost as long as I could remember, my mother had refused to speak his name and had forbidden me to, either. Over the years, time had chipped away at the memories, until sometimes I'd wondered if I'd made it all up.

I hadn't...at least not all of it. As for the whole truth?

The one person who knew that was Rafe.

Now I had to find him. If he was still alive, and still in the area, I had to find him.

Who knew whether he would welcome me, or reject me, or even remember me at all.

After all these years, it was time I found out.

# Chapter 7

Brody

I was mid-workout when I felt Bethany.

It had only been a few days, but I didn't question it. When Bethany was nearby, I knew.

I hadn't expected to see her here, but then again, I hadn't been to the gym since I'd shown it to her on her tour of our building the week before. For all I knew, she'd been here every day since.

I was setting down the weights I'd just finished with when she walked through the door and stopped short. I watched her as I straightened up, catching the flash of dismayed surprise on her face before she smoothed her features into a more neutral expression.

"Good morning," I called across the space, empty except for the two of us. The gym was open to all members of the clan, as well as clan employees, but this early in the day it was rare to see more than a handful of people, if that.

"Morning," Bethany returned, looking around the space undecidedly, and I wondered if she was trying to think of a way to make a graceful exit.

I walked closer, testing both of us, taking a drink from my water bottle as I continued to watch her.

"I didn't...um," Bethany paused as if choosing her words. "I...uh...didn't expect to see you."

If she had, I felt sure she wouldn't be there.

I nodded as I took another drink.

"I'm here most mornings. I've been busy this week, so I've just been getting a quick run in here and there."

Bethany returned my nod as she twisted her workout towel in her hands, looking everywhere but directly at me.

"I can come back later. I don't want to be in your way."

I gave her my best smile, trying to set her at ease as I looked around the gym, arms open wide.

"It's a big place. There's plenty of room for both of us, don't you think?"

I turned back just in time to see her running her eyes across my arms and shoulders, which were exposed by the tank top I wore. When her tongue darted out to wet her bottom lip, I felt a familiar tug in my stomach. I liked her looking at me, liked knowing that there was an attraction there underneath whatever the rest of this was.

It was also nice to know that I wasn't in this completely alone.

And if I wanted her to stay, I needed to back off before she took off back to the changing rooms.

I took a few steps back, pointing off to the side.

"Water and extra towels are over there in case I forgot to show you the other day." With another quick smile I turned and casually made my way back over to the weight area. "Have a good workout."

# Chapter 8

Bethany

I lasted for 27 minutes.

It was ridiculous. *I* was ridiculous.

Brody was just a man – okay, part mountain lion – but still, just a man. Granted, he was an incredibly fit, handsome, hot, smart, gorgeous, stunning man, but even so, I should have had better self-control. I should have been able to keep my eyes to myself and concentrate on my own workout.

I didn't. I couldn't.

No matter how I tried, how many times I told myself not to, I couldn't stop watching him. Like that day at the café, my eyes had a mind and an agenda all their own.

Brody fully clothed and playing with an adorable baby, or sitting across a conference table, or walking next to me down the hallway...those situations were taxing enough. Those, I could handle...barely...even with the hum that was always in the air between us whenever he was nearby.

Brody lifting weights, his muscles bunching and flexing, gleaming with a sheen of sweat? I nearly swallowed my tongue.

The third time I tripped on the treadmill, I shut it down. At that point, I was just asking for a fall, and I could do without the bruises that would leave on both my body and my dignity. I grabbed my towel, sent what I hoped looked like a casual wave in Brody's direction in case he noticed, and left. I'd just take a walk at lunch to make up for the time I'd missed on the treadmill.

I spent the rest of the morning working my way through an online course on social media marketing, picking up ideas and terms here and there to help me fake my way through my job, then sat in on a financial briefing on the clan's current and projected hiking business along with Brody, Rhyne, and several others. Brody wasn't there yet when I got to the conference room, so I made sure to choose a seat between Athena, who, for the most part, ignored me, and Gregory, another of the clan's leaders who I'd met the day before and had a friendly chat with, ensuring there wasn't an empty seat next to me.

Brody arrived just as the meeting started, frowning slightly as he looked between me and Gregory. Then he took the seat to the right of Rhyne, out of my immediate line of sight, and I did my best to focus on the topic at hand.

Once the meeting was done, I slipped out as quickly as possible, and rather than heading back to my office, went out the building's back doors onto the huge terrace. I followed one of several walkways past the wonderfully landscaped pool area and through part of the beautiful grounds and gardens, slowing gradually as I walked, letting the colors and shapes and soft breeze soothe me. I breathed in and out slowly, feeling my mind clear and the tension slip from my shoulders. Sooner than I would have liked, I turned and retraced my steps, feeling more settled than I had for days.

Only to tense up again when I saw Brody leaning in my office doorway, waiting for me.

He didn't smile as he usually did – and didn't return the polite one I gave him – just watched me as I walked closer.

"You didn't stay long this morning."

So, he *had* noticed my abbreviated workout that morning. It would have been hard to miss, I guess, since we'd been the only two in the gym.

I scrambled for an explanation, jumping at the first thing that came to mind. Well, the first thing other than *You were so stunning you nearly made me fall off the treadmill, so I left for my own safety.* "I had a flash of inspiration and I wanted to write it down before I forgot it."

That did sometimes happen. Ideas and solutions to problems often occurred to me when I was running or taking a walk, so it was plausible.

Brody's blank expression gave me no indication whether he believed me or not.

"I hoped to catch you after the meeting, but you were gone before I could."

His voice was...flat, not cold, exactly, but not warm and friendly, which I hadn't realized until now that I'd come to expect from him.

I missed it...and didn't want to think about why.

"I'm sorry, I didn't realize. I wanted to get a quick walk in to make up for this morning." With the added benefit of avoiding him, but whatever. "Did you want me for something?"

There was a flash of...something...in Brody's eyes before he looked down, breaking the connection as he straightened, shoving his hands in the pockets of his dress pants, his shoulders tense.

"What's your schedule look like this weekend?"

This weekend? I didn't remember anything from my interview about working on the weekends.

Or wait...was he asking me out?

My stomach clenched with nerves as I managed to get out, "I'd need to check. Why?"

Brody crossed his arms and shifted his stance and I braced myself for what he was going to say next.

It wasn't what I'd expected.

"Rhyne and Kyra are hosting a reception here Saturday evening for Rhyne's fellow Alliance Council members and the leaders of the region's shifter groups. It's a first for our clan. Rhyne's not much of a social host but since he mated with Kyra..." Brody shrugged, leaving the rest of that thought go unsaid as he shoved his hands back into his pockets. "Anyway, you're welcome to attend. It would be a good opportunity to meet some members of the shifter community."

Some important, influential members was what he meant. Rhyne was a high-ranking member of the region's shifter council – known as the Alliance Council – made up of two representatives from each of the region's recognized shifter groups. Along with the all-human Executive Council and Chancellor, they made up the government of the Central Interior region of our country. The same structure was echoed across the other five regions. Together the six Chancellors governed the country.

These were people Brody's clan did business with, whose cooperation and partnership they relied on, just as those people relied on Rhyne and Brody and their clan.

I didn't want to attend. I was trying to blend, to keep a low profile for however long I was here. Nothing about that pointed to rubbing shoulders with some of the most prominent demi-shifters and shifters in the region as being the brightest of ideas.

Could I say no, though? I knew it wasn't required but Rhyne was my boss, after all.

I nodded at Brody, realizing he'd stood watching me silently as I'd argued with myself.

"I'll be there. Thank you for the invitation."

A short nod was the only response I got before Brody turned and walked away, leaving me wondering whether I'd given him the answer he'd wanted or the one he hadn't.

# Chapter 9

Bethany

"The dark blue one. Definitely."

I gathered my hair in one hand as I turned and looked over my shoulder, checking as much of my reflection as I could see in the large mirror over my bathroom sink.

I wasn't sure I agreed with the opinion of my new friend and neighbor, Andi.

"You don't think it shows too much skin?" I waved my hand at my shoulders and upper back, left exposed by the strapless design.

"Not at all. Your skin is perfect, might as well show it off. It's not like it's low-cut in the front or anything. Here, try these on with it."

Andi tossed me a pair of heels from where she sat leaning back against the wall in the hallway outside my bathroom. The shoes were a loan from her to go with one of the two dresses I'd been lucky enough to find at a nearby thrift store.

When I'd asked Ingrid what I should wear to the reception, she'd simply said "A cocktail dress would be perfect." I hadn't had the heart to tell her that I wasn't sure exactly what type of dress that was but *was* sure that I'd never owned one in my life.

I slipped the shoes on – not that I could see my feet or even the bottom half of my body in the mirror – then turned to face the mirror again, running my eyes over the dress that Andi favored.

I'd met Andi the day I'd moved in when she'd held the door for me as I carried in a load of my things. I'd run into her again a few days later in the building's laundry room and we'd instantly become friends. I'd never had a real friend, so I wasn't sure if I was doing it right, but Andi was more than outgoing enough to make up for whatever I lacked. Whether it was a characteristic of her shifter group – she was obviously a demi-shifter, but she hadn't volunteered what her animal was, and I hadn't asked – or whether it was just her, Andi was anything but shy.

"The gray is more reserved, though." I'd tried that one on first. The dress had small cap sleeves and, unlike the blue one, which stopped an inch or two above my knees, hit right below them. It also came with a long, sheer jacket that would cover my arms. "I'm leaning toward that one. Remember this is a work event for me."

Andi shook her head emphatically, not convinced in the least.

"That gray is a terrible color on you. With your dark hair and eyes, it washes you out. And the style would be perfect if you were sixty-five, but you're not. You're twenty-five, with great boobs and smokin' legs, both of which look amazing in the dress you have on now."

I blinked, not quite accustomed to such personal comments, then shook my head at her blunt assessment.

"Do please say what you think, Andi."

She blew me a kiss. "Always do."

I continued to study myself in the mirror, debating.

"Wear your hair down if you're worried about too much exposure. It will give you a little coverage on your shoulders and back."

"Hmm." She was right about the color. The dark blue of the one I had on did far more for me than the gray.

"Brody will be there, right? You want to look good when you see him."

I kept my eyes pinned on my reflection, not wanting to give Andi any more ammunition than she already had. In a moment of weakness over a carton of caramel fudge swirl ice cream, I'd mentioned Brody and how unsettled he made me feel. I hadn't heard the end of it since.

"He's my co-worker, Andi. That's all."

"Yeah, right," she shot back, unimpressed, as she pushed to her feet. "A gorgeous one who's eye-fucked you several times. Give me a co-worker like that, please and thank you."

"I..." What did I even say to that? "He didn't...there were a couple of looks, that's all."

"He's hot, he's there, I say you go for it."

I didn't respond as I led the way back into my bedroom. Andi collapsed on the air mattress I was currently using as a bed, making herself at home.

"You need to buy a bed. What happens when you get your hot mountain lion man back here and all you have is this blow-up thing?"

"I haven't had time." I hadn't *made* time. The apartment had come partially furnished but those furnishings hadn't included a bed. It wasn't a priority for me, though. The air mattress worked just fine, and, unlike a bed, I could easily take it with me when I moved on, whenever that was.

I didn't share those thoughts with Andi. Instead, I responded to her question. "And the odds of Brody ever even coming to my apartment, let alone sharing my air mattress, are somewhere between zero and never going to happen. He's so far out of my league you can't even see his league from mine."

"Five bucks says you're wrong."

Andi rolled off the mattress and stood, holding out her hand to shake on it. Just to humor her, I did.

"Now hang up your dress and let's order dinner. What do you want on the pizza?"

I reached into my closet for a hanger, telling myself I still had all day tomorrow to decide which dress to wear, and gave her the answer I knew would make her groan.

"Anything but pineapple," I yelled at her back as she left my bedroom, laughing when I heard her grumble in response.

I liked Andi and I was glad to have a friend, but I had to draw the line somewhere. I wasn't eating pineapple on my pizza for anyone, not even my new bestie.

# Chapter 10

Brody

I sipped champagne I didn't want as I ran my eyes over the crowd gathered on the large terrace.

I wasn't looking for Bethany. She wasn't here. I'd know if she was.

I wasn't watching for anyone specific – not really. It was more that old habits died hard. Until recently, I'd been a member of the clan's security team, specifically guarding Kyra, accompanying her in public and serving as her driver whenever Rhyne wasn't with her. In the process, we'd become good friends. It was also thanks to that assignment that I'd met Lacey.

I was no longer a part of the security team – although I still went places with Kyra occasionally, especially when she had Lexi with her – but that didn't mean the ingrained instinct to watch for signs of trouble was gone. This was mostly a group our clan was familiar with, filled primarily with friends and allies, but still, it didn't hurt to be a little careful.

I was talking with Ingrid and Kolborn Evans, alpha of Jackson's bear pack, went I felt it – the sense of knowing, the presence in my brain that told me Bethany was close by. Ingrid and Kole's voices faded as I turned and watched Bethany walk through the door and out onto the terrace. I saw her pause, then, as if I'd called her name, turn her head and look directly at me. As it had in the café, time stood still, everyone and everything fading away until it was just the two of us. My eyes slipped to the hollow of her throat as she swallowed, then rose back up to her eyes, our connection so strong I swore I could feel the beat of her heart alongside mine.

I drew in a sharp breath as the crowd passed between us and I lost sight of her. I shook my head a little, clearing the fog as I turned back to see knowing smiles on both Ingrid and Kole's faces.

At my questioning look, the smiles turned to good-natured laughs.

"Hits you like a brick wall, doesn't it?" Kole asked.

I shook my head again in response.

"I'm not sure what you mean."

Kole's eyebrows lifted in surprise.

"No?" Kole looked at Ingrid and she shrugged lightly, as if she could neither confirm nor deny. "Well, you will, Brody." He clapped a friendly hand on my shoulder. "Believe me, you will. Before long, by the looks of it."

Before I could respond, the beta of Kole's pack and his mate joined us, and the conversation thankfully turned to another topic.

I wandered away a few minutes later, both reassured and keyed up by the fact that I could still feel Bethany close by. I didn't seek her out – not yet – unsure what I'd say to her if we were face-to-face. Instead, I talked with Rhyne and Kyra for a while, then with a Council member and her mate from the local fox pack, then a few others, gradually making my way around the gathering, networking and socializing as was expected of me. It wasn't my favorite thing to do, but I usually had no trouble with it. Tonight, though, Bethany tugged at me, her presence a constant buzz in my brain.

Finally, I let myself look for her. And when I found her, I wasn't happy.

She was, though. At least she looked like it. She was holding a glass of champagne, talking with Gregory, and smiling. At him. With a full, beautiful, genuine smile unlike anything she'd ever sent my way. I got nods, or a polite, reserved, curve of her lips, and sometimes, when I watched closely enough, a flash of heat and interest in her eyes, while Gregory...

Gregory got the gorgeous sight of her radiant smile.

If I'd been holding a champagne flute in my hand at that moment, it would have shattered.

I suppressed the growl that tore through me, knowing in a room full of demi-shifters it would be heard and noted.

There was something between Bethany and me. Whatever it was, she obviously wanted to deny it. Up until now, I'd let her do it, but deny it or not, it was there.

When she said her goodbyes to Gregory and started up the steps to the upper terrace, I saw my opening. It would be quieter up there, with the main festivities concentrated on the first level. I made myself move through the crowd at a reasonable pace, relieved when I made it to the bottom of the steps without being stopped.

When I reached the top, I paused, letting my eyes adjust to the dimmer light, scanning the space for Bethany. I found her, standing at the stone and iron railing, looking out at the darkened grounds. Her dress left the pale, smooth skin of her shoulders bare and her glossy brown hair spilled down her back. As I crossed the space that separated us, I pictured walking up behind her, gathering her hair in one hand, skimming my lips softly across her neck and down her spine, feeling her shiver as I pulled her close against me.

When I'd nearly reached her, I said her name, and she whirled to face me as one hand flew up to press against her chest.

"Brody, you scared the life out of me!" She took a deep breath and blew it out, trying to settle herself. "You were so quiet I didn't hear you."

That was because I'd been stalking her, I realized, approaching her like my mountain lion would its prey. I didn't let myself think too deeply about what that might mean.

"My apologies. I saw you head up here and wanted to check on you. I know this is a lot of new people for you to meet at once. You doing okay?"

Bethany took another deep breath as she nodded and I all but saw the mask she wore around me slip into place.

"Yes, I'm fine. I just needed a little air. Thank you for checking on me."

There was nothing wrong with her reply. Not really. It was perfectly polite and appropriate. It was also bland and emotionless, nothing like what I'd seen in her eyes when she'd first arrived at the reception, or when we'd seen each other at the café.

Still, I could accept her response, leave her to herself as she clearly wished I would, and let it stand.

Then I thought about the smile she'd given Gregory and something inside me snapped.

Fuck it. I was done letting her pretend.

"Do I remind you of someone you hate?"

Bethany frowned at me in confusion, probably due as much to my suddenly heated tone as my out-of-the-blue question.

"I don't know what you mean."

"Exactly what I said." I took a step closer, oddly proud when Bethany stood her ground. "Do I remind you of someone you hate? Or maybe it's simpler. Maybe you just hate me."

"Why would you ask me that?"

Even in her confusion, she was stunning, her brown eyes and perfect lips shaded dark for the evening, tempting me to grab her and cover her mouth with my own. I shoved my hands in my pockets, fighting the need to reach for her.

"Why would I ask you that? Maybe because of the way you stared me down at the café, then very pointedly refused to look at me as I left."

Bethany's cheeks paled as I finally said out loud what had been between us since day one. Did she think I'd forgotten? Or that it didn't matter to me?

"Or maybe the way you go out of your way to avoid me." *That's right, Bethany. I've noticed you practically sprinting out of every meeting we're in together.* "Or the constant expression of...I don't know...forbearance? stoic acceptance?...whenever you're forced to be one-on-one with me?" She looked down at the decorative stones of the terrace, avoiding my eyes. "I've seen you with other people. You're animated. You're interested. You smile." Yeah, that memory would burn for a while. "With me? No matter what I say or do, it's like you can't get away from me fast enough. So, tell me Bethany, what gives? What have I done?"

I made myself stop, crossing my arms over my chest, resisting the urge to step closer to her, trying to give her space to respond.

"I..." she closed her eyes for a second, then opened them as she tilted her face up to look at me. "You haven't done anything. You don't remind me of anyone, and I don't hate you or dislike you."

I simply looked back at her, letting her see the doubt on my face.

"I don't," she insisted. "I'm just...not used to being around men like you. You're...a lot and it makes me nervous, I guess."

Interesting. I made her nervous but Rhyne – our alpha – didn't? She acted fine around him.

I uncrossed my arms and braced my hands on my hips, trying to understand.

"What does that mean – men like me? How am I 'a lot'?"

I was physically a pretty big guy, but again, not much more so than Rhyne, or even Gregory for that matter.

"Just..." Bethany blew out another breath as her cheeks pinked up with embarrassment and she waved her hand in my general direction. "Confident and fit and..." another breath... "charming and gorgeous."

I couldn't have stopped the immediate grin that split my face if I'd wanted to.

"You think I'm charming and gorgeous?"

"Please." Bethany rolled her eyes at me, and I was glad to see a little of the spark I knew she had in her. "Don't act like women don't tell you that all the time."

"Doesn't matter if they do." The only one whose opinion mattered at the moment was standing right in front of me. "Why does that make you nervous? It's just me."

Bethany huffed out a quiet laugh as she shook her head at me.

"This may be news, but 'just you' is pretty intimidating."

It was dangerous how good her words made me feel.

"Would it help if I wore a bag over my head?" I teased.

"Yes?"

I laughed as Bethany looked at me, head tilted to the side as if considering the answer she'd just given.

"No, it really wouldn't. There's still the rest of you to deal with."

And oh, how I'd love for her to deal with me.

"How about this? What if I tell you I think you're gorgeous, too?"

A sudden swarm of butterflies swooped through my stomach as I said the words to her for the first time. I felt like a pre-teen talking to his crush.

She shook her head at me again, but her eyes were lit with amusement. She didn't believe me; thought I really was just saying it to make her feel better. Someday, I'd get her to accept it as true, but for now...

"Tell me what I can do to make this better." I dropped my hands and let myself move a fraction closer. "We need to be able to see each other and work together" – and far more if I had my way – "and I hate that I make you uncomfortable. That's not my intention."

Bethany looked up at me and I realized she was just the right height for me to kiss. We were a perfect fit.

"Just telling you helps, I guess. I'm sorry I've been less than friendly. It's not your fault. Just...maybe turn down the charm a little until I build up some immunity or something?"

I had no clue how to do what she asked, but for her, I'd try.

"Got it. Consider it done."

I smiled at her, and she shook her head at me.

"It would help if you didn't do that either. That smile is powerful."

I immediately did it again as she continued to eye me.

"If you think telling me that is going to do anything other than make the problem worse, you're sadly mistaken."

She sighed. "It was worth a shot."

I sobered a little as I looked at her standing there, so pretty in the soft light.

"I want things to be okay with you, Bethany," I told her honestly. "Are we okay?"

Bethany looked back at me for a moment before nodding. "We're okay."

"No more looking at me like I'm your least favorite thing the next time you see me?"

She winced. "Was it that bad?"

"It wasn't great," I admitted.

"No more looks like that," Bethany said firmly.

"And I'll do my best to be less amazing," I promised with a grin, wanting to see her eyes light up again and feeling prouder of myself than I should have when they did.

"You do that," she responded dryly, then looked toward the top of the steps. "Should we rejoin the party?"

Appreciating her effort to set us back on an even keel, I offered her my arm, satisfaction zinging through me when she took it without hesitation.

As we walked toward the steps, I was keenly aware of her fingers lightly gripping my bicep and the brush of her hand against my ribcage, happy for the moment just to have her by my side.

# Chapter 11

Bethany

As much as I hadn't wanted to go to the reception, I was glad I had. I hadn't made any significant connections for the clan, not that that was my job. What I *had* done was clear the air, at least a little bit, with Brody.

I was still a little embarrassed that my avoidance of him had been a lot less subtle than I'd hoped. I was glad he'd called me out on it. I couldn't believe I'd blurted out that I thought he was gorgeous and charming – my cheeks heated even now just thinking about it – but somehow it had helped. Not that Brody unsettled me any less than he had before, but the urge to run away from it – and him – had diminished. It had made the past week and half since the reception much less nerve-wracking than before.

I'd even gotten a little more comfortable sharing the gym with Brody most mornings. I ogled him as discreetly as possible when I got the chance, which I'd unfortunately missed that morning.

I hurried across the staff parking lot clutching my coffee in one hand and a bag of freshly baked cookies in the other, with my laptop bag and tote bag hanging from my shoulders. I noticed Brody up ahead of me near the front doors. I was a second away from calling out to him to please hold the door for me when he stopped and turned as if I had. It was then that I saw the woman with him – the redhead from the first day at the café.

I felt a pang of disappointment as I realized what that meant – he was involved with her after all. I'd known it was too much to hope that a man like Brody was single. Not that it was relevant to me. I couldn't let it be.

Curiosity filled me as I moved closer, wondering about the woman who had caught Brody's eye. She was cute – a little on the short side for a man Brody's height but who was I to say? – and her smile as they waited for me to catch up was friendly.

I returned Brody's "good morning" as I drew closer to them.

"Thanks for waiting for me." I held up the bag of cookies. "Impulse buy at the bakery this morning. I didn't think ahead to how I was going to open the door with my hands full."

"No problem at all," Brody replied smoothly as I followed the redhead into the building.

As soon as we were inside, she turned to me.

"You must be Bethany. I'm Lacey Torben. Brody's told me all about you. I hear you're doing a great job revamping the social media strategy for the clan's businesses."

The little spark that had jumped to life inside me when Lacey said that Brody had talked about me died a quick and unceremonious death.

Of course, he talked about me. We worked together. I didn't think I'd ever heard him mention Lacey's name but again, I was his co-worker. Not his girlfriend.

I ignored a niggle of disgruntlement at that thought as I answered Lacey.

"I haven't done much yet. I'm still getting the lay of the land." Still trying to get an idea of what exactly I was supposed to be doing, actually, but we didn't need to go into that. "That's nice of Brody to say, though."

"It might be nice but it's also true. You ready for the call with the construction team at nine?"

Strictly speaking, sitting in on calls updating progress on construction of the huts, or finances, or a host of other topics wasn't my core job, but it was giving me a good overall picture of the clan's businesses, so I jumped at the chance whenever I got it. Especially now that I'd stopped avoiding Brody whenever and however I could.

"I will be," I responded to Brody before turning back to Lacey. "Lacey, it was good to meet you."

As I headed to my office I watched out of the corner of my eye as Brody and Lacey paused at the bottom of the main stairs up to the residence. When Brody pulled Lacey close, I turned my head, feeling like a voyeur. There was no need for me to watch a co-worker kiss his girlfriend goodbye.

A few minutes before nine, Brody surprised me when he walked into my office and dropped into the chair near my desk.

"Okay if we take the call together in here?"

I waited a second in case there was more, like maybe a reason to take the call in my office rather than a conference room as we typically did, but nothing else was forthcoming.

"Fine with me," I agreed. It was different, but no big deal, I supposed. I waved to the half-empty bakery bag now sitting well out of my reach near the edge of my desk. "Have a cookie or five and save me from myself. I've had way too many and I'm realizing there's a reason I don't eat cookies for breakfast."

Brody shot me the grin I'd warned him about – the one that had my insides lighting up like a pinball machine.

"No, thanks. Lacey and I had donuts this morning, so I'm already working on my own sugar crash over here."

An unbidden image of the two of them in bed, a box of donuts resting between them as they kissed the sugar off each other's lips filled my mind before I quickly shoved it away.

*Not your business, Bethany*, I reminded myself. *Not your business and not your man.*

It was a relief when the call started.

Ninety minutes and a thousand construction-related details later, we were done. Brody stood and stretched his arms over his head, looking every bit the big cat that he was, while I finished scribbling a random note to distract myself from the peek of tan skin revealed at his waistline as the soft pullover he wore rode up a fraction with his motion.

"I'm glad you got a chance to meet Lacey this morning. She's been curious about you."

*Same, though not for the same reasons.*

"I'm glad I did, too," I responded honestly. "She seems nice."

"She's the best," he agreed, his eyes full of affection.

What would it be like to have a man whose expression looked like that when he talked about you? Lacey was a lucky woman.

"It's a shame she wasn't able to attend the reception with you the other night."

Yes, I was fishing. Like I said, I was curious, too.

"Yeah," Brody shrugged. "I guess she could have. It would have given her a chance to spend some time with Kyra. It was more of a business thing for the clan, though, so..."

I nodded as if I understood, though I wasn't sure what Brody meant. Girlfriends didn't belong at work events? Or maybe clan "things"?

I didn't get a chance to ask, not that I would have. I watched as Brody snagged the bakery bag and held it up with a questioning look.

"Please, take it. It's all yours."

"That's what I like to hear," Brody responded, shooting me a sexy smirk as he left, and leaving me to wonder – again – what exactly he meant.

# Chapter 12

Brody

As I walked toward Bethany's office a week later, that same swarm of butterflies that had hit me the night of the reception reappeared.

I had no reason to be so damn nervous. It wasn't as if I was about to ask Bethany out. It was no different than inviting her to go to the reception. Except that I'd been pissed when I'd done that, still smarting from the fact that Bethany had been avoiding me like the plague.

It hadn't occurred to me to be nervous about it then. Now...

*It's not a date. It's Friday happy hour with co-workers. Bethany's no different than anyone else you've mentioned it to today.*

That last one was a lie. I couldn't act like I believed that even in my own head. The other two things were true, though. This was no big deal.

*No big deal. Just a casual, low-key happy hour.*

I exhaled slowly, then stuck my head around the door to Bethany's office.

Her scent hit me like it always did when I was in her space. It was stronger here than anywhere else due to the amount of time she spent here. I'd even started dropping in for meetings in her office rather than in mine or a conference room, just to give me a chance to breathe her in. As a mountain lion, I wasn't as scent oriented as a bear shifter like Jackson or the wolf shifters in our region, but still, Bethany's scent drew me like no other ever had.

Bethany lifted her head just as I stepped in front of her doorway, and looked at me with tired, slightly glassy eyes. My nerves flipped to concern.

"You okay?"

She blinked her eyes wide a few times, exaggerating the movement, and nodded as she sat back in her chair.

"My eyeballs are about to fall out, but other than that, I'm fine. I've just spent way too much time today looking through images for the hiking service website and other social media."

She'd given me the perfect opening.

"Time to call it a week then. A group is heading out to happy hour. Everybody's been busting their butts with everything we have going on and we need a break. Rhyne is buying."

She looked at me, considering, and I gave her a nudge.

"It'll give you a chance to get to know everybody better. You don't have to stay long if you don't want to. Besides, I may be trained in mountain search and rescue and know advanced first aid, but if your eyeballs fall out, you're on your own."

Her lips quirked up into a momentary smile. Still quiet, she fiddled with a pen for a few seconds, then asked, "You're going?"

My chest tightened a little at her question. That made a difference to her?

"Wouldn't miss it," I confirmed, hoping that made her more likely to go, not less.

She fiddled for another second, then gave me the answer I wanted to hear.

"Okay," she straightened in her chair, stretching her back. "I can stop in for a bit. Thanks for letting me know."

Anticipation rushed through me as I gave her the address. "A bit" was better than nothing. I'd take whatever she gave me and see if maybe I could get her to give me just a little bit more.

• • • •

I WAS WATCHING FOR Bethany when she walked in the bar. I'd been there nearly 25 minutes by then and had started to wonder if she'd changed her mind and decided not to come. The way she hesitated when she walked in told me that she nearly had. That she'd debated with herself whether she could just go home or not. I was happier than I should have been that the side of her that had told her to show up had won.

I waved her over when I caught her eye and she started towards us. When a few of us had arrived earlier, we'd pulled together several tables into one large one. I'd discreetly saved the seat next to me for Bethany, casually draping my arm over the back of it like I was just being comfortable, not staking out my territory. The look Ingrid sent me when she'd noticed told me that she, at least, wasn't fooled, but I also knew she wouldn't say anything one way or another.

The server walked up next to me just as Bethany reached us and Bethany circled around to my side of the table to give her order. When the server moved on, I pulled out the seat next to me.

"Go ahead and take this one."

Bethany boosted herself up on the chair, then laughed a little as I gave her an assist, helping her scoot it closer to the high-top table where we sat.

"Did you have any trouble finding this place?"

I nudged a bowl of pretzels toward Bethany as she returned greetings and a few waves from some of the others seated at the long table or mingling around us.

"None at all. It was easy." She popped a pretzel in her mouth as she looked around. "This is a nice place. I haven't been here before."

I followed her gaze around the building that had once been a manufacturing facility. The huge space should have felt cavernous, but the owners had done a skilled job of making it feel inviting.

"It's owned by several members of our clan. It's not a clan business, per se, but we all try to support it."

"That's nice. Kind of like having a big family behind you."

She sounded so wistful, like that was missing from her life.

"The clan is very much like a family," I agreed. "All shifter groups are. Big, tightknit, sometimes dysfunctional families, complete with all the crazy characters you find in any family."

"Hmm," she murmured, noncommittal. I was about to follow up when Cason stepped up on her other side and asked us a question, drawing us into a discussion with a few people farther down the table. Bethany joined in, not saying a lot but making a comment here and there, laughing along with the group and seeming happy to be there.

Two hours later, our group had thinned out. Those of us who were left moved to a smaller high-top, freeing up seats for the growing Friday night dinner crowd. When Bethany noticed the time and started making noises about leaving, Ingrid did me a solid, persuading Bethany that she just had to stay for dinner and try the food. When Bethany relented, Ingrid sent me a subtle wink. Making a mental note to pick up flowers or chocolate or something for Ingrid on my way into the office Monday morning, I gave her a small nod of thanks.

We'd finished dinner and were standing by our table getting ready to leave, down to only a few stragglers in our group, when Bethany looked toward the entrance and jolted in surprise, her eyes flying open wide before she quickly schooled her expression.

Frowning, my back toward the door, I started to turn to see what had caught Bethany's expression. With a tiny squeak, Bethany latched onto my arm, preventing me from turning, only to jerk her hand back a second later.

"I'm sorry. I shouldn't haven't grabbed you like that." Bethany's cheeks were flushed, her eyes filled with concern. About what, I had no idea. "I just...um..." Bethany's words stalled out as she took a quick peek around me.

I faced her head on, no longer attempting to turn around.

"It's fine." I had zero objection to her touching me, but I was concerned about what the hell was happening. "What's going on, Bethany?"

"I...uh..." She closed her eyes and dipped her head, mumbling under her breath.

*"Of all the places they could have gone, they just had to come here."*

"Who?"

She looked up at me, eyes wide again, clearly surprised that I'd heard and understood what she'd said.

"Mountain lion hearing," I explained quickly, before returning to my question. "Who, Bethany? Who's here that you're so worried about?"

Bethany sighed. My concern deepened as she tugged me down to sit again at the high-top table we'd just vacated.

She stood in front of me, teeth worrying her bottom lip.

"Okay, I'll just say it. Brody, I'm sorry, but Lacey just walked in here with another man."

I couldn't have been more confused.

"Lacey's here. With a man," I repeated, wanting to be sure I'd heard her right.

I hadn't expected to see Lacey, but that didn't explain why Bethany would be worried about it.

"Yes, that's right. She hasn't noticed yet that you're here."

Was that supposed to be a good thing? I was still struggling to understand the problem.

"Is the man she's with big and dark, like you'd think a bear shifter would be, with a frown on his face?"

Bethany's forehead wrinkled with a frown of her own as she focused over my shoulder, presumably watching Lacey.

"Yes. Have you seen him before?"

"Of course. That's Lacey's mate, Jackson. I've known him for years."

Bethany's startled eyes swung back to my face.

"Her mate? As in husband?"

"That, too, yeah."

Staying seated, I swung my head around to look and sure enough, Lacey and Jackson were sitting side-by-side at the bar, Lacey tucked right up against Jackson where he liked her best.

I turned back to Bethany.

"They're probably meeting Rhyne and Kyra here for dinner. Even Jackson, grumpy asshole that he is, likes this place."

"But..." Bethany shook her head as she continued to frown, obviously the confused one now.

Then she looked at me, thoroughly puzzled, her next words sending my brain spinning again.

"She's your girlfriend. Your girlfriend is mated to someone else?"

"My *girlfriend*?" What the...where had she gotten that? "Lacey's my best friend, not my girlfriend."

"But you kissed her."

"No." My denial was swift and decisive. "Never have, never will."

"You did! That morning I met her. At the bottom of the staircase. You stopped and kissed her."

Interesting. Good to know she'd been watching though she'd obviously missed something.

"I hugged her. We do that all the time. If I walk over to her right now, she'll hug me in front of Jackson, and he won't think anything of it."

Bethany looked unconvinced.

"Why did you think she was my girlfriend? Because of that morning you met her?"

"That and the day at the café. I thought...I figured you were with either her or Kyra and when I realized it wasn't Kyra, I assumed...I just assumed."

Understanding dawned. I thought of the way she'd looked at me, the way we'd connected, then her refusal to look at me after Lacey and Kyra arrived.

"You thought I was with flirting with you until my girlfriend showed up." Flirting was a very pale description of the searing, soul-deep look we'd shared.

"I did." Bethany sighed. "I told you I'm not used to men like you. I didn't know what to think, really. Then I got to know you a little better..."

Taking a chance, I reached out and brushed my fingertips across the back of her hand, wanting the zing of the contact, needing her to focus only on me.

"You're right, you didn't know me. I promise you this – I'm not a cheater. I would never cheat on anyone I'm with and would have less than zero interest in a woman who was doing so. There's no one I'm seeing right now."

There was someone I *wanted* to see but I wasn't going to push it. Not tonight. She'd spent way more time with me tonight than I'd hoped, sitting right by my side the whole time. As much as I didn't want to, I needed to let that be enough for now.

"And hey, thanks for watching out for me. I appreciate it."

"I didn't..."

I cut Bethany off, not wanting to hear her dismiss what she'd done.

"You did. You saw something you thought would be tough for me and you had my back. Literally."

Bethany responded to my smile with a small one of her own. It wasn't the full, gorgeous smile she'd given Gregory, but it was real, and it was for me.

"You're welcome. I'm glad it wasn't what I thought it was."

"Me, too."

Bethany took a deep breath and stepped back. I stood, knowing she was about to say her good-byes and wanting to prolong things if I could.

"You want to head over and say hello? Lacey'd be glad to see you again and you could meet Jackson."

Lacey would also blow up my phone the second I left, digging for details about why I was here with Bethany, and how things had gone, and when I was seeing her again, but I could take it. I'd learned long ago that Lacey's love language was being curious enough to kill untold numbers of cats.

Bethany seemed to consider it for a second before shaking her head.

"You go ahead. I'm a little peopled out, so I'm just going to head out. You have a good weekend."

"I'd feel better if I walked you out to your car." I held my hands up in self-defense at her look. "I know you're perfectly capable of walking there by yourself, but it's probably getting dark out. You had my back; let me have yours."

She waffled, then relented.

"When you put it that way, it doesn't seem fair to say no."

"It's not," I agreed and was rewarded with another glimmer of a smile.

After assuring Bethany that Lacey and Jackson wouldn't be mad at me for not stopping, we headed out the front door. It wasn't dark yet, but it was getting there. The lights in the lot were on, but I was glad I was at Bethany's side.

When we reached her car – the practical, gray, 4-door sedan I was familiar with from the parking lot at the office – she unlocked it, then turned to face me.

"Thanks, Brody."

Something about the way she said it made it seem like she was thanking me for more than the unneeded escort to her car.

"For what?" I questioned, knowing it would drive me crazy wondering if I didn't.

"For putting up with how nervous I've been. For helping me get settled in at work. For introducing me to people and telling me about things like the reception and the happy hour tonight. For guarding me against the unknown dangers of a well-lit parking lot."

The spark of amusement in her beautiful brown eyes as she said the last one made me want to push her up against her car and kiss her until she was clinging to me, my hands tangled in her hair and her body pressed against mine.

When Bethany drew in a sudden little breath, I realized my thoughts must have shown in my eyes as I looked back at her.

Going for casual, I pushed my hands in my pockets as I took half a step back.

"You're welcome for all of it. It's been my pleasure."

If I had my way, there would be a lot more to come, but we'd get to that.

She edged her door open, then stood there, looking up at me.

"See you Monday?"

I was starting to think maybe she didn't want to leave any more than I wanted her to go.

"Definitely. Looking forward to it," I responded, hoping she heard even a fraction of what I was saying.

She took another careful breath, eyes still on mine, then nodded.

"Okay. Good night."

I returned her good night as she climbed in her car and let me shut the door for her. I stayed where I was as she pulled on her seat-belt and started the car, then with a cute little wave, drove away.

I watched her until I couldn't see her taillights anymore, then turned and walked to my truck, hoping someday soon I wouldn't be going one direction while she went the other.

# Chapter 13

Bethany

I woke Saturday morning to the chime of an incoming text message. I groaned and rolled over on my air mattress, groping across the floor next to it for my phone. It chimed again as I lifted it up and squinted at it, nearly dropping it again when I saw the texts were from Brody.

I sat up, nearly holding my breath as I tapped the first message to open it.

I was greeted by image after image of a stunning sunrise in the mountains, the beautiful colors growing and shadows receding as the minutes passed. They were breathtaking and I felt tears well up in my eyes just looking at them.

They were followed by other images – a blue and white bird on a slim branch dripping with dew, a tiny lavender flower in a field, an empty trail with a canopy of branches stretched overhead. They were gorgeous, each and every one of them worthy of being framed and displayed.

Then there were the messages.

*Brody: Here are some images to add to the ones you were looking through yesterday. I hope they don't make your eyeballs fall out.*

I laughed as I scanned down to his next message.

*Brody: I just realized what time it is. Sorry if I woke you. Hope you're a morning person.*

I wasn't, especially on the weekend when I could sleep in, but somehow, I didn't care.

*Me: They're beautiful. Where are you?*

Brody must have been watching for my response because he messaged back right away.

*Brody: The sunrise was from one of my favorite spots along the north ridge. The rest are from farther along the trail where the first hut is located.*

Before I could respond he texted again.

*Brody: Did I wake you?*

I debated, then decided to be honest.

*Me: You did, but it's okay.*

The dots popped up and danced as I waited to see what he would say.

*Brody: Dammit, I'm sorry. I've been out since before dawn and I wasn't thinking. I owe you coffee Monday to make up for it.*

He was hiking, before dawn, on a Saturday, for the fun of it? Better him than me.

*Me: No, really. It's fine.*

*Brody: It's not fine. How do you like your coffee?*

*Me: Brody.*

*Brody: Bethany.*

*Brody: I'm bringing you coffee one way or another. You might as well tell me what you want so I don't buy 5 different kinds trying to guess.*

I had the feeling he'd do it, too. Stubborn man.

*Me: I usually get an Americano.*

*Brody: Done. Should I leave you alone now so you can go back to sleep?*

*Me: No, I'm awake.*

It was a few minutes before Brody texted me back. When he did, it was an image of a huge spider web, the sunlight turning the dew to diamonds scattered across its surface.

*Me: I never thought I'd say this but that's an amazing spider web.*

*Brody: Beauty's all around you out here. Got big plans for the day?*

Brody was unlike any other man I'd ever known. Not that I'd known many – my mom had made sure of that – but how many stopped and noticed the beauty of dew on a spider web?

I thought about how to answer Brody's question. I could simply respond, or I could have some fun.

*Me: Absolutely. First, I plan to tour several exciting local sites, gathering goods along the way. When I return, I'll spend the rest of my day engaged in the domestic art of textile cleansing.*

There, let's see what he thought of that.

I waited nervously while the dots danced, disappeared, then danced again.

Was my response fun, as I'd intended, or just plain weird? I wasn't sure. Maybe both?

*Brody: So, you have shopping to do, then you're doing laundry.*

I grinned as I messaged back.

*Me: Well, if you want to make it sound boring, then yes, shopping and laundry. You?*

It took him a minute to reply.

*Brody: Today, nothing but hiking. This evening, though...I'm spending this evening with a beautiful, blue-eyed girl who loves to dance and look at the stars, who looks at me like I hung the moon and never fails to make me smile.*

I frowned at my phone as I read his response. He had a date? Why would he tell me that? I didn't want to hear about him looking at the stars with...

I stopped myself, thinking about how I'd responded and reading his response again before texting back.

*Me: You're babysitting Lexi?*

Once again, I waited nervously.

*Please let me be right.*

My shoulders slumped with relief as Brody's response popped up.

*Brody: Got it in one. Lacey's pissed because it's her turn, but she and Jackson have something tonight, too, so Lexi's all mine. She likes me best anyway.*

*Me: Of course, she does.*

What female in their right mind wouldn't? I mean, Lacey seemed nice, but come on.

I could have texted with Brody all day – which surprised me – but I felt bad about keeping him from his hike, even if he'd been the one to text me first.

*Me: Since I'm up, I'm going to try to hit those exciting local sites early and beat the crowds. More time for the domestic arts that way.*

*Brody: You have fun with that.*

*Me: You enjoy your hike and have a wonderful time with that beautiful baby girl.*

*Brody: Always do. Sorry again for the unplanned wake-up call. See you Monday.*

I set my phone down, pushed myself up off the air mattress and headed for the shower, realizing as I did that I was smiling.

It may not have been the way I'd planned to start my day, but I had to say – it had turned out even better.

# Chapter 14

Brody

I hadn't had any reason to message Bethany over the weekend, not a work-related one anyway. I'd sat there watching the sunrise and thinking about her, taking a few pictures like I usually did when I was hiking. Before I'd thought about it, I'd sent them to her, for no other reason than that I wanted to share the experience with her.

It wasn't until I'd hit send that it hit me how personal that was. I'd been able to save a little face by tying it to what she'd been working on on Friday, though it was flimsy if she thought about it too much. Then I'd realized how early it was and felt like a complete idiot. Luckily, she seemed to have taken it in stride.

Between the happy hour Friday night and our brief text conversation Saturday morning, I'd enjoyed myself more with Bethany this past weekend than I had with any of the women I'd dated. Whether that was more a commentary about Bethany or about the sad state of my past few relationships, I didn't know, but my money was on Bethany.

I'd liked her when she was doing everything in her power to avoid me, as fucked up as that was. Now that we were in a better place I more than liked her. The satisfaction I'd felt buying coffee for her that morning, knowing what she liked and being the one to get it for her, had been over the top. You'd have thought I'd hunted and killed a prize deer and dragged it to her doorway. Even now, the thought of that didn't sound half as crazy as it should have.

There was something about Bethany. I liked women, loved them even. I enjoyed being with them and around them. But Bethany was in a class all her own. No other woman had ever made me wish she were with me while I watched a sunrise or tapped so hard into my need to protect and provide.

Just like none had ever made my mountain lion sit up and take notice whenever she was around.

Like now – I knew the second she stepped through the front door of the building, even though I was in my office. I listened to the sound of her footsteps getting closer as she walked. I made myself wait as she opened her office door and put her things inside, then turned to face my door a few seconds before she stepped into my open doorway.

"Good morning."

Her smile was a little nervous this morning. I leaned back in my chair casually, hoping to set her at ease.

"Hey. Good morning. How was the gathering and textile cleansing?"

She relaxed a little, her shoulders dropping a fraction.

"About as fun as you'd expect. How was your evening with Lexi?"

I grinned thinking about listening to Lexi giggle and watching her get her dinner everywhere but in her mouth.

"About as fun as you'd expect," I echoed.

"I think you win," Bethany said wryly.

"No contest," I agreed, then remembered the stop I'd made that morning. "That's your Americano right there by the way." I nodded to the white cup sitting near the corner of my desk.

"You shouldn't have," Bethany said, even as she stepped forward to pick it up. "But I'm glad you did. I didn't have time to stop this morning."

"No problem." I watched as she took her first sip and closed her eyes in pleasure, hoping I'd get a chance someday to put that same look on her face in a much more hands on way.

"This is perfect." She opened her eyes and looked at the logo on the cup. "I'll have to try this place." Then she switched her gaze to me, her head tilted a little in question. "Do you have a minute?"

"I do, yeah." Even if I didn't, I'd make time. "You want to sit?"

She lowered herself into one of the chairs in front of my desk and sat, her coffee cradled in both hands. I waited, giving her time to gather her thoughts.

"So...I'm not sure what I think of this idea, and I haven't really thought it through. It just kind of popped into my head, but...I don't know if it even makes sense. I mean, it might. It could be the perfect thing, I just..." She looked at me and sort stammered to a halt, then... "I was just thinking..."

When she paused again, I gave her a gentle nudge.

"Not the easiest thing to do on a Monday morning before having your coffee."

"Apparently not," she responded, her self-deprecating smile telling me she appreciated the assist. She straightened a little and went on. "The images you sent me Saturday made me think. I spent hours Friday going through the image files we have, and nothing caught my eye. Don't get me wrong. Everything in there is good, it just all feels a little impersonal."

"You have a good eye," I told her, impressed. "Most of the images, maybe all of them, are stock photos we licensed. I don't think much of anything in there is custom."

"That makes sense then. The ones you sent me had a completely different feel. It got me thinking..." she sat forward in her chair as her eyes lit with interest. "You offered to show me a couple of the shorter trails. Would you be willing to take me up to the first hut instead? I know it won't be as easy, but I think it would really help me with content if I could experience it myself."

Her request surprised me a little, but I did my best not to let that show as I thought about it. With an inexperienced hiker like Bethany, I estimated that the round trip up and back to the first hut would take about six hours. Would I be willing to spend six hours doing something I loved with a woman I couldn't stop thinking about, just the two of us, sharing some of my favorite spots with her and watching her face light up?

Where did I sign?

*Slow your roll, Brody,* I cautioned myself. *She may not realize what she's getting herself into.*

"It'll be about six hours total up and back. The hut sits just off the Horizon Trail. The elevation isn't too bad overall but there are a couple of challenging spots. You can do it – I wouldn't agree if I wasn't confident of that – but are you sure you want to?"

Bethany was nodding even before I'd stopped talking.

"I do. If you'll take me, I want to go."

How bad was it that hearing her say the words "take me", even in this context, gave me a charge? And the fact that she wasn't just asking to go, she was asking to go with me?

There was no way I could say no to that.

"Let's pick a date, then, and get you out on the trail."

# Chapter 15

Bethany

"Hiking socks, two pairs."

"Check."

I put a check next to the item and read off the next one to Andi. "Multi-tool."

"What the heck is multi-tool?"

Andi scanned the items laid across my bedspread, her face screwed up in confusion.

"That thing." I pointed to the small gray and black case Brody had given me the day before. "It's in there."

"If you say so. Check then, I guess." She turned to look at me, hands on hips, her expression doubtful. "Are you sure you want to do this? There has to be an easier way to get this guy's attention than taking a six-mile hike with him."

"Six-*hour* hike," I corrected her.

She threw up her hands and plopped down next to me.

"That's even crazier! I haven't met a guy yet who I'd walk six hours for."

"You're hanging around the wrong guys, then."

"Believe me, that's not news."

She lay back, drawing her knees up and stacking her hands on her stomach. I located the next item on my list and checked it off.

"Besides, I'm not doing it for him. I'm doing it for my job." And if it came with the added benefit of spending a few hours with a man who was taking up an increasing amount of space in my brain, well, yay for me.

Andi rolled her head to look at me.

"They can't make you do it, you know. Just tell them you have allergies or something and you can't be outside that long."

I checked off another item before pausing to look back at her.

"It was my idea."

"You're batty."

I couldn't help but laugh at Andi's unfiltered assessment.

"Believe me, *that's* not news. Are you laying on my shirt?"

Andi arched up, shoved a hand under her back, pulled out a wad of fabric, and held it up.

"One shirt. Check."

"One seriously wrinkled shirt."

I shook my head as I checked off the last item. It didn't really matter if the shirt was wrinkled; it would be rolled up in my backpack for hours, anyway. Most likely I wouldn't even wear it. Most of the things on the list were for "just in case". The odds that I'd need any of them on my hike the next day with Brody were slim, but you should never hit the trail unprepared. You just never knew what might happen. Granted it was much more stuff than I'd ever taken with me when I'd hiked before, but none of my "glorified walks" had been this long, either. Brody and I were also using the list that the hiking service would be providing to its clients, so that was giving me another window into their experience.

I gathered the items, tossed them into the backpack Brody had lent me, and set it next to my hiking shoes by the wall. I'd pack it more neatly in the morning and add in my water bottle and protein bars before I left to meet Brody.

"You sure you're safe with this guy?" Andi questioned from her spot on my floor. "I know he's a hottie, but hotties can also be psychos."

I dropped onto my air mattress and curled my legs under me.

The weird thing was, I did feel safe with him. I could almost hear my mom screaming at me not to let down my guard, but more and more with Brody I wanted to. Besides all that, it wasn't like he was a stranger.

"I work with him, Andi. It's not like he's some guy I picked up in a bar."

"Psychos can have jobs, too. At least the high functioning ones. Then somebody disappears and the police come knocking and all the neighbors talk about how normal the guy seemed and how he went off to his job in accounting or sales or whatever every day just like everybody else."

I eyed her, a little concerned.

"How do you know all this?"

"True crime shows," she said matter-of-factly as she sat up and pulled her phone from her pocket. "You should tell me everything you know about Brody. I'll be your backup. It's not like you have any family to report you missing if you don't come home. I hate my dad and brother, but at least they'd probably tell somebody if I went poof."

I ignored the twist in my chest at Andi's words. She hadn't meant them to be hurtful. Now that my mom was gone, I had no one, not even family I hated. Even if I found Rafe, he wasn't really my family, and it was just as likely he'd want nothing to do with me.

And Andi was right. It was best to be cautious. Even though it probably wasn't needed and reminded me uncomfortably of the type of conversations I'd had with my mom in the past, I was touched that Andi was looking out for me.

I gave her all the info I could think of, including the trail we planned to take and when I should be back, while she noted it in her phone.

"Ok, good. I've got it all down." She nodded in satisfaction and closed the notes app on her phone. "Make sure you tell Brody you told me all that, so he knows he has to bring you back. They love it when no one is waiting at home for you."

Not sure how to respond to that, I just assured her that I would.

She stood and stretched, looking at her phone again to check the time.

"I've gotta get a shower and get ready. You're sure you don't want to come?"

Andi was meeting a couple other people from her shifter group – a "sounder" she'd called it – at a club somewhere and had invited me to tag along.

"I'm sure. I appreciate the invitation but I think I should have an early night so I can be ready for tomorrow."

Brody and I weren't leaving that early – a little later than we'd typically start our workday, actually – but it was a convenient excuse to stay in. Andi was only a few years younger than me, but at 22 she was far more of a party girl than I'd ever been. Honestly, that bar was pretty low, though.

"Alright, then. I'll be at work when you get home tomorrow, so text me, okay? Have fun."

I promised her I would, then locked the door behind her.

There was no question that Andi and I were more different than we were alike, and the way her mind worked was sometimes a mystery to me. Still, getting to know people, and getting to let them know me a little, was new to me. However different Andi and I were, I was glad to have her as a friend.

# Chapter 16

Bethany

When I pulled into the parking lot at work the next morning, Brody was waiting for me, leaning against the back of his truck, thumbing through his phone, looking like an ad for men's hiking gear. The kind of ad that makes you take up hiking just to see if you can find a guy like that wandering around on the trails. The kind of ad that women clip out of a magazine and pin to their inspiration board because if that's not inspiring, nothing is.

He was wearing a long-sleeve sun shirt that matched his turquoise eyes, dark gray hiking shorts and well-worn hiking books. A black ball cap with the logo of the clan's lumber business on the front shaded his eyes and his pack sat next to him on the ground.

The second he saw me he pocketed his phone and stepped away from his truck, sending me a gorgeous smile, while I focused hard on parking without hitting anything. I turned off my car, gave myself time for one last deep breath to calm my nerves, then climbed out to meet him.

"Morning, Bethany. Ready for this?"

I had to smile at the enthusiasm in Brody's voice.

"Someone certainly is," I teased, leaning into my back seat to grab my pack.

"I am," Brody agreed, rubbing his hands together, not daunted in the least. "We've got a beautiful day, and I've got a, uh..." Brody hesitated, then coughed and went on... "a chance to show off all the cool stuff we're planning, so yeah, I'm looking forward to the day."

Almost certain that second part wasn't what he'd been about to say, I let it go.

"Me, too," I agreed. "A little nervous I'll slow you down, but excited to see everything."

Brody waved my concern away.

"There's no slowing anybody down today and we're not in a hurry. Besides, I've seen you burn up the miles walking on the treadmill, with an incline no less." His gaze flicked to my legs, encased in my favorite hiking shorts, then back, his eyes seeming a little darker as they met mine. "You'll be just fine."

Something about the way he said it...my pulse jumped a little, bumping up even faster when Brody's gaze swung to the pulse point in my neck, fixating on it like he could hear my now racing heart. We stood suspended like that, seconds passing, until Brody stepped back, eyes now fixed on the ground as he cleared his throat.

When he looked back up at me, all evidence of whatever had arced between us was gone and his friendly smile was back in place.

"I thought we'd leave my truck and your car here and drive over to the trailhead in one of the work vehicles. We can hit a drive thru on the way if you want to grab some coffee."

"Works for me," I agreed and followed Brody to a nearby SUV. "Though we can skip the coffee unless you want some."

Brody grabbed his things while I got settled in my seat, then we headed to the trailhead. We decided to forego coffee and pulled into the trailhead parking lot just after 9am. We'd chosen to do our hike on a weekday – in this case, a Thursday – because the trail should be less busy, and I was glad to see our vehicle was the only one in the lot. That didn't mean we wouldn't encounter other hikers, but they should be fewer and farther between.

Brody and I checked our packs and water bottles, then headed out on the trail. We started out across a meadow, dotted here and there with tiny yellow and lavender flowers.

"Is this where the picture of the flower you sent me is from?"

Brody paused a second as if he was thinking, then smiled as he nodded. "Yeah, it's here somewhere."

"Perfect." I looked across the meadow, thinking of the image, knowing if I used it at some point, I'd think of standing right in this spot.

"I'm pretty sure it's actually a weed, not a flower."

I echoed Brody's shrug with one of my own.

"Looks like a flower to me."

"Me, too."

After that, I stayed quiet for a bit as we walked, enjoying the sunshine and the view, which admittedly included the man walking in front of me. Eventually we left the meadow and started up into the wooded area.

Brody explained a few things as we went, mentioning the extent of the clan's lands and where they planned to focus the guided hikes and also open up additional space to overnight campers.

His explanation piqued my curiosity.

"Can I ask a shifter question?"

"A 'shifter question'?" Brody grinned at me over his shoulder. "Go for it. You can ask me anything."

I tucked that response away for later and asked my question.

"You were just talking about the clan's lands. This might sound strange, but how do you know they're yours?" Brody shot me a puzzled look, so I tried to explain. "What I mean is, there are a lot of different shifter groups in this region. Some of your land must intersect with some of theirs. It has to, given the amount of land your clan holds. I know not all shifter groups claim land or territory in the same way you and the bears and wolves do, for example, but there must be some overlap."

"There is," he agreed. "The boundaries are passed down, so everybody knows them well. Our biggest areas of overlap are with the eagles and with Jackson's bear pack, and to a smaller extent, with about half a dozen others. There's usually no issue. Most of the groups have been here for generations and co-exist with no issues. The only conflict I've ever seen was the recent one caused by a wild boar sounder that moved into the region last year and started raising hell."

That term – "sounder" – that was how Andi had referred to her group. I wondered if it was the same group Brody was talking about.

"What happened to them?"

"They've been keeping to themselves, but they're still around. You might run into some of them in town. It's not a problem that they moved into this region, per se – it's not like there's an existing wild boar sounder that has a right to object – it's the way they did it that was the issue. We're still not sure if it was just a few out of control members who caused all the issues, or if there's something off about the whole group, but most of the shifter community is still wary of them."

"I can see why," I murmured, thinking. "So, no other mountain lion clan has ever tried to move into this region?"

Brody shrugged as he continued walking.

"Not in my lifetime. At least not in the way I think you mean. Our clan is large and dominant. There are several smaller clans who have essentially merged into ours – even a few from different regions – but no one has been unwise enough to challenge our alpha in generations, if then."

Brody paused as we reached the edge of a stream.

"This is one of the spots I told you about that can be a little challenging. It's not bad right now since the water level is moderate, but we'll still need to watch our footing. If you want to go upstream a little ways, there's a small land bridge that crosses part way and makes it a little easier. What do you think?"

I looked across to the other side of the stream, thinking over the options. It wasn't deep; the worst thing that would happen if I slipped off the rocks while crossing was I'd get a little wet and my pride would be a little bruised.

"Let's cross here."

Brody's eyes gleamed with satisfaction at my response.

"Perfect. There's a great spot right up here that we'd miss if we went the other way, but I didn't want to influence you one way or another."

Brody pointed out the best route to get across, then went first as I watched him carefully. Not letting myself overthink it, I started out right after him. With the exception of one spot where his long legs had given him a distinct advantage and I had to take a small leap of faith from one rock to the other, I made it without incident.

I was rewarded soon after when we came around a bend in the trail to see nearly the full length of the stream we'd just crossed stretched out behind us. From this vantage point we could see the way the water tumbled over the rocks in its path, and the play of light and shadow on its surface as the sun streamed through the branches of the trees overhead. As I stood and took it in, hearing only the rush of the water and the rustle of the breeze through the leaves, and feeling the presence of the man beside me, I felt something open inside me that had been closed off for a long time. I didn't examine it too closely – didn't want to spoil the moment by dissecting it – instead just enjoyed the feeling of being able to simply breathe for the first time in forever.

Quietly I slipped my phone from my pocket and took image after image, knowing they wouldn't fully capture the magic of the spot, but also knowing that I had to try. Minutes later, when I zipped my phone back in its spot, I looked up at Brody to find him watching me, that same satisfaction from earlier along with a touch of something else I couldn't decipher in his eyes.

After a few seconds, he broke eye contact, turning his head to take in the view.

"This is one of my favorite spots." His soft words felt weighty, like he'd shared a deeply personal part of himself with me by saying them.

"I can understand why," I returned, my voice equally hushed. He turned to look at me again, his eyes intense and I nodded slowly, not really knowing why, only wanting to acknowledge that whatever was in the air between us in that moment, I felt it, too.

Finally, Brody turned, leading our way up the trail again, and I followed, knowing that something between us had just changed. Time passed as we followed the trail up and around, leveling off in spots, climbing or descending a little in others, passing in and out of wooded areas and across hillsides. Brody pointed things out as we went along, patiently answering my questions and pausing while I took photos.

It was during one of my many times doing so that my stomach growled loudly, making me jump and Brody laugh.

"Sounds like you're ready for lunch."

I looked at my watch, surprised to see that it was already a little after 11am.

"I guess I am."

"Okay, then, decision point again. I was originally thinking we could eat once we got to the hut, but that's an hour or so away. A possible plan B is there's a good spot about 20 minutes from here off a short side trail. It's nice and flat with a view most people don't get to see because you kind of have to know it's there. It'll add an hour or so to our overall time, though, so I'll leave it up to you."

"Plan B," I responded without hesitation. "I want to see all the best spots while you're here to show them to me. As long as you don't mind taking the extra time."

Brody spread his arms wide with a smile.

"I'm all yours for the day."

And my, didn't that sound a little too nice.

By the time we reached the spot Brody had mentioned my stomach had set up a constant commentary about the fact that I wasn't meeting its demands. When Brody pulled a stuffed cooler bag out of his backpack and started setting out its contents – pita bread, hummus, smoked turkey, veggies, olives, pickles, and dense chocolate cookies, along with two sports drinks – I could have hugged him.

We made our pita sandwiches then sat looking at the pretty little valley spread out below us. I looked over at Brody and he just looked so right in that spot that I spoke without thinking.

"You love it out here, don't you?"

Brody glanced back at me with a small smile, then looked back at the view.

"I do, yeah. I've been hiking since I was a kid. I try to come out at least every couple of weeks. It centers me in a way. My mom used to say it got my head back on straight and she's right."

"Moms usually are," I said, giving the expected response, although I didn't know that I believed it. I'd wondered most of my life if my mom was right about some fundamental things. I was finally so close to finding some answers and, if I was being honest, hoping with everything in me that "mom's always right" turned out to be a fallacy in my case.

And now wasn't the time to think about any of that.

I helped Brody gather our garbage, then took the opportunity to take a few photos as he packed up our leftovers. I noticed that the once clear sky now featured a few heavy looking clouds, a somewhat dramatic effect that I hoped my pictures would capture. When I mentioned it to Brody, he scanned the sky with a slight frown.

"It looks like we might get some rain. It wasn't in the forecast for today, but up here things can be unpredictable."

I shrugged, unconcerned. We both had rain jackets with us to protect us from the worst of it. So what if we got a little wet?

The drizzle started when we were about a half mile from the hut. We picked up our pace and reached the hut just as the drizzle turned into a steady rainfall. We stood on the tiny, covered porch of the wood structure and shook ourselves off the best we could.

"Hopefully it'll blow over before long. In the meantime, welcome to hut number one."

Once we stepped inside, the tour didn't take long. The space made me think of a small, bare bones, studio apartment. It was one room, with space for what Brody mentioned would be half dozen or so cots. The metal frame of one cot leaned against the wall, looking less than comfortable to my inexperienced eye, but what did I know? A simple table with benches was built into one wall next to a tiny kitchen, and two sturdy-looking lockers provided what Brody described as "pissed off bear"- proof food storage. There were also two propane stove burners, a propane heater, and a solar operated ceiling fan, none of which were hooked up yet, and a cistern-fed sink that was. A small outbuilding housed a composting toilet, completing the set up.

I stood in the middle of the space, taking it in. It was basic, no question, but the wood smelled fresh and the windows on either side would provide a nice breeze and plenty of daylight when it wasn't raining. Camping in general wasn't my thing, but with the hut I could see the attraction.

I shared my thoughts with Brody as he lounged, arms crossed, his hip resting against the kitchen counter.

"That's what we're banking on. It's a lot less hassle to hike hut to hut or use a hut as a base for day hikes, than it is to carry overnight gear with you. There will always be people who want to tent camp, and there will be plenty of opportunity for them to do that, but for those who that doesn't appeal to, we're hoping they'll give the huts a chance."

I took a bunch of photos, noting as I did that not only didn't the rain seem to be slowing, it seemed to be coming down harder.

I must have looked worried, because Brody walked over to join me.

"It's going to be a messy hike back. Sorry about that."

I couldn't help but smile at his regretful tone.

"The next time you order up the weather I'll expect you to do better, but just this once I'll give you a pass."

"Noted," he returned, playing along. "I don't mind hiking in the rain, but a downpour is no fun."

We delayed a little longer, still hoping the rain would let up, before Brody reluctantly said it was time to go.

"It's going to be slow going and we don't want to lose whatever daylight there is."

We were pulling out our rain jackets, knowing full well we would still be soaked through before long, when Brody's pack began to ring. He pulled his phone out and answered it, and I realized it was Cason. When Brody looked at me again, I knew we weren't going anywhere soon.

# Chapter 17

Brody

I could see on Bethany's face that she could read whatever was on mine.

Not that I was going to be able to hide the news from her. It wasn't like she'd miss the fact that we weren't leaving the hut right then.

I switched to speaker so Cason could tell both of us what was going on.

"I put you on speaker, Cason. Bethany is here, too."

"Okay, that's fine." Cason, being Cason, didn't waste words. "You got to hut one, right?"

"Yeah, we're here." At least I'd done that right today.

"Good. That's good. You're gonna want to sit tight right there for a bit. We've got a small slide on the lower part of Horizon." Bethany looked at me, puzzled. I mouthed "rockslide" to her, and her expression cleared as she nodded that she understood. "We're gonna try and get it cleared quick for you. You got headlamps?"

I did; Bethany didn't. Not unless she'd brought one of her own, which was doubtful given that we'd planned on a daylight hike.

"One. And flashlights."

Cason grunted in acknowledgement.

"Good," he said again. "You're gonna need 'em. I'll let you know when the trail's clear enough you can set out."

We said our goodbyes and I disconnected, not wanting to look at Bethany, knowing everything Cason had refrained from saying. Bethany and I had several hard hours of hiking ahead of us. Unless we got very lucky and Cason and his team cleared the rockslide at lightning speed, part of that hike would be in the dark. Night hiking in the rain was treacherous at best. The only thing in our favor was that we weren't on a difficult trail. It would be doable, but just.

Whatever was going through her head, Bethany seemed to be taking the delay better than I was.

"So...we just wait now, right?"

"Yeah." I scrubbed my hand over my hair, wishing I could think of a way out of this. "We wait."

Bethany headed for the table, pulling her phone from her pocket as she walked.

"Do you want to help me sort through the pictures I took to-day?"

Glad for something to take both our minds off the wait, I joined her. She slid over on the bench she sat on, making room for me to sit next to her rather than across from her.

"It's easier for both of us to see the pictures this way."

I couldn't have agreed more, enjoying the barest touch of her leg against mine as a bonus. She scrolled through image after image, each one better than the last, capturing different angles and light, turning views I'd seen a hundred times into something interesting and new.

"You have a gift, Bethany."

I loved it when she blushed like she was now, her cheeks pinking up as she dipped her head. I'd love it even more if I could brush my lips across the soft spot just behind her ear, wisps of hair escaping her ponytail, enticing me to see if it was as silky as it looked and maybe make her blush deepen in the process.

"It's just that it's so beautiful out here. The pictures practically take themselves."

"I'll agree to disagree with you on that. I'll just say you have a ca-reer as a photographer if you ever decide to ditch the whole social media thing. Not that I hope you do that any time soon."

Now Bethany did flush more, but not for the reason I'd hoped, stiffening a little as she pulled away a fraction, putting just a little more space between us.

Before I had time to think about her reaction, my phone rang again. Bethany's expression lit with hope, but when I checked the time, I knew it couldn't be good news. Less than an hour had passed, not nearly enough time for the team to clear even a small slide.

Not wanting to be the one to burst Bethany's bubble, I answered and put it on speaker again.

"Hey, Cason. You're on speaker."

"Alright, well, sorry to say it but all the news I've got is bad." I heard Bethany's soft exhale and knew that the bubble was officially gone. "We have a report of another slide right where Horizon intersects Stable Falls. It sounds like it's impacting both of 'em, but we won't know until somebody can get up there to assess the situation."

Which may not happen until the morning if the rain didn't clear up. Even if it did, the trail wouldn't be cleared tonight.

There was no way around it. Bethany didn't know it yet, but she and I were stuck right where we were for the night.

"Okay, thanks for the update, Cason."

"You kids okay? Got water and food and all?"

Cason wasn't worried about me; he was worried about Bethany. He'd seen me in far rougher conditions during rescue operations. I might have been offended that he thought I wasn't taking care of her, but I knew that wasn't what this was. If anything, I think she reminded him of his daughter.

"We're okay." I looked over at Bethany, checking with her, and she nodded in agreement. "Is there anybody else on the mountain that you know of?"

If there was a chance of anyone else needing to stay in the hut with us, I wanted to know.

"Group of four, all adults. They're how we knew about the second slide, saw it on their way down. They're holed up in the cave right near Stable Falls and checked in as okay for overnight."

It sounded like an experienced group. They'd known enough to call in the rockslide and had been smart enough to take shelter rather than trying to hike out.

"Thank God this isn't the weekend, or we'd have people everywhere."

I agreed with Cason, then signed off, knowing he'd update us when he could.

"Unless I completely misunderstood that entire phone call, we're here for the night, right?"

I reluctantly faced Bethany, wondering how I could make this better for her.

"We're here for the night," I confirmed. "We probably were anyway with the first slide, but with the second one, plus the fact that it's still raining like it's the end times, yeah, we're not going anywhere. If we had a medical emergency or were in some kind of danger, Cason would send a team up after us, but as it is...I'm sorry, Bethany."

"It's okay. It's not worth risking anybody being injured." She sat down at the table, her expression thoughtful as she set her backpack on the top. I was wondering what she was thinking when she jumped, shaking her head like she was clearing it as she reached for her phone.

"I need to let my friend know I won't be home. She made me promise. I'm also supposed to let you know that she knows all about you in case you decide not to take me home."

Not taking Bethany home sounded perfect under other circumstances, but I was sure that wasn't what her friend meant.

"Um...okay." This friend of hers sounded interesting. Still... "I'm glad you have somebody watching out for you."

"Me, too." Bethany tapped to send her message, then sat still looking at her phone, her top teeth worrying her bottom lip, making me want to run my tongue along it to soothe it. "I wish I could be sure she got that. Messages can be unreliable, and I'd hate for her to freak out and send the police after you."

"Not a good outcome," I agreed. "You want me to have Cason or somebody on the team call her to let her know what's going on?"

"Would you?"

Those damn brown eyes of hers. Little did she know I'd do much more for her than that if she asked.

Message sent to Cason, and his return message received saying the call had been made, I pocketed my phone and looked around the space.

"Let's see what we're working with in terms of food and water." I crossed to the storage lockers and undid the series of latches designed to make them accessible to people without needing a key, but impenetrable to even the hungriest of bears, even if they did happen to catch the scent of the contents. I didn't expect to find any food, but I was hoping for...

"Perfect."

A case of canned water sat in the first locker, giving us plenty in addition to what Bethany and I had carried with us for the day. The second locker netted us two battery-operated lanterns complete with batteries. For food, we had the leftovers from lunch, along with four protein bars, trail mix, and dried fruit. It wasn't gourmet, but all in all, we were in pretty good shape.

Bethany and I finished going through the images on her phone, picking a few to feature on our various sites. We talked a little about our favorite movies, music, and books; each read for a while on our phones; and relaxed as much as we could, listening to the rain on the roof.

It wasn't until we'd eaten dinner and the light had faded that I felt the tension begin to build between us. Up until now, we'd both carefully avoided the elephant in the room. But with darkness falling, we needed to talk about it.

I looked at Bethany, standing at the window watching the rain, the light from the lantern brushing her with gold, and bit the bullet.

# Chapter 18

Brody

"We need to talk about sleeping arrangements."

Bethany hesitated, then turned to face me. The way she looked at me – cautious, tense – told me I was right, she'd been thinking about this, too.

We had a blanket and compact, lightweight sleeping bag I'd carried attached to my pack. That was it. I hadn't had an extra so Bethany hadn't carried one. I hadn't seen the harm – day hike, right? – but now...

There was only one way I could see this working.

"I was thinking, if we put the sleeping bag on the cot frame and you sleep on top of it like you would a mattress or pad, you should do okay with that and the blanket."

"Where will you sleep, though?"

"I'll be fine here." I indicated my spot on the floor, leaning against the wall.

"Brody, no. You can't sleep sitting up against the wall while I use both the sleeping bag and the blanket. You carried them – it's only fair you use them."

"Not gonna happen. You're using them."

Bethany crossed her arms and shook her head as she frowned at me.

"I can't use everything and be comfortable while you're sitting here on the hard floor. And it feels like the temperature's dropping. What if you get cold?"

She was right; there was a chill in the air that hadn't been there earlier. Not that it made a difference.

"I'll be fine," I repeated. "And I wouldn't overestimate how comfortable that cot frame is going to be with only the sleeping bag to cushion it. You may be less comfortable than I am."

I hoped that wasn't true, but it might be. Unfortunately for us, the mattress and remaining cots hadn't made it up to the hut from our warehouse yet.

Bethany looked from the sleeping bag to the cot like she'd think of another way if she just tried hard enough.

She wouldn't, not one she liked anyway.

The only other option I could think of had my shorts growing uncomfortably tight in a hurry. Sharing the cot with Bethany, her soft curves pressed against the length of my body, legs tangled together, her hands on me and mine on her...

I bit back a groan just in time.

All I was doing was torturing myself. It wasn't going to happen.

I stayed where I was while Bethany fought the inevitable. My shorts didn't give me much camouflage and the last thing I needed was for Bethany to see how hard I was for her.

After a few minutes, Bethany gave in and admitted defeat. When she headed out to the outbuilding, I grabbed the chance to set up the cot for her while I did my best to talk myself down. I pulled my extra shirt from my backpack and tossed it toward the corner, figuring I'd roll it up as a makeshift pillow to lean my head against the wall, just as Bethany came back in.

She frowned at my shirt as it lay in the corner but said nothing. She walked slowly toward the cot, seeming reluctant to get anywhere near it, as I retreated to the corner, wanting to give her space.

I rolled my shirt up with far more precision than was needed, keeping my eyes glued to it as Bethany flicked glances my way. Seemingly reassured that I wasn't watching, she turned away from me, did that magic maneuver where women remove their bra without taking off their shirt, and shoved her bra quickly into her backpack. She sat down gingerly on the cot, slipped under the blanket, and lay down, straight and stiff as a board.

"How is it?"

She wiggled a little, shifting this way and that, like she was assessing.

"It's okay." She sounded like a kid trying a new food and trying to decide whether to spit it out or not.

"You sure about that?" Not that there was much I could do to make it better for her. If there were, I already would have done it.

Other than letting her sleep on top of me and that wasn't on the program for this evening.

"Yes. It's better than I thought it would be."

That would have to do.

"Fair enough. I'm going to turn the lantern off, okay?"

"Okay. Good night."

"Good night, Bethany."

I flicked the lantern off, then sat staring into the inky darkness, letting my eyes adjust. Like all mountain lions, I couldn't see in complete darkness, but I could make out details in much lower light than humans can. I sat, my back against the wall, legs stretched out in front of me, and leaned my head back, trying to clear my mind and relax.

As quiet descended I focused, searching through the myriad muted sounds for the sound of Bethany breathing. It was there, soft and even, but not regular enough for her to be asleep. I sat and listened to it, hoping she'd be able to drop off at some point.

A minute later her breathing pattern changed, and I could tell she was about to get up. I stayed still, watching her outline across the dark cabin.

Just to feel my own breath stutter in my chest as I watched her stand and slip her shorts off, no doubt believing that I couldn't see her in the dark. She turned to set her shorts on her pack, treating me to a heart-stopping view of her in nothing but a t-shirt and tiny little white panties, then climbed back under the blanket.

I sat frozen as she tried to get settled, the blanket rustling as she tried to get comfortable.

Something that was now completely out of the question for me. I was maybe fifteen feet away from the woman I wanted more than I could remember ever wanting anyone, and she was just barely half-dressed.

I took a careful breath, testing to be sure my lungs still functioned. The urge to cross the room, pull away the blanket, and strip off the flimsy barriers that stood between me and Bethany's beautiful body was so strong a low growl slipped out. I stilled again, hoping Bethany hadn't heard me, relieved when she didn't react.

I was strung so tight my body felt like granite. I listened for Bethany's breathing again, willing it to help me settle. The hike back was going to take focus tomorrow; I didn't need to be doing it on zero sleep.

I matched my breathing to Bethany's, wishing I was holding her against me, feeling her heartbeat and her breath against my skin. Slowly, inch by inch, I relaxed.

When Bethany's soft whisper came out of darkness, I responded without thinking.

"It stopped raining."

"Yeah, a little bit ago."

Bethany rolled to face me, though I doubted she could make me out even with a small amount of moonlight now brightening the space a fraction.

"How did you hear what I said?" she asked in the same barely-there murmur.

"Mountain lion hearing is hyper-sensitive. It's like scent for a bear or a wolf."

Bethany was quiet for a moment, then...

"That's how you heard me when I made that comment about seeing Lacey at happy hour. You said something about it, and I didn't quite understand." I waited, sensing the wheels spinning in her head. "I guess I still don't. I mean, I get that you heard me that night, but how? There was a lot of noise in there. Doesn't it all sort of blend together?"

"Sometimes, especially when you're young, but you learn to filter it out as you get older. There are certain things that are always clearer, like the voice of your alpha or beta or your mate or offspring, and anything that might signal trouble or danger, like a growl or even a twig snapping, or other sounds you learn to focus on."

I stretched my arms over my head, trying to ease the tightness in my back and shoulders. Talking with Bethany, hearing her voice, had helped me relax a fraction, but my muscles were still in knots. I wanted to keep talking to her, but she wouldn't thank me for that in the morning, or whenever we got the green light to head out.

"We should try to get some sleep. With the rain gone, Cason and the team will be out early to clear the trail. We'll need to be ready when we get word that we're good to go."

# Chapter 19

Bethany

I knew Brody was right, but...

"I'm not sure I can."

He sighed and I immediately felt guilty. Here I was, the one with the sleeping bag, blanket, and cot, laying down, for heaven's sake while Brody was trying to sleep sitting up, and I was whining about not being able to sleep.

I was about to apologize when his voice came to me through the darkness again, not sounding the least bit angry or annoyed.

"I wish I could think of a way to make things better."

I'd thought of nothing else since I'd realized our situation.

It kept circling and circling in my brain, keeping me awake and on edge. There had to be a way, except...

One sleeping bag plus one blanket divided by the two of us...I couldn't make the math work.

I let the idea flirt at the edges of my mind again, afraid to let myself consider it. It didn't work unless...

Unless we slept together.

Me. Brody. Same cot. Together.

Sleeping, I mean. Of course, just sleeping, but...

I thought again of lying next to Brody, pressed right up against him given the size of the cot.

Would it make things better, or much, much worse?

I couldn't believe what I was about to say.

"I can maybe think of a way."

My breath rushed out of me as I finished my sentence. Brody went so still I could feel it from across the room. I waited, heart pounding, wondering if Brody could hear it.

"What's that?"

Just two words, deep and gravelly, told me he could.

"I think we should share."

Brody grunted, almost like I'd punched him. I swallowed hard and forced out the rest of it.

"I know there's not much space, but..." I paused, then lost my nerve in the face of the absolute silence from the corner of the room where Brody sat.

"Brody?" I sounded every bit as hesitant and unsure as I was. Had I embarrassed him? Made him mad? What?

"Baby, I can't. Fuck, I'm sorry. I didn't mean to call you that." Fabric rustled and I could see faint movement in the moonlight. Brody was on his feet and pacing.

"I can't, Bethany. I wish I could, but...that's the one thing I can't do."

"Why?" I whispered before I could think it through and make myself not say it.

Brody's laugh was short and rough.

"Do I really need to explain it, Bethany? Do you really not know?"

I hated that I couldn't see his face, his eyes.

"Tell me."

Brody stopped moving and I could feel him watching me.

"You need to hear me say it? I want you more than I want to breathe, Bethany. More than anyone or anything I can ever remember. I know we work together. I know you're a pure human and I'm not. None of that matters. You're all I can fucking see. The possibility that I can lay there tangled up with you and not touch you..." Brody's voice was harsh, strained... "I'm not strong enough, sweetheart. I can't do it."

He blew out a breath. "I'm sorry for laying this on you. You didn't ask to be stuck here with me overnight. And I'm sorry for calling you 'baby' and 'sweetheart'. I don't have the right. I know that."

He'd given me so much of himself; I needed to give him something back.

"Don't apologize. I like it."

Brody grunted again like he'd taken another blow.

"Bethany, help me here." He paused and I heard skin sliding over skin, as if he was rubbing his face. "You can't tell me things like that. You need to tell me to leave you the fuck alone and keep my hands and all the things I want to do to you to myself."

My core heated at his words, and I shifted restlessly under the blanket. I felt reckless, free in a way I never had.

"What if I don't want to? What if I don't want you to keep your hands to yourself?"

I could swear I heard Brody growl. Goosebumps ran across my skin in anticipation at the sound.

"You're killing me, Bethany." Brody's words sounded strangled, nearly desperate. "I'm trying to be a gentleman and do the right thing, but I'm hanging on by a thread."

Was that what I wanted? For Brody to be a gentleman?

It had been so long since I'd wanted to be anywhere close to a man, since I'd felt safe enough to. Did I want to deny that, push it away like I had been since I'd met Brody? Or did I want to see where this went?

It was no contest; I wanted, *needed*, to do this.

I climbed off the cot and crossed to the shadow I knew to be Brody, feeling his eyes on me as I drew closer. I'd nearly reached him when the moonlight hit his face, turning his eyes fiery gold. My breath hitched and he held out his hand.

"Your eyes..." I whispered, and he nodded his understanding.

"It's just my mountain lion, sweetheart. Just me." I put my hand in his and he drew me closer. "You don't have to be scared. I'll never hurt you."

"I know." Our bodies brushed, so close as I looked up at him. "I know you won't." I took a breath and said the words that I knew he needed to hear. "I don't want you to be a gentleman, Brody."

I felt his heart race under the hand I'd rested on his chest.

"Tell me, Bethany."

I knew what he was asking me for.

"I want you, too, Brody. I know we work together." I echoed his words. "I know I'm fully human and you're not. None of that matters."

I could feel Brody fighting, felt it in the tension that ran through his body and his tight grip on my hips. He dipped his head, his breath rough and warm against my lips, and I waited, hoping...

He slid one hand up my back and into my hair, tugged me closer with the other, and his mouth descended on mine. I slipped my arms around his neck, melting against him even as I opened for him and felt the warm slide of his tongue against mine.

His kiss was slow and hungry, as if I was his favorite treat and he was savoring the first taste of me after a long while of being denied. With his hand cupping the back of my head, he tilted it just so, taking the kiss deeper as I followed, pressing against him, needing to feel every inch of his hard body against mine. When his lips left mine, only to slide softly across my cheek and down my neck, I shivered, clinging to him as my nipples pebbled to hard points and my center ached.

Finally, he circled his arms around me and rested his forehead against mine, my heart squeezing at the gesture, so full of tender affection.

"I don't want to stop." The low rumble of Brody's voice rippled along my skin, and his eyes, so intense in the dim light, burned into mine. "I don't want to let you go. But I don't have protection with me."

I looked back at him, thinking, weighing, considering. Deciding.

"I'm on birth control. And I've been tested and I'm clean."

Brody's arms clenched, squeezing me tighter for a second as his eyes flared. I watched him fight himself again as he weighed my words.

"I am, too," he gritted out. "You're safe with me."

He was fighting, but he was wavering.

I needed him to give in to what we both wanted.

"I know that. I know I'm safe with you."

I lifted my chin a little, brushing my lips across his, tilting my hips just a fraction to press against his hard length.

He swallowed hard as he slid one hand down to trap my hips against him.

"Are you going to let me have you, Bethany?"

I brushed my lips across his again, then across his cheek to his ear, and whispered, giving him the question back...

"Are you going to let me have you?"

I felt the growl in Brody's chest even as I heard it.

"Fuck, yes."

His mouth slammed down on mine again as he lifted me up and my legs circled around his waist. He carried me to the small kitchen counter, setting me on the edge, his mouth never leaving mine. I tunneled my hands under his shirt, loving the way he rumbled as I ran my hands over the smooth, warm skin of his sides and back. He slid his mouth to my neck, nipping and kissing and licking as I tilted my head, giving him better access. I shivered, as I had earlier, as I slipped my hands out from under his shirt and up to his face, bringing his mouth back to mine, while he pressed me into him, one hand on my lower back holding me firmly against him, my center against his steel hard length. When he pulled his mouth from mine, I whimpered, a sound I couldn't remember ever making before, and his harsh breath echoed in my ears.

He tilted my chin up so my eyes met his, dark now and blazing with desire.

"Have you ever been with a demi-shifter, Bethany? Ever done this with someone like me?"

It was on the tip of my tongue to tell him there *was* no one like him, demi-shifter or not, but I just shook my head, not trusting myself to form words.

"You need to know I'll shift a little. Not to my full extent, but some. With the way I want you, there's no way I won't. There's nothing you have to do, just don't be scared. No matter what, it's always me. I'm the one touching you, the one inside you."

Moisture flooded my core as I imagined Brody pushing into me, filling me.

I repeated the words I'd given him earlier.

"I know I'm safe with you, Brody."

Brody surged forward into me, his mouth coming down hard on mine, our tongues tangling, before he pulled back again.

"I'm so fucking hard for you, sweetheart. I need to touch you."

He slid his mouth back to that oh so perfect spot on my neck at the same time he slipped his hand into my panties. I gasped, holding tight to his biceps as his fingers parted me, slipping through my wetness. He groaned into my neck, biting down lightly as he pushed two fingers into my core, wringing an echoing groan from me. It had been so long since a man had touched me this way, so long since I'd wanted one to. Even then, nothing I'd ever experienced with a man came anywhere close to Brody's touch, to the feel of his broad fingers stroking in and out of me.

Feeling utterly shameless, I widened my legs for him, urging him deeper.

"You're so wet, sweetheart. So tight. You're going to feel amazing on my cock."

I arched into him, nearly detonating as his thumb stroked back and forth over my hard little bundle of nerves. I rocked with his hand, feeling myself inch closer and closer to the edge with each stroke.

Then he captured my mouth with his again, taking possession. When he curled his fingers, hitting that spot inside me just right, I came apart.

I tore my mouth from Brody's, wrapping my arms around him, needing an anchor in the sensual storm that swamped me, threatening to carry me away. Holding me close, one arm banded around me, he pumped his fingers in and out of my center, wringing every possible bit of pleasure from me, then slowing as the frenzy inside me calmed. I took a breath, then another, feeling boneless, making a small sound of protest as Brody slowly pulled his fingers away.

I watched as he sucked them clean, turned on and a little fascinated, the look of proud satisfaction on his face making me smile.

"You look like the cat that ate the canary."

Brody shook his head as he pressed kisses along my jaw.

"More like the mountain lion who finally got a taste of the woman he can't get out of his head. As far as the eating part..." Brody paused and my core clenched as I imagined his blond head between my thighs, his hot tongue stroking me, sending me into oblivion... "As much as I want that, if I don't get inside you, I'm going to lose my mind." He dropped a hard kiss on my lips then drew back a fraction to look at me. "Raincheck on eating that sweet pussy of yours so I can give you my cock?"

A shiver rippled through me at the thought of Brody inside me, filling me. A raincheck meant we were doing this again. No smart woman in the world would turn that down.

I gave him a soft version of the kiss he'd given me.

"Yes, please."

He chased my mouth as I pulled away, kissing me deep and slow as the hunger built inside me, then pulled back with a wicked grin.

"Since you asked so nicely..."

He stepped back a fraction, pulling my shirt up and off before doing the same with his own. I'd never seen him with his shirt off, and even in the dim moonlight he was captivating. I ran my hands over his chest, loving the springy texture of his light covering of hair, up over his muscled shoulders and down his strong arms, reveling in the chance to touch him the way I'd wanted to. I ran the backs of my fingers across his hard abs, loving the way they tensed at my touch. Brody's breathing picked up and I looked up at him, only to be met with the stare of a predator, eyes glittering with need.

"I'd love to let you play. And later I will. But right now, I need you."

Holding his hot gaze, I slid my hands down a fraction, feeling his abs tense again as I slipped my fingers in the waistband of his shorts and popped the button open. His hand covered mine as together we lowered the zipper, Brody groaning as the back of my fingers brushed against his hard length.

Then he pushed down his shorts and boxer briefs and stood naked in front of me, his body tense and his manhood proudly erect, mind-blowingly gorgeous even in the dim light.

I stared at him, running my eyes over him, nearly stunned by his beauty.

"Bethany...sweetheart." Brody's voice was raspy and deep. "I fucking love the way you look at me."

Stepping closer, he put his hands on my hips and boosted me up to pull away my panties. He moved back between my legs, the bare skin of my inner thighs nestled along the smooth, warm skin of his hips. Seconds later, I felt his hot, hard length against my center. "I hope to hell you're ready for me."

"I am. Please, Brody."

I sounded needy, my near-desperation matching Brody's.

I held tight to his shoulders as he gripped my hips, slipping through my wetness again and again, torturing us both.

Just when I thought I couldn't wait another second, Brody reached between us, positioned himself just where I needed him most, and pushed steadily inside me.

Not thinking, I gripped down on him with my inner walls, loving the way he stretched me.

Brody groaned in reaction, dropping his forehead against mine.

"God, Bethany. You feel so good." He drew out a fraction and pushed back in, testing us both. "You're perfect. Hot. Tight. Perfect," he growled out, punctuating each word with small thrust that made me desperate for more.

"More, Brody," I pleaded, swiveling my hips a fraction against his tight hold and digging my nails into his shoulders lightly, not wanting to hurt him.

"All yours, baby. All yours."

Slipping his hands lower on my hips, Brody began stroking into me in earnest, setting the perfect pace to make me lose control. I clung to his wide shoulders, throwing my head back, lost in the feeling of him inside me, his hands gripping me, our bodies pressed tight as he drove me closer and closer to a place I wasn't sure I'd ever been before.

I could feel it waiting for me, a climax so huge it threatened to obliterate everything I'd known before. I opened my eyes, wanting, needing, a connection with Brody, only to find the face of a changed man in front of me.

His cheekbones, always defined, had sharpened even more. His eyes seemed rimmed in black, his cat-like oval pupils wide in the dim light. His body seemed sleeker, his muscles rippling under his hot skin, the sprinkling of chest hair now a light covering of soft fur.

Brody stared at me, breathing hard, and I caught just a glimpse of sharp canines behind his lips.

Maybe I should have been startled, afraid, but I wasn't. Whatever the physical changes, the man, the...being, holding me, watching me, stroking inside me again and again, was Brody. Our connection, the thread that I felt stretching between us when I allowed myself to acknowledge it, was the same, stronger even.

Then I noticed something else, another change, and felt my lips curve with a smile.

"Brody...your ears." I reached my hands up, running my fingers over his ears in wonder, unable to resist their slightly pointed shape or the hint of silky fur that covered them.

The growl that emanated from Brody told me all I needed to know about what my touch was doing to him.

"You're playing with fire, sweetheart. Keep that up and I'll fuck you so hard you won't be able to hike out of here for days."

"Promise?" This wasn't me. This teasing, flirting woman, especially during sex, wasn't me. But somehow, with Brody, it was.

Brody's mouth slammed down on mine, his deep, hungry kiss and driving thrusts obliterating everything else from my mind. Before long I was clinging to him, shuddering through a devastating climax, gripping down on him fiercely with my inner walls, pushing him over the edge right behind me. He surged inside me, holding himself there, burying his face in my neck as I felt his heat fill me. Gasping for air, we held each other for long moments, neither of us seemingly willing to let go.

Finally, Brody pressed a kiss to my neck, then my shoulder, then leaned back a little to look at me. I studied him, a little bemused that mountain lion Brody, or at least most of the physical signs of him, were gone, and human Brody was back in place.

"You okay?"

"I'm okay," I reassured him. "You?"

"Not sure." The hint of vulnerability in both his answer and his eyes made my heart squeeze. "I think my world may have just shifted on its axis."

"I know," I agreed, unable to hold back even if I probably should. "Mine, too."

Brody leaned in and gave me a soft kiss, one that had nothing to do with desire and everything to do with whatever was making the butterflies dance in my stomach.

"We should get some sleep."

I felt as much as heard the words Brody murmured against my lips.

I nodded in response, then came full circle to the invitation that had started all this, or at the very least had fanned the embers that had been burning between us for weeks.

"Share the cot with me?"

"Yes." His response was immediate, decisive. "Now that I've touched you there's no way I'm sleeping across the room from you."

We cleaned ourselves up the best we could, then after several hilarious minutes spent trying to figure out how to fit two grown adults on a cot meant for only one, ended up spooned together with me as the little spoon, not a whisper of space between us.

Was it the most comfortable I'd ever been? Far from it. Would I have traded places with any other woman in the world at that moment? Absolutely not.

Brody grumbled as he shifted positions a little, draping one big leg over mine, enveloping me in his warmth. He kissed the side of my neck as I wiggled a little to find my spot, finally settling into him with a satisfied sigh. As he held me close, I couldn't resist one last whispered comment.

"You know, this camping thing isn't so bad after all."

I drifted off with Brody's soft laughter in my ears.

# Chapter 20

Brody

I woke the next morning with Bethany draped on top of me, her head resting on the center of my chest and one of my legs tucked between hers. Her body felt perfect on top of mine, her sweet curves pressed into me from head to toe. I vaguely remembered lifting her on top of me sometime during the night. She'd protested a little, then snuggled in and settled down. Though I'd prefer it to be on a softer surface, waking up tangled up with Bethany was something I'd be more than happy to get used to.

My phone chirped and I reached for it just as Bethany stirred. I slid a hand up onto her cute little ass to make sure she stayed where she was and answered my phone with the other.

Based on the sunlight beginning to peek through the windows, I was sure the call was from Cason. I was proven right when Cason's voice answered my good morning.

"Good morning, yourself. You kids do okay last night?"

Bethany stacked her hands on my chest and grinned at me as I answered.

"We did fine, yeah." Damn fine, actually.

"Good, that's good. We should have the bottom slide cleared in another 30 minutes or so, then we'll head up to the upper one. Give us another 30 on that one, and you should be good to head down. We'll have it clear by the time you make it down that far. Oh, and take the upper crossing on the stream. The way it's running now there's no way Bethany will be safe coming across the lower one."

The lower crossing was the one we'd taken on the way up. Bethany had done fine then, and I'd likely be fine to do it now, but without the natural agility and sure-footedness of a mountain lion, Bethany would find it difficult if not impossible with the higher water and faster current.

I thanked Cason for the heads up, then disconnected. I folded my arms under my head and looked back at Bethany as she looked at me, her brown eyes still sleepy, but curious.

"So, we can head back in an hour, and we need to take the other crossing through the stream."

"You got it."

I pulled her forward for a kiss and she surprised me by readily sliding up a little to accommodate me. As we kissed, I felt my cock swell and harden until it pressed urgently against Bethany's inner thigh, making its demands known. I groaned as Bethany pressed her hips into me, the pressure feeling so fucking good I was close to coming in seconds.

"Baby, stop. That feels too good. If I come, I want it to be inside you."

"If?" Bethany's eyebrow cocked up and she glanced down toward where my rigid cock was trapped between our bodies. "I'd say it's definitely when."

I loved it when she gave me attitude.

When she tilted her hips into me again, grinding on me, I reached down and gripped her hips to stop her.

"Fuck, Bethany. The feel of you on top of me alone has me on the edge. I can't take you moving on me like that. If we had a decent bed, I'd flip you over and give you everything you're asking for. But this cot isn't up to it, even if we could manage to stay on, and I don't want to have to explain how we broke it."

Bethany stayed mercifully still as she looked around the hut, surprising me with her next words.

"What if we put the sleeping bag on the floor? Could we...?"

Bethany's voice trailed off as I shook my head.

"It'll be hard, baby."

Her eyebrow tilted up again.

"It already is if you haven't noticed."

I gave her ass a firm smack as she jumped and laughed.

"I noticed, believe me. I was talking about the floor, smartass. We'd have to spread the sleeping bag out and it won't be much cushion. I want to, sweetheart. I really fucking want to, but it won't be what you deserve."

Bethany pushed herself up until she was straddling me, her hot center cradling my cock like she was made for me. The only thing that kept me from lining myself up and pushing deep inside her was the creak of the cot. Even now we'd be lucky if we didn't end up in a pile of cot pieces.

Then Bethany ran her hand up my chest, tugging lightly on my chest hair, and I forgot all about the cot.

"I know it won't be perfect, but I need you, Brody. I need to feel you inside me."

"Get up, sweetheart."

There wasn't a single chance in hell I was saying no to that. No matter what I had to do, I was giving my woman what she wanted.

Bethany climbed off me carefully as the cot groaned ominously again. The second she was fully on her feet, I pushed up off the cot, dragged the sleeping bag off it, unzipped it, and spread it out on the floor.

I took Bethany's hand and pulled her down along with me, lying on my back and settling her on top of me, straddling me as she had on the cot.

"I promise you a bed next time." I gripped her thighs, loving the feel of her and the stunning view I was being treated to. "This time..." I slid my hand up and cupped her right breast, running my thumb across her nipple as I watched her eyes glaze with pleasure... "this time I just promise to make you feel so good you come loud enough to scare the animals for miles around."

"Is that all?" she teased softly, even as she arched her back to get closer to my touch, making my cock swell even harder with the innocent sexiness of the move.

She dropped her head back, moaning softly as she felt me press against her.

"That's a start." I lifted her a little, positioning her so I was notched right at her entrance. "I'm all yours, sweetheart. Take what you need."

She braced her hands on my abs and slid down, inch by agonizing inch until I was fully seated inside her.

She moaned again, a little louder this time.

"You feel incredible, Brody."

"Right back at you, baby. You're perfect. Now..." I rested my hands at her waist, bracing her as I thrust up into her, loving her little gasp. "Ready to scare the wildlife?"

She nodded as she rose up a little, wringing a groan from me this time as she slid back down.

"I'm ready."

# Chapter 21

Bethany

The hike out was much harder than the hike in.

The trail was okay in some places; in others, it was a slippery, muddy mess.

Brody went slowly, moving with infinite patience as I gave over my entire focus to staying on my feet. Despite that, even with Brody's help, I'd fallen three times by the time we reached the stream. When I saw the lower crossing – with the rocks we'd used to cross it the first time now wet and slick, and several submerged altogether – I thanked what luck I had that there was another way to get across.

We made our way upstream a little and I was grateful to see the land bridge Brody had talked about. It wouldn't get us all the way across, but between it, a couple of logs that sat at an angle across the stream, and a big, flat rock jutting out of the bank on the other side, we could get across without going in the water.

Assuming all went well.

Brody stood behind me as I took in the path we would need to take, giving me time to look it over. He squeezed my shoulders in reassurance as I blew out a breath.

"Just follow me and step exactly where I do as much as you can. There will probably be a few slick spots, but I'll warn you, okay? You're going to do great."

He gripped my chin, gently pulling my face around and up to meet his kiss. His eyes met mine, asking if I was okay, if I was ready, and I nodded. The only way to go was forward and the sooner we got started, the sooner we'd be done.

"Good girl." Brody dropped another kiss on my lips, then stepped around me. "Here we go."

We got to the end of the small jut of land with no problem at all. Next came the two logs that sat nearly side-by-side. Brody took one step onto the logs and frowned, holding up his hand to me to stop. He took a cautious step, then another, then shook his head.

"These logs are slippery as shit, I'm not gonna lie. It'll probably ruin your shorts, but I think your best way across is to slide across on your butt."

I couldn't care less about my shorts at that point. They were covered in mud and who knew what else anyway.

Slowly, cautiously, I lowered myself to sit on the logs. I waited for Brody to finish walking across, his innate balance and agility allowing him to do what I couldn't. When he reached the end and jumped across what now seemed like an impossibly wide space onto the flat rock beyond, I started to move.

I inched my way forward, not allowing myself to acknowledge the water rushing by a foot or so below me or think about what would happen if I fell. I just focused on the logs and Brody's voice, encouraging me every inch of the way. I was so intent, I surprised myself when I reached the end. I looked at the space between me and the rock where Brody stood, wondering how I was going to jump across it, my tired legs feeling both weak and heavy.

"If you can stand up and get just a little closer, I can lift you across."

I looked at Brody, then at the space between us. "It's too far, Brody. I don't know how you'll even reach me, let alone be able to lift me over."

"Look at me, Bethany."

I did as he asked, his eyes glowing bright as he looked back at me.

"Do you trust me?"

"Of course." The answer still shocked me, but it was true.

"Just get a little closer and reach for me. Watch your footing. I swear to you I won't let you fall."

I swallowed hard as I braced myself to push carefully to my feet. I crept forward – one inch, two, three, stretching out my hands toward Brody – then suddenly, impossibly, he was tugging and lifting, pulling me across the space into his arms.

I wrapped my arms around him and held tight, more grateful than I'd ever been to have both feet on solid ground. Brody held me close, wrapping me in his warmth, and I soaked him in, reveling in a sense of security I hadn't felt since I was small.

Far too soon, he loosened his grip and looked down at me with a grin.

"See? Piece of cake."

The man was just far too charming for his own good, or for mine.

"That's one way to describe it." I leaned up and gave him a small kiss. "Thanks for getting me across."

"Anytime, baby." He returned the kiss, then turned toward the trail and held his hand out for me. "It should be smooth sailing from here."

This last part of the trail was wide enough for us to walk side-by-side. We made our way across the muddy meadow, hand-in-hand, while I marveled at how much had changed in such a short time. If someone had told me when we'd set out the day before everything that would happen, I would have been convinced that they either had a wildly active imagination or a very serious drug problem.

When we reached the parking lot at the trailhead and saw the clan's vehicle sitting there waiting for us, I could have hugged it. How you hug an SUV, I don't know, but I was that happy to see it.

Now that we were down the mountain, out of the woods, and back at the trailhead, every remaining ounce of energy seemed to drain out of me. I slipped my backpack from my shoulders and leaned back against the SUV as I breathed a sigh of relief.

Brody stood in front of me and nudged my chin up to look at him. "You did great, Bethany. That wasn't easy, but you hung in there like a pro."

I gave a short laugh as I looked down at myself. "A mud-covered pro with my pride bruised only slightly less than my backside from all the spills I took, maybe."

Brody looked down at my mud-coated legs and feet along with the mud streaking across my shirt and backpack and shrugged. "I'm wearing my share of mud, too."

"Ha, no." I eyed his boots and legs. There was mud, true, but he was practically pristine compared to me. "I think I'm wearing mine, yours, and that of half the town's population."

Brody crowded in closer and set his hands on my hips. "It looks good on you."

I shook my head at him even as I felt my lips curve in a smile. "Nice try, but that's a bit much, even for you."

Brody moved in another inch.

"It's true. I hope this doesn't make you decide hiking isn't your thing. There are too many beautiful spots I still need to show you."

My heart thumped hard at the implication, or more, the statement, that he wanted to spend more time with me. Did that mean...?

Before I could respond, Brody gripped my hips more firmly, closing the last tiny space between us as he went on.

"I also hope you don't plan for us to go back to just being co-workers. I gotta tell you – if that's what you're thinking, I plan to do everything I can to change your mind."

The hunger in his eyes told me everything I needed to know, but I asked anyway.

"You don't want to be just co-workers?"

Brody shook his head slowly as he slid his hands up to cup my neck, his thumbs lightly stroking my jaw. "Not even close."

Craving his kiss, I let my eyes slip down to his mouth, then back up to meet his gaze again.

"What do you want to be?"

"This."

He tilted my face up, bent his head, and kissed me, slow and soft at first. Then he tugged my chin down with his thumb, parting my lips for him, and took possession. He slanted his mouth over mine, taking the kiss deeper as he slipped one hand into my hair, holding me captive right where he wanted me. I hung on, gripping his forearms as I leaned into him, holding back nothing from him. His chest rumbled with a low growl as he hauled me against him and drove everything but his mouth on mine completely out of my conscious mind. Then slowly, slowly, he softened the kiss again, brushing his lips across mine one final time before drawing back.

"I want to be all that and more. We can take it slow from here if you need to or want to. I just want to be with you. If you want that, too, we can figure out together how it works and what it all means."

I wanted that so much. I shouldn't – I should stay focused on what I was here to do – but in that moment, with Brody looking at me as if I was all he'd ever wanted, I couldn't.

"I want that, too," I admitted, watching as Brody's expression flooded with satisfaction and relief at my response.

He kissed me on the forehead, then the tip of my nose.

"You let me off easier than I thought you would. Especially considering I just got you stuck overnight in a basic cabin on your first hike with me. I was prepared to use all my powers of persuasion if I needed to."

Well, *that* piqued my curiosity.

"You wouldn't consider that kiss 'all your powers of persuasion' then? I found it pretty convincing."

Maybe I shouldn't admit that, but on a scale of one to ten, it had been at least a 20. Possibly a 25.

The sexy grin Brody gave me made my heart give a little bump again, and that was before he responded in that low, rumbly voice that never failed to send a shiver through me.

"Baby, you have no idea."

"Hmm." I narrowed my eyes, pretending to mull over his answer. "Maybe I should consider being a little less agreeable in the future."

Grin still firmly in place, Brody tugged me closer.

"Please do." He dipped his head to skim his lips across my neck, right up to the sensitive spot behind my ear, as my nipples pebbled up in response. His warm breath brushed across my ear as he went on. "I'd be more than happy to spend as long as it takes showing you everything I've got."

It was a wonder I didn't melt into a puddle at his feet.

With a final kiss to my neck, he pulled back a little.

"I'd love nothing better than to show you right now, but given that we're both tired and dirty, I also realize this isn't the best time."

Sadly, he was right. We'd barely gotten any sleep, had spent several challenging hours hiking down the side of a mountain, and I, for one, was essentially covered waist to toes in a layer of rapidly drying, itchy mud.

I straightened up from the truck as Brody grabbed my backpack. I opened the passenger-side door, but hesitated before climbing in.

"What's wrong?"

I looked from my mud-covered self to the passenger seat as he set our packs in the back of the SUV and hit the button to close the back liftgate.

"I'll get the seat and floor all muddy."

Brody shook his head, unconcerned as he crossed to my side and held the door for me. "Not an issue. We use these vehicles for the lumber business and search and rescue all the time. Mud comes with the territory."

Still a little hesitant, I went ahead and climbed up into the seat. As we drove, a wave of tiredness hit me, and I found myself fighting to keep my eyes open. I startled at the feel of Brody's hand on my thigh.

He glanced at me, then back at the road as he gave my thigh a gentle squeeze.

"I think I should drive you home. It's not safe for you to drive as sleepy as you are, and you'll just get your own car muddy, anyway. I don't want to take a chance of you having an accident and why clean up two vehicles when you don't have to?"

What he said made sense, but...

"I don't want to trouble you. And I'll need to get my car at some point."

"We'll figure that out." Brody glanced over at me again. "It's no trouble at all. I'll worry anyway until I know you're home safe. I might as well take you there myself, then drive the SUV home so I don't get my truck muddy either. We'll deal with getting our own vehicles back when we're not tired and dirty. We'll both be home sooner, and I'll know you haven't fallen asleep and driven off the road into a ditch somewhere."

I was too exhausted to argue with him, so I just nodded my agreement.

"I don't know why I'm so wiped out all of a sudden. I feel like someone drugged me." I gave up the fight to keep my eyes open and leaned my head back against the headrest.

"A bit of an adrenaline crash, I'm betting. Give me your address so I can put it in the GPS, then go ahead and check out if you want to."

I gave Brody my address, then before I knew it, Brody's hand was on my shoulder, gently shaking me awake.

I yawned, realizing we were in the parking lot of my apartment building as Brody opened his door and climbed out. The back of the SUV popped open so he could pull out my backpack, then he met me at my door as I opened it. Surprising me, he slung the strap of my backpack over his shoulder, then reached in and lifted me into his arms.

"Brody, I can walk," I protested, even as I admitted to myself that being cradled against his broad chest, held securely in his strong arms, was an extremely nice place to be.

"You'll track in less mud this way," Brody answered matter-of-factly. "Close the door, sweetheart."

When he put it that way...

I did as I was told, then reached out and opened the building door when we reached it, wondering at the frown that flashed across Brody's face.

"Is this door always unlocked?"

"As far as I know." I settled against him again as he crossed to the slow-as-molasses-in-winter elevator, which I avoided except when going back and forth to the ground floor with big loads of laundry. "I've never found it locked, and I don't have a key for it."

The frown reappeared on Brody's face when the elevator finally arrived, and we began our slow ascent to my floor.

Worried that I might be getting too heavy, I told him he could put me down if he wanted to.

"I've got you," he responded absently while he looked around the elevator car, scanning for who knew what.

When the elevator reached my floor, Brody strode out into the hallway, and I pointed the way to my door.

"You'll have to put me down so I can get my key out."

Brody lowered me to my feet in front of my door, holding the backpack for me while I fished around inside it until I found my key. I unlocked it and stepped inside, holding it open as Brody followed me in.

I took the backpack from him, setting it carefully on the rug by the door, then removing my hiking shoes and placing them alongside it, all while watching Brody as he ran his gaze around my space. It didn't take long. I had a miniscule kitchen that flowed right into a small sitting area, which was taken up almost entirely by the world's hardest couch. Down a short hallway, out of Brody's current line of sight, was my bedroom and the apartment's one bathroom, consisting of a tiny tub/shower combo, pedestal sink, and toilet.

It wasn't much, but it was everything I needed, and, most importantly, I could afford it.

The longer Brody didn't say anything, the more nervous I got. Finally, I couldn't take it anymore.

"That bad, huh?"

"No." Brody shook his head, still looking around. "I just wouldn't have pegged you as a fan of the minimalist look."

The glint of humor in Brody's eyes as he turned his head to look at me sparked an answering smile from me.

"Yes, well, I prefer my space to be uncluttered."

That was an excuse. The lack of decorations and extra furniture, even a TV, had nothing to do with a chosen aesthetic and everything to do with portability and permanence, or lack thereof. If I didn't need it or couldn't move it easily by myself, I didn't own it. But teasing with Brody felt good, so I gave myself a pass on the little white lie I'd just told.

"I can see that." Brody pushed a hand through his hair as he turned toward me, and for the first time I noticed how tired his eyes looked. Guilt swamped me when I thought of the way he'd taken care of me and watched over me from the second we'd set out the day before, right up to him carrying me up to my apartment. "I guess I'd better get going so you can get cleaned up and get some rest."

"You could stay."

The words flew out of my mouth before I even realized I was going to say them. Once they were out, though, I liked the sound of them.

Brody didn't seem as sure. He stilled, simply looking at me, his expression unreadable.

"You should stay." I rushed on, wanting to convince him. "You can use my shower, then take a nap with me. That way, I won't have to worry about you driving tired either."

Brody dropped his head, staring at the floor, still saying nothing.

"Just a nap, Brody. I'm not expecting anything else."

Brody's head came up and he locked eyes with me.

"I'm not worried about that." If I'd thought he was going to share what he *was* worried about, I was wrong. Instead, he focused back on me. "Are you sure about this?"

I stepped closer, leaning up to press a kiss to his scruff-covered jaw.

"I'll take a quick shower, you can do the same, then we'll crash for a little bit. Come on."

I held my hand out to him, gratified when he reached for it without hesitating. I started to lead him toward the bathroom, but he tugged me to a stop so he could remove his hiking boots and line them up next to mine. He followed me to the bathroom, and I showed him the cubbies where I kept towels and an extra toothbrush, then he stepped out, giving me my privacy. I stripped quickly, leaving my muddy clothes in a heap to take care of later, and stepped into the stream of wonderfully warm water. I brushed my teeth then lathered up my hair and body. I rinsed off quickly, resisting the urge to linger, mindful of Brody waiting for his turn.

I stepped out, dried off, spritzed leave-in conditioner on my hair, then stopped, realizing I hadn't brought any fresh clothes into the bathroom to put on.

I debated for a second, then wrapped my towel around me and cracked the door open. The coast was clear, so I dashed the few feet to my bedroom, yelled down the hall to Brody that the bathroom was free, and closed myself in my bedroom.

As I changed into a soft t-shirt and a pair of loose shorts, I heard the bathroom door close and a minute later, the shower turn on.

While I reveled in the luxurious feel of a clean body and clean hair, I searched through my things for something for Brody to wear. I pulled out a pair of men's shorts I'd bought for a dollar at a thrift store and held them up, trying to picture them on Brody. They were big enough on me that they just might fit him. They were a little shorter than the ones he typically wore in the gym, and they might be a tiny bit tight in the booty, but they would be better than putting his dirty hiking shorts on and would give him something to wear while I did our laundry later.

I carried them down the hall and was setting them outside the bathroom door when the shower shut off.

"Brody, I left some shorts out here that I think will fit you. Just leave your clothes in there and I'll do laundry when we wake up."

I waited until I heard his "thanks" through the door to be sure he'd heard me, then headed back to my bedroom. Once there I changed the sheets on my air mattress and flipped the blinds closed. Then, all my energy spent, I lay down on top of the comforter to wait for Brody.

# Chapter 22

Brody

I stopped short as I walked into Bethany's bedroom, taking her in. She was asleep, curled up like a kitten, and I huffed out a quiet laugh when I saw what she was laying on.

The whole time I'd listened to her in the shower, picturing the water streaming down her beautiful body, over her mouth-watering breasts and strong, toned legs; as I'd rushed through my own shower, talking myself down, reminding myself that she'd made sure to assure me this would only be a nap; as I'd imagined pulling her close, wrapping around her, feeling her body against mine the way I had the night before, and drifting off with her... it had never once occurred to me that she might not have a bed.

The air mattress she was laying on was a huge step up from both the cot we'd slept on the night before and the hard wood floor where we'd had sex just that morning. There was no question about that. It was bigger for one thing, probably full-size from what I could tell, and had to be softer. It would still be a cozy fit, but I couldn't say I hated that. Still, I couldn't wait to get Bethany in my queen-size bed. The things I wanted to do to her...well, they required room to stretch out.

For now, though, I'd take what I could get.

I lifted Bethany enough to free the covers from underneath her, chuckling again as she gave a little grunt of protest, then immediately burrowed into my chest like she couldn't get close enough. I slipped under the covers as best I could with her in my arms and settled on my back with her tucked in at my side. My heart bumped hard when she nuzzled her face against my chest, gave a sigh of what sounded like contentment, and relaxed fully against me. As I drifted off, the thought slid through my mind that if I could have just this every day

– Bethany by my side, wanting to be with me, trusting me – I'd be a very happy man.

• • • •

I WOKE HOURS LATER to the sound of Bethany moving around somewhere in the apartment. I sat up, running my hands over my face as I listened, just as Bethany popped her head around, then stepped fully into her bedroom doorway.

"Hey." She gave me a shy smile as her cheeks pinked up a little and I wondered what she was thinking about. "I was just about to leave you a note. I'm going to throw our clothes in the washer. The laundry room is on the ground floor, so I'll only be a few minutes."

"Sounds good. Thanks for doing mine, too."

"Sure." She gave me another smile and a little shrug. Damn, she was cute.

I pushed up off the mattress and stretched, loving the way her eyes swept over me as I did. The shorts she'd found for me to wear didn't leave much to the imagination, and she took full advantage of that, not that I minded in the least.

I crossed to her and brushed a kiss across her cheek just as my stomach protested the fact that we'd had a minimal breakfast and missed lunch altogether.

"While you're downstairs I'll look around your kitchen for something to make us for dinner if that's okay."

"That's fine, if you want to. There might be some soup or something."

She didn't sound optimistic, but I wasn't worried.

A few minutes later, I had sausage and onion sautéing on one of Bethany's two stovetop burners, and a pot of water ready to boil on the other. I'd found a box of spaghetti and a can of tomato sauce in Bethany's pantry, and a package of breakfast sausage and half an onion in her fridge. I'd stripped the casings off the sausage, broken it up, and tossed it in Bethany's lone skillet with some chopped onion to cook. Along with the tomato sauce, it would do fine for the spaghetti.

I was about to add the tomato sauce to the sausage and onions when I heard a knock on the apartment door. Assuming Bethany had forgotten her key or had her hands full, I crossed to open it, then stopped short as I reached for the doorknob.

My mountain lion stirred, and I felt a low growl rumble through me. Whoever was on the other side of the door, it wasn't Bethany.

And they weren't fully human.

I stilled, opening my senses, letting my mountain lion lead, trying to figure out what it was about the person that had made him take notice. They didn't feel like a threat per se, so not a predator, but there was something...

There was another knock, then a female voice.

"I know you're in there, Bethany; I can smell that amazing dinner you're making! You need to share with me and spill all the details about your hot mountain lion man."

My mouth quirked up in a smile. Hot mountain lion man, huh? Yeah, definitely not a threat. Shoving down whatever had made my mountain lion overact, I reached for the door again. Keeping my expression as impassive as possible, I pulled it open.

"I can't believe you...oh!"

The young woman now gaping up at me was unquestionably a wild boar shifter. I could sense that now that the door no longer stood between us, even if her close-set eyes and slightly upturned nose, both characteristic of her sounder, hadn't given her away. It probably wasn't anything to worry about, but it was something to note.

"Can I help you?"

She blinked at me once, twice, as she seemed to gather herself. "Wow. You aren't Bethany."

"I'd be the hot mountain lion man, I believe." At least I damn well better be. "And you are?"

She had the grace to look chagrined, though as she took in what I was wearing, or maybe what I *wasn't*, she recovered quickly enough.

"I'm Andi," she responded, holding her hand out to shake mine even as her eyes caught somewhere around my mid-section, hopefully on my abs and not a little lower.

"Brody," I returned, shaking and releasing her hand, though I doubted she noticed. I was on the verge of reminding her that my eyes were up here, when I heard Bethany.

"Andi, oh my gosh!" She rushed up, the empty laundry basket dangling from her hand. "I'm so sorry! I completely forgot to text you when I got home."

"You're forgiven." She eyed me again as she gave Bethany a quick hug. "I can see why you were distracted."

It had been fatigue that had distracted Bethany, not me, but I wasn't about to correct her. I was a little surprised when Bethany didn't, either.

"Yes, well…" A little frown appeared on Bethany's face as she noticed Andi ogling me. "Have you two introduced yourselves?"

I confirmed that we had, then stepped back, letting Bethany into the apartment, not overly surprised when Andi followed right along behind her.

I crossed back to the stove to stir the tomato sauce into the sausage and onion mixture and turn the burner on under the water for the pasta.

"That smells heavenly."

I shrugged as I turned to face Bethany and Andi again. "Thanks. It's just spaghetti."

If Andi was angling for an invitation to stay for dinner, and she was, it wasn't going to come from me. If Bethany wanted to invite her, well, it was her apartment and Andi was her friend. She could do what she wanted.

I leaned a hip against the counter and folded my arms across my chest, waiting to see what Bethany would do. She set the laundry basket in her hallway then stepped back to the kitchen.

"Like I said, I'm sorry I forgot to text you. Thanks for not being mad at me. Are you going to be around tomorrow?"

Andi shoved her hands in the back pockets of her jeans casually, probably beginning to realize that an invitation to share our dinner didn't sound likely.

"I'll be around," she confirmed.

"Okay, good." Bethany pushed her hair back behind her ears as she looked over at me, then back at Andi. "I think we're just going to eat dinner, then crash for the night. I'll text you when I'm up and moving tomorrow, okay?"

It was a polite dismissal, but a clear one.

One that Andi accepted gracefully.

"That works. Also..." Andi crossed to the apartment door, pausing to shoot Bethany a sly grin as she was closing it behind her... "you owe me five bucks."

Bethany huffed out a breath, then turned back toward the kitchen, her expression so disgruntled, I had to laugh.

She looked at me, puzzled.

"What's funny?"

I reached for her, pulling her into my arms.

"You are." I kissed her forehead, smoothing the wrinkles out, then looked down at her. "You look like a kitten who's gotten its feathers ruffled."

"I'm not quite sure that metaphor works, but I am. Ruffled, I mean." She avoided my eyes, running her fingers lightly through my chest hair, making me crazy. "I didn't like how Andi was looking at you."

Really? This was interesting.

Careful to hold back my satisfied grin, I leaned back a little and tipped Bethany's face up to mine.

"Yeah?" I said mildly. "And how was that?"

Bethany narrowed her eyes at me, and my grin fought hard to break free.

"You know exactly how it was. Like you were a tasty snack and she wanted to lick you."

I not only grinned, I laughed.

"So descriptive." I leaned down and kissed her before cradling her face in my hands. "You mean the same way all those men looked at you at the shifter reception that night?"

"They did not," she denied, and I knew she believed that. She had no idea of her allure.

"They did," I insisted, my voice a little rough. "Watching them watch you was hard as hell."

She frowned up at me, still not understanding. "You were mad at me that night. Why would you..."

Her voice trailed off as I shook my head.

"I wanted you. I wasn't mad, I was frustrated. Not only would you barely give me the time of day, you practically ran from me every time I got close. So, watching the other men, knowing what they were thinking as they looked at you, and not having the right to do anything about it..." I blew out a breath, remembered tension swirling through my body... "once I talked to you, got you on my arm, it was better. They could still look, but I could make sure they didn't come near you."

I watched her think about it, remember the way I'd stayed close to her the rest of that night, not always touching her, but always by her side.

Her dark eyes full of apology, she pulled me to her for a kiss. "I'm sorry. Andi was bad enough. If we were in a whole roomful of women looking at you like that? I'm scared to think what I might do."

I liked that way too much. The thought of her throwing down with another woman over me? I'd never want her to do it – would never give her cause to do it – but I couldn't deny that touch of possessiveness lit me up.

I pulled Bethany against me, letting her feel how her little declaration had affected me, loving the way her eyes sparked with heat when she felt me against her.

"I don't care if they look. You're the only woman I want licking me."

It made her laugh, even if it was dangerously close to a statement I wasn't ready to make yet. I needed her to know, though. If she thought I was looking around for anyone but her, she was dead wrong.

"I don't care if the men look, either. I only care if you do."

I turned to the stove and flipped off the burners. Dinner would have to wait. All I wanted right then was Bethany, her soft body under mine, her sweet, tight heat surrounding me as she moaned my name.

I swept her up and over my shoulder, squeezing her cute little ass, carrying her toward her bedroom as she wiggled and laughed.

Dinner, when we had it, was very late that night.

# Chapter 23

Bethany

Monday morning, I was still the best kind of sore. Just a little, a twinge now and then, but enough to remind me of the many times Brody had been inside me over the past few days. If I was being honest, I probably should have told him I was too sore the last time on Saturday morning, or even the time before that when he woke me up in the middle of the night, but I hadn't wanted to. What I *had* wanted was Brody. With his talented hands and mouth all over me and his hard, perfect cock inside me, it had been impossible to remember all the reasons I shouldn't.

There were plenty – reasons I shouldn't let myself want him and reasons I shouldn't let him close. I was here to find answers, not to get involved with someone, no matter how amazing and irresistible he was. I didn't know who I could trust, not really. I didn't know how long I would or could stay. And once I found my answers – which I was determined to do – I had no idea what they would mean, for me or for my future.

It wasn't safe to get too close to Brody. And it wasn't fair to him. I was lying to him, every single day. Each time we kissed, each time I took him inside me. I was lying about who I was and why I was here. He deserved better.

And yet...

As I made my way into work on Monday morning, feeling the butterflies swoop and soar in my stomach at the thought of seeing Brody, I knew I wasn't going to pull back from him. There had never been anyone in my life remotely like Brody. For better or worse, I couldn't make myself push him away. I was going to ride this wave as long as I could and when it crashed, as it inevitably would, I just hoped there would be enough pieces of me left to pick up.

I crossed the lobby to the office wing, watching for any sign of Brody as I waved across the space to Ingrid and Kyra heading the opposite direction. I was all but holding my breath as I turned down the hallway to my office and Brody's just beyond it. I'd nearly reached my door when Brody stepped out of his office, devastating in a navy-blue suit and crisp, white shirt, just a hint of blond scruff lining his perfect jawline and the color of his suit turning his eyes bluer than usual. He looked like he'd stepped off the pages of a "sexiest man" calendar and I couldn't help but stop and stare.

"Morning, Bethany."

His smile was knowing as he ambled toward me, the mountain lion inside him evident in every step he took. It wasn't fair, really. The combination of those looks and that sexy, prowling walk would make any woman stupid, and I was far from immune.

He stopped in front of me, leaving a little space between us, though still far too close for mere co-workers, and brushed the tips of his fingers across my cheek.

"You okay?" he asked, a hint of real concern in his voice, and I realized I hadn't returned his greeting.

I took a breath and nodded. "Good morning. I'm okay."

"You sure?"

"I'm sure," I confirmed. "It would help if you could try to be a little less spectacular. Maybe shoot for merely 'attractive' rather than 'stunning' on some days."

The huge smile that crossed his face didn't help in the least.

With a hand behind my neck, he pulled me forward gently and pressed a kiss to my forehead, then bent his head next to mine.

"You need to do the same," he said in a low murmur, doing his best to keep his words for me only, surrounded as we were by mountain lion shifters. "That dress you have on makes me want to push you against the wall and see what you have on underneath it."

It was a simple sweater dress. I loved the deep ruby red color and the way it skimmed my curves without being too tight, but I wouldn't have considered it sexy or provocative. I wouldn't have worn it to work if I did.

Brody, however, had ideas of his own.

"I can't find out for myself, so I need you to tell me. What do you have on under here, Bethany?" He tugged lightly at my dress, pulling it up just a fraction.

I could have told him the truth – that I had on serviceable black panties and a matching bra. Sure, they were the same color, if that could be considered sexy, but that was as far as it went.

I didn't tell him that, though. That wasn't what he wanted to hear, and it wasn't the answer I wanted to give.

I turned my head a little, speaking directly in his ear. "I guess you'll just have to wonder and use your imagination."

A low growl rumbled through him as I felt his body tense.

"I'm about two seconds away from pinning you against this wall, pulling your dress to your waist, dropping to my knees, and shoving my tongue in your sweet pussy."

Heat rushed through me at his words, and I felt the cotton of my panties grow damp.

That was one thing he hadn't done for me yet, and that I hadn't done for him. Just the mental image was almost enough to make me come right then and there.

My breath caught in my chest, and I very nearly whimpered. "We have to stop, Brody. We're at work."

Brody stilled, inhaling deeply as if he was breathing me in, before stepping back, the banked fire and reluctance in his blazing blue-green eyes telling me how very much he didn't want to.

He cleared his throat and pushed a hand through his hair, giving us both a moment to regroup.

"Are you free for lunch?" His voice was still husky with the aftereffects of our exchange.

I shook my head, not trusting my voice at first, but giving it a try. "I have a meeting with Cason and Athena."

I'd happily skip it if I could. Though I liked Cason, I found Athena stern and intimidating, and I avoided her whenever possible. Unfortunately, this wasn't one of those times.

"Okay." Brody let out a slow breath as he focused on the floor for a few seconds before bringing his eyes back to mine. "I'm booked solid today other than lunch, and I'm attending the Alliance Council meeting with Rhyne tonight. It will be late by the time we finish." Body shook his head in frustration. "Dammit, I wanted to see you today."

Warmth buzzed under my skin at the thought of Brody being disappointed that he couldn't be with me.

"I wanted to see you, too. Lunch tomorrow?"

It wasn't what either of us wanted, but at the moment, it was the best I could do.

"Lunch tomorrow," Brody agreed. He ran his eyes over me. "Just the two of us. Somewhere private."

I laughed even as heat filled my core. "You have a bit of a one-track mind, Mr. Klein."

"Your fault, Miss McKay." He lowered his voice again. "If you weren't so damn tempting, I might be able to think of something else."

"Right back at you, Mr. Klein," I whispered back and watched his eyes flare.

"Be careful, Miss McKay. There's a ravenous animal inside me that's fighting to get free. I only have so much control and it's close to breaking."

I leaned into him, just a little, enough that our bodies barely brushed, and felt his muscles lock tight with tension.

"I'd love to find out what happens when it does."

His tortured growl ringing in my ears, I stepped into my office and closed the door behind me. I leaned back against it, breathing hard, unable to believe how I'd teased Brody, almost daring him to take me right where we stood. I listened, trying to hear over the rush of blood in my ears, feeling his presence on the other side of the door.

Just when I thought he was going to walk away, his voice, low and tight, whispered through the door to me.

"I can't wait to show you, baby. I cannot wait."

I swallowed hard as a thrill shot through me. I'd baited the mountain lion in its cage, as it were. It was only a matter of time until I found out what happened when it broke free.

# Chapter 24

Brody

It was Thursday before I saw Bethany again. An issue with one of the contractors working on the huts kept me out of the office all day Tuesday, making me miss our lunch date, and I'd spent the day Wednesday buried under all the work I hadn't gotten done Tuesday.

We'd texted back and forth, nothing heavy, just checking in with each other. It helped to know I was on her mind like she was on mine, but what I needed was to be close to her, to see her and touch her and breathe her in.

By the time she knocked on my door Thursday evening after work, I was practically coming out of my skin. The hours between when she'd agreed to let me make her dinner – at my place this time, where, unlike her place, I had not only multiple burners and pans and a working oven, but also a big, soft queen-size bed – had crept by like the hours before Christmas morning when you were a kid.

I couldn't wait to unwrap my present.

Seeing Bethany's smiling face, her cheeks pink and her eyes bright, when I opened the door sent a surge of emotion through me that I didn't want to examine too closely. There was want, desire – hell yeah, there was – but there was something else there, too. Something bigger and deeper, and too much to think about when I finally had Bethany close to me again.

I reached out and pulled her inside, my mouth descending on hers before I even got the door closed. When it was, I leaned her back against it, tunneling my hands into her hair, slanting my mouth over hers, our tongues tangling as she circled her arms around me. She slipped her soft, cool hands under my t-shirt, running them over my back and along my sides, the feel of her skin on mine making my cock swell and harden. I groaned into her mouth and pressed against her, letting her know, letting her *feel*, what her touch and taste did to me.

When breathing became an urgent necessity, I ended the kiss, pulling back just enough to let us both draw in much-needed oxygen.

As our breathing settled, I smoothed her tousled hair and slipped my hands down to her hips, while she slid hers out from under my shirt and around to rest on my chest.

"Hi." Her swollen lips and dazed eyes made me want to roar with triumph. If that made me a primitive asshole, so be it.

"Hi," she returned with a small smile, sounding a little shy, and I had a sudden worry that my... *enthusiastic*... welcome may have overwhelmed her.

"Sorry I practically mauled you the second you stepped in the door. I guess I missed you." More than anyone or anything I'd ever known.

"It's okay. I liked it. I guess I missed you, too."

Bethany scraped her nails across my chest lightly, dragging them across my tight nipples as she went, and I swear I nearly passed out as all remaining blood in my upper body rushed straight to my cock.

I got the shock of my life when Bethany reached down and cupped me through my jeans. My eyes slammed shut and my breath stuttered in my lungs as the sensation of her hand holding me, squeezing me gently, nearly took me to my knees.

"Bethany," I managed to wheeze out, "baby, you can't do that if you want..." I swallowed hard and tried again. "There's...dinner...I..."

Another light squeeze, the firm slide of her hand down my length and back up, and I knew, just *knew*, that I'd die if I didn't get inside her.

Eyes still closed, I dropped my head forward to rest against hers. "Baby, you have to stop. I can't hold on with you touching me like that."

"I don't want to." She sounded breathless and more turned on than I'd ever heard her. I opened my eyes to find hers, dark and hot, on mine. "I don't want to ruin dinner, but I don't think I can wait."

I'd died and gone straight to heaven. A hot, perfect heaven where Bethany was as desperate for me as I was for her.

It was the only possible explanation.

Lucky for me, dinner was in the fridge, waiting to go into the oven. It could sit there all night if it needed to.

With the way I wanted Bethany, it just might.

I swung her up into my arms and headed for the stairs as she held tight to me. Once in my bedroom, I tossed her on the bed, then stepped back, tearing at my clothes as she tore at hers.

She'd gotten her shoes, sweater, and leggings off and was reaching for her panties when I stopped her.

"Leave your panties on," I ordered, my cock surging as her hands fell away from them immediately and her eyes flew to mine in surprise. I'd never talked to her in that tone, never commanded her to do anything. Given her reaction, it seemed she liked it. I filed that bit of information away as I went on. "Those are for me to take off you."

She nodded, eyes fixed on me as I pushed my briefs down, baring my rigid cock to her gaze, then stepped out of them along with my jeans.

Her breath whooshed out of her as she stared at me, and I swore I felt her eyes on me like a touch. Knowing I was already skating close to the point of no return, I climbed onto the bed with her and helped her with her bra. As I tossed it to the side, I treated her to the same stare she'd given me, drinking in her beauty, reveling in the fact that, at least in this moment, she was all mine.

I dragged the bedspread out of the way, then pushed her on her back and angled my body over hers, swooping in for a kiss, devouring her mouth as she wrapped one leg around my hip. I broke the kiss, sliding down a little to take one of her nipples in my mouth, playing with the other while she arched into me, her arms wrapped around me in a death grip as if she was afraid I'd try to get away. I could feel the heat of her on my abs as I lay between her legs, and finally it was too much to resist.

I slid down her body, pressing kisses along her ribs and across her stomach as I trailed my hands down her sides, loving the feel of her silky skin. I ran my nose across the waistband of her panties, then careful not to scrape her delicate skin with my rough stubble, nudged her legs farther apart and nuzzled my face into the crease of her inner thigh. I inhaled her delicious scent, feeling my canines start to drop as my mouth watered in anticipation of her taste. I'd gotten a first tiny taste up on the mountain when I'd licked my fingers clean of her sweetness; I couldn't wait any longer for my feast.

Mindful of my sharp canines, I gripped Bethany's panties with my teeth and dragged them down, revealing her sweet, wet center. I pulled them off the rest of the way and threw them, wholly focused on the gorgeous sight in front of me. I felt myself shifting as I looked at her, my muscles growing lean and taut and my senses of hearing and sight heightening. A light layer of soft fur covered my chest and back. I felt my facial bones and then the tips of my ears sharpen, taking on the classic, feline look of the animal that was so much a part of me. I knew if I looked in a mirror, my eyes would be glowing, tipped up slightly at the corners, my pupils oval. Unlike many other members of my clan, my claws rarely extended unless I shifted to my fullest extent, a fact for which I was grateful as I continued to run my hands over Bethany's hips and abdomen.

Tipping my head down, I took long, leisurely licks of Bethany's center, relishing each millimeter from bottom to top. I flicked the tip of my tongue across Bethany's swollen clit again and again as she gasped, her hands fisting in the covers at either side of her hips. I pulled her little bundle of nerves between my lips and sucked as she moaned, then clamped an arm across her hips, holding her down as

I licked down to her opening and shoved my tongue as deeply as I could inside her. When her legs began to shake, I licked back up to her clit, torturing it for a moment, holding her on the edge, listening to the sweet sounds of her panting over the thump-thump-thump of her racing heart. She keened, sounding desperate, and I gave in and gave her what she needed. I sucked her clit between my lips, slid two fingers into her tight channel and she exploded. I held her tight to the bed, making her take it all, feel it all, as her inner walls clamped down on my fingers as I repeatedly thrust them into her, and her pussy pulsed against my lips. I watched her lose herself in pleasure, knowing I'd been the one to give it to her, and that I'd give almost anything to be able to do it again and again.

As she started to come down, I pushed to my knees and wiped my face with the crook of my arm. Gripping Bethany's legs, I pulled her to me, draped her thighs over my own, and leaned over her, entering her with one smooth thrust. Her quick intake of breath made me pause and look up into her eyes.

She looked perfect – satisfied, a little sex-drunk, so beautiful it made my heart hurt.

"Okay, baby?"

"Fantastic." She lifted her hips, eyes closing with the sensation, taking me in a little deeper and making both of us groan. "You feel so good inside me. You fill me up like I was made for you."

My heart slammed harder in my chest as I thrust into her, feeling her words to my core. "Maybe you were, baby. Maybe we were made for each other."

I pushed into her over and over – hard thrust in; slow, tortuous drag out – as Bethany shook, arching her back, her nails digging into my forearms. Too soon, I felt the telltale sparks at the base of my spine and knew I wouldn't last much longer.

"Touch yourself for me, Bethany. I need you to come for me; to come with me. Let me see you come apart again, baby."

Bethany moved one hand to her clit, stroking it hard, her eyes locked on mine. I saw her orgasm coming the second before it hit, her inner walls tightening on my cock, triggering my own release. I pressed into her one final time, holding myself there as I came so hard, I nearly blacked out. Muscles shaking, I pulled out of Bethany slowly, levering myself to the side to lay next to her. I felt her hand brush mine and I reached for it, notching our fingers together as we lay on our backs, our breathing and heart rates slowly returning to normal.

When I thought I could stand, I left the bed, and cleaned myself up quickly in the bathroom. I took a warm cloth back the bed to do the same for Bethany, loving the way she always blushed a little as I took care of her. Then I climbed back on the bed, grabbed the covers from where they'd ended up on the floor, and pulled them over us. Bethany snuggled into my side, and I let out a long breath, feeling more settled, more peaceful than I had in a long time.

# Chapter 25

Bethany

"Can I ask you a shifter question?"

Brody gave me the same answer he always did as he gathered up the remains of our lunch. "Of course. Ask me anything."

We were sitting in the spot Brody had shown me on our first hike together, the same place we'd eaten our lunch that day. It was the second time we'd made the hike up in the weeks we'd been together, and it was quickly becoming one of my favorite things to do with Brody.

I loved being with Brody anywhere doing anything – our lunches together, the times we'd hang out and relax or cook together, the nights and mornings we'd lay in bed talking – but out here he was different. He was in his element, his love for the great outdoors front and center. He seemed so relaxed, so open when we were up here or on one of the shorter hikes we'd taken, as if everything other than joy at being out in nature melted away for him.

He sat down next to me, his thigh touching mine as we sat side-by-side, facing the view of the valley below us.

"What do you want to know?"

His question brought my mind back to what I'd wanted to ask him.

"I've lived around demi-shifters my whole life, but I've never had one as a close friend or anything, so I've never been able to ask this. I've always wondered how the whole demi-shifter thing works. I know some of you are 'stronger' than others but I'm not sure I 100% understand what that means."

Brody picked up my hand, playing with my fingers as he answered.

"Every demi-shifter is a little different, just as every full shifter and every pure-bred human is. There's a wide spectrum. Some demi-shifters are close to being able to shift fully. Those are the ones considered the 'strongest'. Ingrid, Rhyne's assistant, is a strong demi-shifter, the strongest in our clan. On the other end of the spectrum are demi-shifters who barely have any characteristics of their shifter animal and don't shift at all, at least not in any noticeable way. Most of us are somewhere in the middle."

"Can you shift when you're born, or do you grow into it, or...?"

"Some characteristics are there at birth. Like with Lexi – those eyes of hers are a dead giveaway that she's got mountain lion in her. As far as how fully she can shift? We won't know that until she's a little older, probably around 11 or 12, maybe a little younger."

"Okay, just one more."

Brody tugged on my hand, pulling me close for a kiss. "Ask as many as you want."

"If you start to shift, can you stop it? Can you shift on purpose, or does it just happen?"

He pulled me close again and kissed the tip of my nose, making me smile. "That's two questions."

I stuck the tip of my tongue out at him, and he gave me a sexy grin.

"I have better uses for that tongue."

I rolled my eyes at him, fighting another smile as he answered.

"Can I stop it? To some extent. Control is something every demi-shifter learns as they mature. A shift can happen fast, though, and talking yourself down doesn't always work. Can I make it happen? No. That's something only full shifters can do."

I bumped my shoulder against his, loving our closeness. "Thanks for telling me. It's hard to imagine what it's like having an animal that's part of you."

"It's hard to imagine what it's like *not* having an animal that's part of you."

Brody stood, holding his hand out to me to pull me to my feet. "It's probably time we head back. How's this...I'll race you to the stream. First one there picks our first position tonight."

A small thrill went through at the thought of the night ahead with Brody. Still, I propped my hands on my hips and gave him an exaggerated pout.

"That hardly seems fair, Mr. Mountain Lion."

"All's fair in love, baby. Besides, it's only our first position. Loser picks the second one. We can pick the third together."

Mmm, I loved it when he grinned at me like that, his beautiful eyes burning with the heat of his desire for me.

"Well then." I dropped my hands, slid my pack on my shoulders and sauntered toward the trail, letting my hips swing a little, making him groan. "If you're promising me three positions, it sounds like I've already won."

I squeaked as Brody gave my butt a light smack, coming up behind me. "At least three positions, sweetheart; at *least* three. And I would say we've both won."

# Chapter 26

Bethany

The text from Will, the investigator I'd hired, came as I was unlocking my apartment door after work one night a couple weeks later. It had been nearly a month since I'd heard anything from him at all, and I had been starting to worry that he'd forgotten about me.

I dumped my things on the floor, closed my door, then read through his text.

*Will: I have information. 9pm at The Big Read Bookstore. See email for instructions.*

9pm? I checked the clock. I had just over two hours to read his instructions, figure out where this bookstore was, and get there. I had no plans for the night – Brody was at another Alliance Council meeting with Rhyne, and Andi was working – so I should be fine.

A half hour later, my phone pinged again, only this time it was a message from Brody. My heart sank as I read it.

*Brody: Hey sweetheart, it sounds like the meeting won't go as late as I thought tonight. We should be done by about 8pm. I could be there to pick you up by 8:30.*

Brody and I almost never stayed at my place; his was just so much nicer. I looked at the clock, scrambling in my brain, trying to figure out how to bend space and time to make it all work.

It was impossible. There was no way I could go home with Brody *and* meet Will and I couldn't miss a chance to get more information on Rafe.

Hating what I was about to do, I did it anyway. Brody knew I didn't have plans with Andi that night and I could think of only one other plausible excuse not to see him.

*Me: I wish I could, but I think I'm coming down with something. I'm already in my pajamas. My plans for the night include my bed, a cup of tea, and a book. Can I have a raincheck?*

I set my phone down, feeling physically ill from the lie I'd just told. If there was a hell, I was going to burn in it.

I sat, head buried in my arms, and waited for Brody's reply.

Only to feel even worse when I read it.

*Brody: Of course, sweetheart. Always. If you need anything at all, let me know. Feel better, baby.*

Damn it. Why did he have to be so sweet to me when I was being anything but to him?

I texted him a simple "good night" then set my phone down again and walked away from it. I needed to pull myself together, get ready to meet Will, and I couldn't do that thinking about Brody.

# Chapter 27

Brody

I glanced at the parking lot of the bookstore as I went past, the full lot and lit up interior signaling that tonight was their once-monthly late-night sale. I was almost by it when something that shouldn't have been there caught my eye. I jerked my steering wheel to the right, making a hard turn into the parking lot of the closed business just beyond it. The driver behind me laid on their horn at my sudden maneuver, but I barely noticed, all my attention focused on Bethany's car sitting tucked away in the corner of the bookstore's lot.

There was no doubt it was hers. The half scratched off sticker in the back window would have told me that even if I hadn't been able to see her license plate. The question was, what was it doing here?

What was *she* doing here?

A couple hours earlier she'd said she was in her pj's and headed to bed with a cup of tea and a book. What had happened since then?

Had she suddenly felt better and wanted a different book? And decided to get out of bed, change, and drive halfway across town to get one?

It didn't make sense. Yet I couldn't deny that, for some reason, she was in the bookstore.

I climbed out of my truck, not sure what I was going to do, only knowing that I needed to find Bethany and figure out what was going on. This felt wrong, and I knew I wouldn't rest until I had some answers.

I strode toward the front doors, but stopped short when I spotted Bethany through the big front window. She stood with her back to me, looking at a shelf of books like she was scanning the titles. People milled all around the space, the event obviously popular, but Bethany seemed completely focused on the books in front of her. As

I watched, she pulled one out, seemed to check the title, then walked away.

Was it really as simple as her wanting a book? It still felt off, but it wasn't like she had to report her whereabouts to me or that she couldn't change her mind. If she wanted...

Then I saw the sign hanging over the bookshelf where Bethany had made her choice.

It read "Military History."

There was no way Bethany was here to grab a book on that topic. I was right...something was up.

I continued on into the store, moving around the stacks looking for Bethany, feeling the hum that told me she was somewhere nearby. I spotted her in a small alcove, her head bent over the open book. I was just about to call her name when she slipped an envelope from between the book's pages and quickly pushed it into her shoulder bag. My confusion grew as she pulled a similar envelope from the oversize pocket of her jacket, stuck it between the pages, and closed the book firmly.

She stayed where she was as she glanced around nervously. I instinctively stepped behind a stack, needing to see how this situation would play out. There was a suspicion forming in my mind, one I hated, but I had to know.

I watched her through a gap between the books as she checked the time, flipped the book over like she was reading the blurb on the back, seemingly stalling, waiting for who knew what as inconspicuously as she could. A moment later, she checked the time again, straightened her shoulders, and began moving back the way she had gone.

Which would take her right past where I was standing.

I moved to the far end of the stack, away from her direct path, and tracked her step by step. Just as she started to pass the stack, I slipped around the end and into the aisle she'd just passed. She hesitated, frowning, looking down the empty aisle where I'd been a split second before, and I wondered if she could feel my presence the same way I could feel hers. She glanced directly behind her, then down the aisle again, before shaking her head a little and moving on.

She went straight back to the section on Military History, reshelved the book as if she'd decided against it, then spun to her left and began scanning titles in the Political Philosophy section.

When a man immediately stepped up to the military history shelf and pulled out the book Bethany had just reshelved, my heart sank to the pit of my stomach. It sank even further when he moved over to stand at her side, looking at the books along with her.

"You're interested in Political Philosophy?"

His demeanor was non-threatening, his tone exactly what you would expect for one booklover casually speaking to another in the midst of a bookstore. From the feel of him, he was a boar demi-shifter, but nothing else about him stood out.

"I am, yes." To me, Bethany sounded nervous, on edge, but that may have been because I knew her.

Or had thought I did.

The man pointed out a book on one of the lower shelves. "I'd highly recommend you take a look at that one."

Bethany smiled at him politely. "Thank you. I appreciate your help."

She could have been talking about the book recommendation – her comment fit – but I couldn't help thinking that she was thanking him for something else.

Like whatever was in the envelope she'd pulled from the first book.

"Always glad to be of service." The man gave her a small nod, then turned and meandered away.

Bethany bent and pulled out the recommended book, moved to another out-of-the way spot, and repeated the steps she'd done with the other. This time, though, she didn't place an envelope in the book once she'd pulled one out. She simply placed the book on a small table and walked away from it.

When she headed for the front entrance, I made a beeline for the one on the side of the store. I needed to confront her and find out what the hell was going on, but this wasn't the place.

I sprinted to the truck, then drove toward Bethany's apartment as fast as I could without being a complete asshole, using every shortcut I knew to get there first. As I drove, my head spun, searching for a logical reason for what I'd seen, circling back again and again to the one thing that made any kind of sense.

The one thing I didn't want to believe.

When I reached Bethany's apartment building, I drove past, her empty parking spot confirming that I'd beat her there. I parked around the block so she wouldn't notice my truck, then ran silently through the back yards of the adjacent buildings, using my night vision to navigate. I slipped in the unlocked back door of her building and raced up the stairs, taking them three at a time. Once I reached her floor, I eased open the stairwell door just a fraction. Her hallway was empty, quiet, with no sign of anyone moving around. I hurried to her door and paused, listening for any hint that someone was inside. Hearing and feeling nothing, I took a few seconds to jimmy open the cheap lock, slipped inside the dark apartment, and re-engaged the lock.

I crossed to her front window and nudged aside the curtain, just in time to see her car pulling into its spot. Letting the curtain fall back in place, I settled in the darkest corner of her apartment to wait.

# Chapter 28

Bethany

My stomach was churning as I stepped off the elevator onto my floor. The whole drive back to my apartment from the bookstore was a blur. Somehow, I'd made it safely, even though my mind hadn't been on driving. My attention was focused on the two envelopes I'd gotten from Will, along with a persistent niggle of guilt at the back of my mind over the way I'd lied to Brody. I did my best to push that aside. I'd done what I had to in order to get the information I needed. Brody never needed to know.

I hurried to my door, hoping against hope that Andi wouldn't somehow pop up and intercept me. I unlocked my door, fumbling it twice because my hands were shaking, then finally, blessedly, stepped inside.

I closed the door behind me and leaned back against it. Eyes closed, I took a breath for what felt like the first time in hours as my shoulders slumped and relief poured through me.

"Did you think I wouldn't find out?"

I screamed, the voice in the darkness catching me completely off guard. I whirled and grabbed for the doorknob, my mind screaming at me to run. I pulled the door open a fraction just to feel it slam closed again as a big hard body barreled into my back crushing me against the wood surface of the door. I opened my mouth to scream again only to feel a hand clamp tightly over it.

"Don't scream. Don't make a sound. And I'll say this only once. Do. Not. Run. I will chase you down and I will catch you. I promise you, I will. My mountain lion will make it impossible not to. I'm just barely in control, Bethany. Do not test me."

Brody.

It was Brody who held me, if that was what you wanted to call the way his arms banded like steel around me. I took a deep breath in through my nose and released it, trying to slow my heart that was racing like a jackrabbit.

"Do you understand?"

His voice, rough and tight, rumbled directly in my ear and a shiver ran through me despite myself.

I nodded – all I could do with Brody's hand still covering my mouth – and felt his arms loosen a fraction. I squeaked, startled, when he spun, placing himself between me and the door, obviously not trusting me despite my agreement not to run. I heard the deadbolt lock into place, then Brody released me.

I took a few steps, then turned to face him, barely able to make out his features in the dim light, yet knowing he could see me much better. I was already at a disadvantage; I didn't need his night vision working against me, too.

"Will you please turn the light on?"

Brody hesitated and I thought he was going to refuse, then he reached one hand behind him and flipped the switch.

When I saw his face – his eyes – in the light, I regretted asking him to turn it on. His eyes were blazing turquoise, so much like they were when we were tangled up together, skin-on-skin, but oh so different. This time they didn't glow with desire. No, this time it was anger, and suspicion, and worst of all, betrayal. The way he stood, his back against the door, feet braced and arms crossed, completed the picture of a furious, hostile male.

"In your pj's headed to bed with tea and a book? Wasn't that what you said?" He looked me up and down, eyeing my street clothes and jacket.

It was obvious I'd lied. There was no use denying it or trying to make Brody think he'd misunderstood me.

The best I could do was damage control.

"I did say that. I got a call from a friend who needed to see me tonight."

Brody shook his head, his expression stony. "Strike two. You didn't go to bed, and you didn't go to help a friend. Wanna try again?"

Brody's biting sarcasm and the disbelieving smirk on his face made my heart twist. Even back when I'd been avoiding him, he'd never spoken to me or looked at me that way. I searched for something to say, anything but the truth.

There had to be some way to...

"I saw you at the bookstore, Bethany. You can stop trying to make up some other bullshit story. I saw you, and the man you met, and your whole little game with the books and the envelopes. So cut the crap and tell me what's going on."

Dammit. I closed my eyes as the last of the fight drained out of me.

"That's right, sweetheart. Whatever it was, your scam is over. Time to try something different and tell me the truth."

There was no way out of this. I could refuse to tell him, but it wouldn't matter. He wouldn't let this go.

I turned and walked to the couch, lowering myself slowly as I thought about how to say what I needed to.

Brody, anger rolling off him in waves, didn't wait for me to figure it out.

"Who is the man you met? What is he to you?"

That was easier than answering the "why" though I knew that was coming next.

I braved a glance at Brody.

"An investigator." I cleared my throat, my nerves making it hard to form words. "He's a private investigator that I hired."

"To do what?" Brody demanded.

"To help me find someone."

Brody pushed a hand through his hair, agitated, so different than his usual calm stillness.

"Dammit, Bethany, this is like trying to get blood from a stone. To find who? What the fuck are you up to?"

I took a deep breath, my hands clenched in my lap, my nails biting into my palms.

Here it was, the moment of truth. I could only hope I didn't come to regret it later.

"My father." My breath hitched as I said the words out loud. "I'm looking for my father."

# Chapter 29

Brody

Her father?

My mind slammed to a halt as I tried to process what Bethany had said.

I'd been so sure – 100% certain – that she'd been passing confidential clan information – selling it – to either the wild boar sounder or someone they were working with. The group had been laying low lately, but with the trouble they'd caused in the past...once I'd realized the man was a boar demi-shifter, no other thought had entered my mind.

So, to have Bethany say what she had...

"Why are you looking for your father? Why do you need an investigator to find him?"

Bethany's eyes dropped to her hands clenched together in her lap. I ruthlessly shoved away my instinct to comfort her. This was hard on her, but that was just too fucking bad. I hadn't asked her to lie to me and do whatever shady shit she was doing behind my back.

"He...it's a long story."

"I've got all night. Spill it."

Her cheeks pinked up a little, whether in embarrassment or anger I didn't know and didn't care. I needed to know what was going on. I wanted to cross the room, sit next to her, take her hands in mine, and beg her to trust me.

Which was why I stayed exactly where I was. Letting Bethany close without knowing more about her had been a mistake – one I needed to stop making.

Bethany pushed to her feet, and I tensed. I watched her warily as she crossed to her tiny kitchen, pulled a glass from the cabinet, and filled it with water from the tap. She took a few sips, set it on the counter, her hand still wrapped around it like a lifeline, then turned toward me. Her eyes flicked up to mine, then away to some seemingly random spot on the wall as she began to talk.

"He's not my actual father...not my biological one. I don't know who is. He's just the closest thing I ever had."

Taking her glass of water with her, she resettled herself on the couch. "I lived here, in this area, when I was little, until I was about four or five. The man I'm looking for was my mother's boyfriend when we lived here. We lived with him, and he took care of me, of us. My mom is..." she paused, her hands tightening around her glass... "was...scattered...flighty, I guess you might say. When I was growing up, she'd forget to pay bills, or forget to make dinner, or even forget that a day was a school day and take me off on an errand to some random town for something that had popped into her head. She also had bouts of paranoia. I guess my childhood could best be described as chaotic."

She stopped, took a sip of water, then shook her head before glancing up at me again. "I'm sorry. You didn't ask for my life history."

I hadn't asked for it, no. But despite everything – her lies, my anger, the fucking hole she'd torn in my heart – I ate up every crumb she gave me like a starving man who hadn't seen food for days.

"So, for a little while, we lived here with him. Then suddenly, one day, literally overnight, we didn't anymore. My mom moved us to the South Coastal region, far away from here, in an area where we knew no one. And that was where we stayed. I remember asking about him a few times after we first moved. My mom got angry – almost panicked – and told me never to say his name again, that he was dangerous and knew dangerous people; that if he or they found us, they would hurt us. Finally, she told me that wasn't even his name, that it was made up and the person I thought I knew was someone else entirely. As the years went by I just...stopped. Stopping asking, stopping wishing, stopped everything."

Bethany shrugged and I could feel how hopeless and lost she had felt, maybe still did.

"Mom and I kept to ourselves, and I grew up. She never wanted me to have friends, never let me do any after-school activities or date. It wasn't until I started at the community college a few years ago that I ever had a job, and even then, it was only because it was part of a co-op program."

Bethany blew out a long breath, her shoulders slumped as she went on.

"She passed away about a year ago. She got pneumonia somehow and just never..." Bethany's head dipped, and she took another breath, a shaky one this time. I wanted more than anything to scoop her up, hold her in my arms, and absorb her pain, but I didn't. I couldn't.

When she lifted her head, Bethany's eyes were glassy, but her voice was even. I admired her strength even as I fought my resentment that she hadn't trusted me enough to share any of this with me until I'd forced her to.

"I was going through her things when I found an old, cancelled check with his name on it. I was so shocked at first that I dropped it like it might bite me and just stared at it. Then I realized I not only had his full name, I had an address, and banking information. For the first time, I had what I needed to find him. Or I thought I did. I couldn't stop thinking about it so eventually I looked him up. And it was like he had never existed. The bank had gone out of business years before and the address on the check was a parking lot. A search of his name turned up nothing. So, I told myself to forget it, that what my mom had told me when I was little must have been true – that the man I knew was a phantom, and a potentially dangerous one at that. I set it aside, but then the dreams started."

Bethany stood and crossed to the sink again. She set her glass down and turned to face me, her hands gripping the counter on each side of her. "I dreamed about sitting on his shoulders, feeling as tall as the tallest tree; of him making me peanut butter and butter sandwiches, and of falling asleep snuggled between him and my mom. It was like a movie reel that played over and over in my head until it nearly drove me crazy. I had to know."

She looked directly at me and held my eyes for the first time tonight. "I have no one, Brody. My mom is gone and I'm alone. I had to know."

*She was wrong. She'd never be alone.*

I bit back the words just in time. A few hours before, I'd known they were true. As long as I was alive, Bethany would always have me. I'd never told her that, but it was true.

Or it had been then. Now...

I didn't know how I'd walk away from her, but her lies had shaken me up. How could I ever be sure of her when she'd had me completely fooled?

"So, you came looking for him." My voice sounded rough, tight from the control I was still exerting.

"I came looking for him. I knew I'd need help, so I contacted the private investigator, and he agreed to do some digging for me."

"What was in the envelopes he passed to you?"

"I don't know." Bethany glanced at her bag where she'd dropped it just inside the door. "I haven't opened them yet."

"What was in the envelope you left for him?"

"Money. He split the information he had for me into two envelopes and wouldn't tell me where the second one was until he had his money."

What the hell kind of sketchy PI had she gotten tangled up with? I pushed that away, trying to focus.

"Say you find your father, or this person who was like one to you. Then what?"

Bethany spread her hands wide as she shook her head slowly. "I don't know. My mom thought he was dangerous, that he would hurt us. Maybe I should listen to that, but something just tells me that's wrong. I barely remember him now, but when I think of him, of that time, I remember feeling happy. Safe. Maybe something changed, though. He may not even remember me or want anything to do with me."

"Let's assume he does. Do you stay? See if you can build a relationship with him? Or are you just here to satisfy your need to know, then take off?"

I didn't know why I was pushing her so hard on this.

Fuck that. Yes, I did.

If she didn't plan to stay, I wanted to know. I was already too far gone to make it matter, but...yeah, I wanted, *needed*, to know.

"I..." she ran her gaze around her space, avoiding mine again. "Don't know."

She did, though. I could feel it.

"I think you do. That's why this place looks like it does. You've been here for months and there's not a single thing that marks this place as yours. Not so much as a picture on the wall or a blanket on the couch. That's why you don't even have a damn bed."

She didn't push back, didn't even meet my eyes, telling me everything I needed to know.

Here I'd been – idiot that I was – planning my future around this woman, thinking about the mate bond, and babies, and forever, and all this time, she'd practically had one foot out the door.

Bile burned in my throat as I realized what a fool I'd been. I paced the tiny space, needing movement, something, to help me contain the anger and hurt that threatened to spew out of me.

I turned and pinned Bethany with a look, ignoring her pale face and the haunted look in her eyes. There was one more thing I needed to know, and she was damn well going to tell me.

"Is that it then? Are those all the lies you've told or is there more?"

# Chapter 30

Bethany

I needed to tell him the last of it. He could hardly get more furious with me than he was already.

I forced myself to look at him and just say it straight out.

"I lied on my job application. I needed a job, and I saw the one the clan posted..." I broke off. Brody didn't care about the details, only the fact that I hadn't been honest. "I did work in the marketing department, but I have no social media experience. I've just been winging it since I started."

I swore I felt a weight fall off my shoulders as I said the words. Brody's expression hardened a little, but he said nothing as he stared at me.

I knew the answer to what I was about to ask him – of course, I did – but I had to ask.

"Are you going to tell Rhyne?"

He wouldn't willingly lie to his alpha; if I knew anything about shifter culture, I knew that.

Brody choked out a harsh laugh, scrubbing his hands over his face before pushing them through his hair, leaving it disheveled.

"You know I have to." He shook his head, and my chest tightened at the resentment in his eyes when he looked at me. "Is your name even Bethany or is that a lie, too?"

His biting tone hurt, but I deserved it.

"That's my real name."

Brody didn't respond, just exhaled roughly, looking around my apartment again as if trying to figure out what to do next.

Hands on hips, he turned to face me. "Be at the office at 7 o'clock tomorrow morning. We'll catch Rhyne before his first meeting of the day and tell him together."

"Okay." Nausea swirled in my stomach as I agreed, but I knew it had to be done.

"Be there, Bethany," he demanded, his voice harsh. "Do not think you can fuck with me, or with my clan. I will personally hunt you down and drag you back here if I have to. Don't think I won't."

I'd never been afraid of Brody. Even knowing a predator lived inside him, even in the early days when I didn't know him and was nervous around him, I hadn't been afraid. I'd never worried he'd hurt me or wondered if he might be a danger to me. Now, as he stared me down, his turquoise eyes that had looked at me with such heat and affection burning with anger and betrayal, I wondered if that had been a mistake.

"You promised you'd never hurt me," I whispered, watching as Brody's eyes hardened even more, if that was possible.

"And you never said it back, did you? I guess I should have paid more attention to that."

He stalked to the door, pulling it closed behind him as he left without looking back. I sat on my couch, listened to his footsteps as they faded, and wondered how I'd managed to mess up the best thing in my life so completely.

• • • •

I WALKED INTO THE LOBBY of the clan's offices at 6:50 the next morning, not wanting to take the chance of being late and making things worse.

Brody was waiting for me. He watched me with his characteristic stillness as I crossed to him, eyes flicking over my outfit with no comment. I'd chosen to wear my ruby red sweater dress, both the color and the fit giving me a boost of desperately needed confidence. I wondered if Brody remembered our exchange in the hallway outside our offices when need had blazed between us, and it had been all we could do to keep our hands off each other. From the barely civil way he looked at me, it seemed the answer was no.

Had it only been a few weeks? Right now, it seemed like a lifetime ago.

My thoughts were interrupted by the tap of Ingrid's heels on the polished floor as she approached.

"Rhyne's ready for you."

Her tone was polite, and the look in her eyes as they met mine was...if not warm, at least not unfriendly.

I sighed, wishing I could undo the damage I'd done, but unable to see any other way I could have proceeded. I knew I could trust Brody, and Rhyne, and Ingrid, and their clan *now*, but I'd had no way to know it *then*.

I followed Ingrid to Rhyne's office, feeling Brody's presence at my back as I walked, no doubt ready to intercept me if I decided to bolt. He didn't need to worry; there was no chance of that. I just wanted to get this over with, put it behind me, assuming Rhyne would allow me to, and figure out what to do next.

Rhyne rose from behind his desk when Ingrid ushered us in, and I was struck once again by the aura of power that permeated the air around him. I thought, not for the first time, that his mate, Kyra, must be a special woman to have captured his absolute devotion the way she had. He was attractive, yes, though my eye was always drawn straight to Brody, and confident, but there was something more. Something that left no doubt he was the one in charge in any situation he was part of.

"Bethany, Brody, good morning. Ingrid, I think we have everything we need for now."

I felt a modicum of stress leak away at Rhyne's greeting. I had no idea what Brody had told him, but he didn't seem angry, at least not yet. Not the way Brody had been, and still was, though he seemed to have tamped it down a bit.

Rhyne waved me to a small seating area, lowering himself into the wingback chair across from mine after I'd seated myself.

"Coffee?" Rhyne offered, glancing from me to Brody where he stood across the room, his shoulder braced against the wall between two tall windows, as if he wanted to be as far from me as possible.

Shaking that thought away, I declined Rhyne's offer, worried that with the nausea already flipping my stomach end-on-end, coffee would only make things worse.

Rhyne poured a cup for himself, then sat back. "I want you to know that this office is sound-proofed, Bethany. Anything you say in here will only be heard by me and Brody. Whether I choose to share that information with anyone else once I've heard what you have to say remains to be seen. But for now, it's just you, me, and Brody. Understand?"

"Yes, I understand." I wished my voice was stronger, less timid, but at least I'd gotten the words out.

"Alright, then. Tell me what's going on."

I took a breath, dared a glance across the room at Brody, who stared back at me impassively, and launched in. I repeated what I'd told Brody the night before, even admitting the fact that I'd lied to get my job. Rhyne listened without interrupting, and also without showing any surprise, making me wonder how much he'd already heard from Brody. Nonetheless, I spilled it all, holding nothing back.

When I was finished, I sat back, waiting to hear my fate as Rafe continued to look at me, saying nothing, his expression unreadable. He still didn't seem angry exactly, but other than that, I had no clue what was going through his head. The silence stretched out. By the time Rhyne spoke, I was sure I was about to be escorted off the premises and told in no uncertain terms never to return.

"I don't think I have to tell you how serious this is. At the very least, I'd normally terminate your position with the clan immediately for lying in order to get it. Then there's the separate matter of the fact that you deliberately mispresented yourself, not only to us, but to everyone we introduced you to in the shifter community. If that were to become known – that we'd allowed you access to confidential clan information and trusted someone we shouldn't have – it could damage the reputation of our businesses and our clan."

Rhyne's words hit me hard. I'd never considered the possible ramifications of my actions for the clan.

"That wasn't my intention." That was no excuse, I knew.

Rhyne released a slow breath. "I believe that. I don't think you set out to deliberately do harm to the clan or any of its members."

If only certain members felt the same way. I resisted the urge to chance another glance at Brody, staying focused on Rhyne as he went on.

"As it is, I think we can minimize the possibility of any repercussions by keeping this information to just a highly trusted few. I'll allow you to remain in your position, as well."

There was no way I could hide my shock. I hadn't thought there was the slimmest possibility of not being fired. As for the rest of it...

"I...thank you. For allowing me to keep my job, although I know I don't deserve it, and most of all for allowing me to keep my true reason for being here mostly private."

"As for the job, you've done well, and removing you would only cause questions." Rhyne sat forward, resting his elbows on his knees, pinning me with the full weight of his intense alpha stare. "As for the rest, I'm taking a chance, possibly a foolish one. Don't mistake it for weakness. If there's any more dishonesty, you'll be dealt with accordingly with no hesitation."

I nodded my understanding, not trusting myself to form words.

Rhyne straightened and I drew in a careful breath, relieved to have the force of his powerful focus off me.

"You mentioned working with a private investigator. Is he the only other one who knows about your search for your father?"

"As far as I know. I haven't told anyone else."

Rhyne watched me, his expression thoughtful, as he ran his thumb back and forth across his bottom lip.

"Who's the investigator you're working with?"

"His name is Will Wyland. I have his contact information in my phone if you want it."

Rhyne nodded but didn't give any indication he wanted the information. "What information has he uncovered for you so far?"

"Not a whole lot." I let my frustration show. "Before last night, he'd found an old rental car contract that at least told me the name I remembered was right, and that it belonged to a real person. The information he gave me last night, though..." I shook my head, remembering how disappointed I'd been. "It was just a copy of a utility shutoff notice for an apartment that doesn't exist anymore, and banking information similar to what I already had. It gave me no new information at all. With the way Will was acting, insisting that we go through the whole process at the bookstore, I thought for sure it was something big."

"You said you've confirmed your father's name?"

"I have. It's Rafe Logan."

If Rhyne didn't show surprise before, he did now. Brody turned from where he'd been staring out the window, his eyes locking with Rhyne's for a moment before they both looked back at me.

"What?" I was suddenly breathless and wasn't sure why. "Do you recognize his name?"

With another glance at Brody, Rhyne looked back to me and nodded.

"Not only do we recognize his name, we know him."

# Chapter 31

Bethany

They *knew* Rafe? Not just knew *of* him, but knew him?

I stared at them both as unbidden tears welled up in my eyes. I swallowed hard, willing them away as Brody straightened and looked away, obviously uncomfortable with my emotional display.

"So, he's still here, in this area? He lives here?"

After the disappointment and anxiety of last night, I'd been losing hope. The information Will had provided to me – and that I'd paid a lot of money for – had led me nowhere.

"He does," Rhyne confirmed. "He's reclusive, keeps to himself, but both Brody and I have met him."

I released a slow breath, struggling to believe that I wasn't dreaming. "Do you...could you tell me how to get in contact him, maybe meet him?"

Something passed between Rhyne and Brody again, some unspoken discussion that ended with a nod of agreement from them both. I knew shifters couldn't communicate telepathically, though that was a persistent myth among full humans, but something had clearly been discussed and decided in those few seconds.

"We can arrange a meeting, if that's what you want."

If that was what I wanted? My mind swirled with confusion. "Is there a reason I shouldn't?"

My mother had told me Rafe was dangerous, violent, even. I'd never quite believed her, but had she been right?

"No, it's just that the decision is yours and yours alone. If that's what you want, we'll set it up for you."

Rhyne's mild response eased my fears. I didn't know him well, but I knew that he'd never put me in a situation to meet Rafe if he thought I'd be in any kind of danger. Even Brody, as mad and disgusted as he was with me, wouldn't do that. His protective instincts, like

Rhyne's, wouldn't allow it. It was nothing to do with me personally. If that thought made me a little melancholy, well, it was what it was.

"I want to meet him, yes."

"Okay, fine." Rhyne sat, gazing at nothing, expression thoughtful as if he was thinking through next steps. "It's probably best to start with his alpha, Asher. From there..."

Rhyne cut off at my sharp intake of breath, looking at me with concern.

"He's a shifter? Rafe, I mean. He has an alpha, so that means he's a shifter, right?"

Rhyne frowned as he nodded slowly. "You didn't know that, then."

"I...no." Suddenly I felt foolish. How could I not know that? "I was so young, and my memories..." I shook my head. My memories were vague, fuzzy, more impressions than anything. "My mom would never talk about him and...I guess I never considered it."

"He's not just a shifter; he's rumored to be a full shifter. One of the few full shifters who still exist. Some say that's why he's so reclusive, but I don't know that to be true." Rhyne watched me closely and I wondered what he was looking for. "Does that change your mind about wanting to meet him?"

"No. Not at all." My answer was immediate, decisive, even though I was puzzled why it would make a difference.

Something made me look at Brody where he still stood across the room. He was watching me with an expression I couldn't read, and I looked away, too flustered to try to figure it out.

"Understood. I'll get in touch with Asher and explain the situation, then we'll go from there." Rhyne stood and crossed to his desk. "In the meantime, I'll have Ingrid look at my calendar and find..."

"I'll take her."

They were the first words Brody had said since we'd entered Rhyne's office. They sounded forced, reluctant, as if he'd rather not have said them.

"I can take care of it." Rhyne's tone was neutral, not dismissing or denying what Brody had said, simply stating a fact.

"You could." Brody pushed a hand through his hair, suddenly restless after his stillness of the past hour. "But think about it. If you take her, some may see that as an official clan action. If Rafe wants to refuse the meeting, it will be a lot more difficult for him if it's with you. If I do it, they'll know she has our support, but there won't be implications beyond that. It makes sense for you to reach out to Asher, alpha to alpha, but it would be less complicated if I go with her when they meet."

Rhyne leaned a hip on his desk, considering Brody's words. "You may be right. Even though it wouldn't be official business, some in the shifter community may see refusing a meeting with me to be an insult. We don't want to force his hand and the last thing we need is to have to do damage control."

Rhyne's attention swung to me as I stared at Brody, shocked by his offer.

*He's doing it for Rhyne, for his clan, not you. Don't go getting the idea that it means anything other than that.*

"Is that okay with you, Bethany? If Brody goes to meet Rafe with you, assuming a meeting happens?"

"I..." I hated that I was putting him in this position, forcing him to be around me. I didn't want that, but...

If the hard look he shot my way was any indication, my hesitation had made him even angrier. "I could just go by myself."

"No." Brody's response was as immediate as mine had been a few moments before and ten times more forceful. "That's not an option. You go with one of us or you don't go."

I waited for Rhyne to respond, maybe to intervene, but he said nothing.

"Okay, I...it's fine." I looked at Rhyne, then back to Brody, or more precisely at Brody's back, since he had now turned away from me. "Whatever you think is best," I finished weakly, not wanting to make things any worse.

"Brody has a valid point. Potential complications will be kept at a minimum if he takes you, and you'll have the security of knowing he's there. He's right that you shouldn't go on your own, not because you wouldn't be safe, but Rafe would no doubt be wary of who you are and what you want. There's no need to set him on edge if you can avoid it."

I simply nodded in agreement, still a bit stunned that we were sitting here talking about arrangements for me to see Rafe again, not *if*, but *when*, assuming he agreed.

The goal I'd set for myself nearly a year before was about to happen. No more clandestine meetings with an investigator, no more lying to people I cared about – all that was left was to see Rafe again. What happened after that was anyone's guess.

# Chapter 32

Brody

I was late for my donut date with Lacey.

I'd slept like shit – which was par for the course these days – woken up late once I did get to sleep and made a mad dash out of the house to meet Lacey.

I could have cancelled, probably should have. But I'd done that too often lately and needed some perspective from my best friend. If anyone could help figure out the shit show my life had turned into, it was Lacey.

She was sitting in our normal spot, scrolling through her phone when I walked in, with our regular order already sitting on the table in front her. She gave me a little wave and set her phone aside, then leaned her forearms on the table, watching me as I came closer.

"Morning, Lace. Sorry I'm late."

She waved that away as I picked up my coffee to take a sip. "You already apologized in your text. You look terrible."

Trust Lacey to put it right out there.

I shot her my best smile. "Thanks, sweetheart. I love you, too."

There was no answering smile from Lacey. "I do love you, and I'm worried about you. Kyra told me a little about what's going on with Bethany" – she held up her hand before I could protest – "Rhyne told her she could because he knows how close you and I are. I don't know all the details, but I know enough."

I set my coffee down and sat back, scrubbing my hands over my face like that would clear the fog from my brain. "Yeah, it's fucked up."

I shook my head as I stared off at nothing, running the past few weeks with Bethany through my mind. "She completely fooled me. I can't believe I didn't see it, or at least sense that something was off. I was blind-sided and I still have no idea how it happened."

"You're being too hard on yourself." Lacey reached across the table and gave my hand a squeeze. "I know she lied about a few things, but I liked Bethany when I met her. Kyra said the same thing."

"She didn't lie about a few things, Lace, she lied about everything. Or at least all the important things." Like who she was and why she was here. And our time together...her wonder at the beauty we'd experienced the times we'd gone hiking, her smiles, her need for me, the way she responded to my touch...had those all been lies, too? All calculated to distract me from what she was really here for? Was any of what we'd had together real?

"So, what's next?"

I thought about the evening ahead. "We meet with Rafe tonight. Kole agreed to let us use his pack's meeting hall so we're on neutral ground that's private." Kole, alpha of the bear pack to which Lacey's mate, Jackson, belonged, was also Rhyne's closest ally. "Asher will be there, too, so Rafe has backup if he feels like he needs it."

"He's the wolf who helped me and Jackson, isn't he? Rafe, I mean."

Some months before, Lacey and Jackson had had some trouble with the wild boar shifters and Rafe had stepped in to help.

"He is, yeah."

"He has my vote as a good man, then. He jumped in where he didn't have to. I'm sure he knows Jackson, but he didn't know me from any other human woman. I've never even spoken to him, before or since. But he still helped."

"Everything I know about him, which isn't much, sounds like he's a decent guy who keeps to himself. I don't know how this thing with Bethany is going to go, though, how he's going to react to her popping up out of nowhere after 20 years."

It could be a disaster. Who knew what her mother may have pulled before she took off with Bethany? What if Rafe wanted nothing to do with Bethany and rejected her? Or didn't remember her?

She was pinning so much hope on this meeting, what if it blew up in her face?

That was a big part of why I'd insisted on being the one to go with her. If it all went to hell, I'd be there for her. As pissed as I still was at her, I couldn't stand the thought of her going through that alone. Her tears when she'd found out we knew Rafe had nearly ripped my fucking heart out, what was left of it anyway. If she was hurting and I wasn't there? I wouldn't let that happen.

"Hopefully it will go fine."

"Hopefully. I don't know how much detail Asher gave Rafe, but he agreed to the meeting, so..."

"What happens after that? After tonight, I mean. What then?"

I shrugged, picking up my coffee again. "It's up to them. Bethany doesn't seem to expect much from him."

"That's a little sad, but I wasn't talking about Bethany and Rafe, I was talking about you and Bethany."

My heart squeezed in my chest as I carefully swallowed the drink of coffee I'd just taken. "I don't think there is a 'me and Bethany,' not anymore."

Lacey's eyes softened and I looked away, not wanting to see her feel sorry for me.

"Are you sure, Brody?"

"Yes. No. Fuck." I jammed my hand into my hair, frustrated. At this rate, I was going to end up bald. "How can there be? I can't trust her, can't trust my judgement when it comes to her. How can we have anything without that?"

"Do you love her?"

There it was. The question I'd been working hard not to think about. Ignoring it, shoving it down, hadn't made it go away. I looked my best friend in the eyes and told her the truth I'd known for weeks.

"She's my mate."

Lacey knew what that meant. She and Jackson were bonded mates; she knew exactly what I was saying.

"Oh, honey." Concern filled Lacey's expression as she reached across the table for my hand. "Maybe it will all work out. You don't have to decide anything right now. There's still a chance if you want there to be. I know Bethany messed up. She messed up, she confessed" – she raised her hands, forestalling my objection – "after she was caught, and she asked for forgiveness. We all do stupid stuff. Some more stupid than others, I get that, and what Bethany did was right up there. But she was scared, Brody. She was alone and she was scared, with all that craziness her mother dumped on her over the years filling her head. I know this is hard for you but give yourself some time. This can all still be okay."

I loved Lacey more than anyone other than my mom and Be...I stopped that thought in its tracks. I loved her and I wanted to believe her, but I just didn't know if I could.

I squeezed her hand and let go. "I don't know. It's like this whole thing has knocked me on my ass and I can't get my feet under me again. The past three days since I found out the truth...I don't know. I was so sure of what I wanted with her, but now? I can't see a way back there."

"I know. I know right now it seems impossible. Be mad if you need to, no one will blame you in the least, just...don't do anything that can't be undone, okay?"

It was good advice; I knew it was. But could I follow it? Should I?

Should I hope? Try? Or was I just setting myself up for more pain?

# Chapter 33

Bethany

This was it. In less than – I checked my phone for the thousandth time in the past hour – 15 minutes, I'd see Rafe again.

I moved restlessly in the passenger seat of Brody's truck, his silent, brooding presence next to me ramping my nerves up even more. I'd been grateful he was the one going with me, but now? The tension stretching between us was nearly unbearable. I was so nervous, I was shaking.

I closed my eyes and breathed, trying to calm down and keep my heart from beating out of my chest.

"Relax." Brody's voice startled me, and my eyes flew open. He'd said only a handful of words to me for days, and nothing at all tonight when he'd picked me up or during the drive. "You're going to hyperventilate if you keep it up."

"I'm trying. Sorry."

There was no response, only more stony silence as we drove on.

A couple minutes before we reached our destination, Brody spoke again. "When we get there, let me go in ahead of you."

I looked over at him, surprised, but he resolutely kept his eyes on the road.

"Do you think there could be a problem?"

"No."

Then why...? I pressed a little more. "Why do you want to go in first then?"

"Because it never hurts to be careful. Just do as you're told. The way things are going with you, this will turn into a huge cluster, and I'll be the one who has to clean up your mess."

This wasn't the time, or the place, but the combination of nerves stretched to the breaking point and the cold resentment in his voice pushed me over the edge.

I turned in my seat to face him. If he didn't want to look at me in return, so be it.

"I get it, Brody, okay? I lied and I suck and you're mad and you hate me. I get all that, loud and clear. There's no need to keep saying it."

There was a moment of strained silence, then a quick glance at me before he looked away again. "I don't hate you."

But apparently, he did think I sucked and was still mad at me. Somehow that didn't make me feel much better.

"You have a strange way of showing it." I waited...no response, verbal or otherwise. I straightened in my seat, turning to stare out the windshield at the darkness, seeing only what was illuminated in the beam of the headlights. I couldn't stop the deep sigh that slipped out of me. "Look, Brody. I don't want to fight with you. I know I shouldn't have lied and I'm sorry. I did what I thought I had to at the time. It was unnecessary; I know that now, but I didn't know that then."

I wanted to say more, to ask him straight out if he could ever forgive me, but I couldn't go there right then.

"I appreciate you being willing to bring me tonight. I'm glad it's you." Brody gave a soft grunt, but I kept going. "Can we have a truce? Just for tonight?"

I saw him look over at me and turned my head to look back. His eyes were dark, unreadable.

"Truce," he agreed, his voice rougher than it had been a moment before. Then he looked away, nodding his head at a building up ahead of us. "We're almost there."

• • • •

AS INSTRUCTED, I LET Brody go through the door ahead of me. He hesitated for only a moment, seemingly scanning the area inside the building, then stepped back, holding the door open so I could pass him.

As I stepped inside, I got the impression of a big, open space, with a long bar at one end. The details were lost on me, though, as every bit of my attention focused on one of two men sitting at the bar.

Both stood as Brody and I entered, and I froze, riveted by the man on the right. He was big, as tall as Brody, but broader through the chest and shoulders, his dark hair and beard sprinkled with touches of gray.

He seemed as arrested by me as I was by him. Our eyes locked across the space, and seconds ticked away. I wondered idly if either of us was breathing.

Breaking out of the trance that held us, he took one halting step toward me, then another.

"Bex?" His voice was hoarse, tight, and the name he'd choked out nearly took me to my knees.

All I could do was nod as tears welled up and spilled over. He took one more step toward me, and I was moving.

I didn't even remember crossing the space between us. Suddenly, I was slamming into him, my arms around him as his clamped around me. He held me so tight I could hardly breathe, and I loved it.

He felt right. He smelled right. This was Rafe.

After 20 years, I was finally home.

# Chapter 34

Brody

If there'd been any doubt, there wasn't anymore. This was the man Bethany had been searching for.

I stayed where I was near the door, trying to give them space while still keeping an eye on Bethany. Asher walked over to join me, watching them, as well.

"I guess that answers that."

"Yeah, I'd say so." I folded my arms over my chest, watching them both wipe their eyes, bracing myself against the storm of emotions swirling through me – relief and happiness for Bethany, gratitude that I was here to witness their reunion, and a whole host of other emotions I wasn't sure I could even name. "It answers a lot of things."

"Thank God it's really her," Asher said, keeping his voice low, though I doubted they could hear us even if they were aware we were still in the room. "His face when I told him it might be... I'm not sure he'd have recovered if she'd turned out to be a fraud."

My hackles rose a little at the suggestion that Bethany may be a scam artist, but I reeled that in fast. Hadn't I thought the same thing when I'd witnessed the scene in the bookstore? And I knew Bethany far better than Asher. His highest responsibility as an alpha was to protect his pack and its members. It was only natural for him to have had his suspicions.

We gave them a couple more minutes, then joined them. The pure joy and happiness radiating from Bethany made my heart squeeze tight in my chest. I wanted that for her so badly – for her to feel that every single day. Now that she had the man she considered her father back, maybe she could. Whether I still wanted to play a part in that – whether she'd allow me to even if I did – was another question.

Asher clapped Rafe on the back as we stopped beside them. I shoved my hands in my pockets, fighting the instinct to pull Bethany out from under Rafe's arm and into my own. I knew it was different for him – she was his daughter, not his mate – but I couldn't stop my primal reaction to seeing another man touching her.

"So...you two know each other?" Asher asked blandly, ringing laughs from both Bethany and Rafe, and lightening the mood.

"We do," Rafe confirmed, eyes shining with happiness that mirrored Bethany's. "Though she's a little taller than the last time I saw her. You look just like her, Bex, just like your mom."

"I do," she agreed. "And you look just like I remember. You haven't changed at all."

Rafe huffed out a laugh. "I have wrinkles and a few gray hairs that say different, but I'm not going to fight you on it." Rafe sobered, the light in his eyes dimming a little. "How is she, Bex? Your mom. Does she know you're here?"

Bethany swallowed hard, looking at the floor, and I was surprised a second later when her eyes swung to me. I looked back at her, not sure what she needed from me. Whatever it was, she must have gotten it, because she looked back at Rafe with a sigh.

"She's gone. She died a little over a year ago."

Rafe's expression filled with concern and something that looked a lot like regret. He reached out and smoothed his hand over Bethany's hair, seemingly seeking comfort as much as giving it.

"I'm sorry to hear that. I know you were the center of her world."

Bethany nodded, acknowledging his words. "Thanks. It's been a hard year. But it's better now."

Her small smile sparked an answering one from Rafe.

"Best it's been in a long while." He stepped back and motioned toward the bar where he and Asher had been sitting when we'd come in. "You want to sit? Fill me in on the last 20 years of your life?"

If I'd ever heard a laugh as beautiful as Bethany's, I couldn't remember it. Her face lit up again as she nodded. "Maybe just the highlights for tonight."

For the next two hours we sat and talked. Bethany and Rafe included Asher and me, and we each made a few comments here and there, but mostly it was the two of them, laughing, sharing memories, asking questions, and making up for years of lost time. As I watched them together, I realized I'd never seen Bethany this way – so happy, so open and free. Even in our best times together, I understood now that she'd kept part of herself closed off. I'd thought I'd had all of her, and it was a bitter pill to swallow realizing I never had.

I shook that thought off, not wanting Bethany to pick up on my mood.

Finally, the two wound down. Bethany sat looking at her hands for a moment, then back up at Rafe.

"This may be too much for tonight, but I want to understand why my mom did what she did. Why she moved us away so suddenly and never looked back."

Rafe's jaw tightened. When his hands gripped down on his thighs, I shot a look to Asher and got a brief shake of his head in return, telling me we didn't need to intervene.

"That's too much for tonight, you're right." I relaxed. Rafe sounded sad, maybe worried, but not as if Bethany's request had made him angry. "Let's plan a time to get together. I don't have all the answers, but I'll tell you what I know."

By unspoken agreement, we stood and headed for the exit together. Once outside, I shook Rafe's hand, then Asher's, as Rafe swept Bethany up in hug.

When she stepped back, her eyes were glassy again.

"None of that now," Rafe chided, touching her cheek. "You've already made this old man tear up once tonight. Any more and you'll damage my reputation."

Bethany gave a watery laugh. "We wouldn't want that." She wiped her eyes and sniffed, giving a little shake of her head. "I can't make myself leave. It's like I'm afraid you'll disappear again if I let you out of my sight."

"I get that, believe me." Remembered pain tinged the edge of Rafe's words. "Just remember, I've been here the whole time. And this is where I'll stay. No matter what, you'll always be able to find me, just like you were brave enough to this time."

Bethany launched herself at him, hugging him tight before stepping back again. "Okay, okay." She flapped her hand at her teary eyes and blew out a breath. "I know we have to go. I'll talk to you tomorrow?"

"Tomorrow," Rafe confirmed, as he took a reluctant step back, looking like he was no more eager than Bethany was to leave. "Sweet dreams, Bex."

"You, too."

After a "good night" to Asher, Bethany followed me to my truck. A minute later, we were turning out of the lot going one way, while Rafe and Asher went the other.

I glanced over at Bethany. She was quiet, watching the darkness go by out the passenger-side window, and I wondered what she was thinking.

"Happy?"

She turned her sweet smile on me, making my stomach tighten in reaction.

"Happy."

"Everything you hoped it would be?"

"It's funny, but..." she titled her head, thinking... "I never pictured what it would be like seeing him again. How it would play out. I was just so focused on finding him, I guess I never thought beyond that."

"The name he called you, 'Bex'. Is that just a nickname?"

"Mostly. I guess when I was little – like *little* little – I couldn't pronounce 'Bethany', that it came out more like 'Bexy'. So, that's what my mom and Rafe called me, mostly shortened to 'Bex'. When he called me that tonight...I haven't heard it in so long. After we left here, my mom used to slip every once in a while at first, but mostly it was just 'Bethany'.

She fell quiet again and I let her be, knowing she was replaying the evening in her head, thinking through all the things she and Rafe had said.

I pulled up at the door of her apartment building and it took her a minute to realize we'd stopped; she was so lost in thought.

"Thank you for taking me. I...it would have been a lot harder without you there."

Not wanting to read into that, I just nodded and told her, "You're welcome."

I expected her to get out of the truck, but she stayed, strangling the strap of her purse.

"Would you..." she stopped and cleared her throat... "when Rafe tells me what happened with my mom, would you be there with me? I know it's a lot to ask," she rushed on, "but from the way he reacted when I asked, it seems like it might be something big, and it's just...I feel better when you're there, like I can breathe better." She shook her head. "I don't know what it is exactly, and I know you're angry and I shouldn't ask, but...I'm asking."

I sat in stunned silence, trying to hide my shock. She didn't know it, but she was describing the mate bond – the sense of being complete, whole, settled in a way – that came only from being with your mate.

I'd felt it with her almost since the beginning, even if I hadn't recognized it at first. I'd had no idea that she felt it, too.

It wasn't until she spoke again that I realized I hadn't answered her.

"Never mind." She gave me a smile, a forced one that didn't come close to reaching her eyes. "I shouldn't have asked. Good night."

She was climbing out of the truck before I had the presence of mind to grab her arm, stopping her. It was the first time I'd touched her in days, and I knew from her gasp that we'd both felt the spark. She turned to look at me, half in, half out of the truck, those beautiful brown eyes of hers making my heart stick in my throat.

"I'll be there," I heard myself say, knowing I shouldn't dig myself in any deeper, but incapable of denying her. "You just surprised me. I'll take you. Just let me know when."

Her eyes warmed and the small smile she gave me this time was real. "Thank you. I'll let you know. Good night."

I watched her climb out the rest of the way – realizing belatedly that I should have held the door for her and helped her out – then go through the door to her building with a little wave.

I swung the truck back out onto the street, my mind still swirling. I'd told myself that Bethany had never truly been mine, yet she'd just told me that she felt our bond. She didn't understand it, but she felt it. The question I couldn't answer was...did that mean nothing, or did it mean everything?

# Chapter 35

Bethany

I was getting ready to meet Rafe when I heard a knock on my door. Surprised, I checked the time on my phone.

It was too early to be Brody. He was picking me up, and I knew he wouldn't be late, but it's not like he'd arrive early to hang out with me for a while either. Those days were gone.

We'd gotten through the past two days at work being civil. His communication with me had consisted mostly of nods, and chin lifts, and grunts, but at least he hadn't frozen me out completely. The others obviously knew something was up – the change in the dynamic between me and Brody was too blatant to miss – but nobody asked questions or commented, at least not to me.

For my part, I kept my head down and did my job. I was grateful and surprised to still have it, and equally grateful and surprised that Rhyne and Brody had apparently kept everything I'd told them to themselves. Not that I'd expected them to spread it around, but I'd fully expected that at the very least I'd be fired.

The knock came again as I left my bedroom. It wasn't Brody, so it could only be one other person. I opened the door to find Andi standing there, her eyes open wide in mock surprise.

"She lives! I'm in shock!

I groaned; eyes closed as I sagged against the doorframe. "I know, I'm the worst friend ever."

Since the night Brody had pulled all my secrets out of me, I'd been terrible about keeping in touch with Andi. Our schedules had been opposite and with everything that had happened in the past few days, it had been a whirlwind.

I stepped back to let Andi in. I didn't have time to talk with her, but I didn't want to hurt her feelings by telling her that.

"Maybe not the worst *ever.*" She threw herself down on the couch as she tended to do on furniture and frowned down at it. "Though you do own the worst couch."

"It came with the apartment," I reminded her. "I'm really sorry, but Brody's picking me up in a few minutes. You can keep me company while I get ready if you want to."

"And have a chance to get an eyeful of that beautiful mountain lion man of yours? Sign me up."

I hadn't told Andi that Brody and I were no longer together, and I wasn't going into it now. Letting her assume what she would, I lead the way to the bathroom. Andi perched on the side of the tub, while I worked on my make-up.

"So, what are you and Brody up to tonight?"

I could at least catch her up on this – the very short, very simple version. "I found out someone I used to know still lives in the area. We were close when I lived here before, so it was great to find out he's still here. Brody and I are going to spend some time with him tonight, just hanging out and catching up."

And finding out why my mom ran from this place and never looked back, but that was way more than I wanted to go into.

Andi looked up at me, her lips pursed, and brow wrinkled in thought. "Did I know you used to live here?"

Oops.

"Sure," I lied smoothly, then paused as if I were thinking. "I mean, I think so. I'm sure I mentioned it at some point."

"Probably," Andi agreed. She straightened, stretching her back as she covered a sudden yawn. "These crazy shifts I'm working are turning my brain to mush. So..." she leaned on her hands and studied me. "This guy...former friend, former boyfriend, human, shifter, none of the above, all of the above?"

"Uh..." I thought about how to respond as I swept on mascara. "None of the above on the first two, and shifter."

She perked up a little. "Yeah? What kind?"

It took me a second, but I followed her. With Andi, it wasn't always easy.

"Wolf."

"Mmm, the wolves are sexy."

I shot her a look. "Is that all you think about?"

"Given the lack of action I'm getting these days, yeah, it's on my mind. So, not friend, not boyfriend, then…?"

She let her question hang as I again thought about what to say.

"He was like a father to me."

Andi's eyebrows arched up. "This is a story I know I haven't heard."

"It's a long one." One I didn't want to share with anyone – other than Brody, I supposed, since I'd all but begged him to go with me to hear it – until I fully understood what had happened, myself.

I was saved from saying anything else by another knock on the door.

"That must be your hottie," Andi teased, wiggling her eyebrows and making me laugh. I needed to work on being a better friend to her. "That's my cue to get lost."

She followed me to the door, shooting Brody a flirtatious smile when I opened the door. She got no reaction, but that didn't deter her.

"You lovebirds have a great time." She slipped past Brody and down the hall, calling over her shoulder, "Don't do anything I can't afford bail money for!"

Which, given that Andi was perpetually broke, would be nearly anything.

Brody frowned down the hall after her, then looked back at me. "Is she always like that?"

I grabbed my bag from the hook near the door, then followed him out into the hallway. "She can be a little…"

"Obnoxious? In-your-face?"

"I was going to say 'enthusiastic' but she's a nice person."

Brody looked doubtful. "I'll take your word for it."

He held the stairway door for me, and we jogged down the stairs to the ground floor. When we reached his truck, I was surprised when he held the door for me and gave me a hand up. He didn't let his touch linger like he had when we were together, but still, it was a courteous gesture he hadn't shown me a few days before and one that I hadn't expected. I was probably reading too much into it, but it gave me a tiny bit of hope that he wouldn't stay mad at me forever.

We pulled out onto the street, and I was wondering how to break the silence between us when Brody spoke.

"You doing okay?"

I nodded even as my stomach jumped. "Mostly, yeah."

"Nervous?"

"Nervous, excited. Scared a little," I confessed.

Brody glanced over at me. "Scared? Of seeing Rafe or of what you might find out?"

"The second." I took a breath, forcing myself to stop twisting the strap of my bag into knots. "I've wondered about this for most of my life. I just hope I don't hate the answers."

"It's better to know, though, right?"

"It is," I agreed. I knew that, I believed it, but it didn't make me any less nervous.

Half an hour later, we turned off the paved mountain road onto a gravel drive. As we bumped along, I made a mental note not to attempt it in my sedan. Brody's truck handled the ruts fine, but my car would be toast long before I ever got to Rafe's house, which we did a few minutes later.

It was nice, simple – a modified A-frame with a deck that circled the house. Rafe opened the front door as Brody brought the truck to a stop in a small gravel-lined spot to the right of the house. The driveway continued on around the house, leading to what I assumed was an attached garage.

As Brody helped me down from the truck, Rafe came over to join us. As soon as Brody backed away, Rafe swept me into a hug.

"Good to see you, Bex." He shook Brody's hand. "You, too, Brody. Thanks for coming all this way."

"That's thanks to Brody. I never would have made it down the driveway, and that's if I'd even found it."

Brody pushed his hands in his front pockets and looked away, as if my thanks made him uncomfortable. "It's no trouble."

We followed Rafe into the house, and I looked around curiously, never having been inside an A-frame. It was more spacious than I'd thought it would be, the décor leaning toward "comfy woodsy male", but not so much that I felt like I was in a hunting lodge. I had an impression of one big space, with the great room flowing directly into the kitchen, and a huge stone fireplace centered on one wall, a small fire crackling away within the grate.

"I can give you the full tour now or later, if you're even interested."

"I am, but let's do it later if that's alright. I'm too nervous about what you're going to tell me to appreciate it right now."

Rafe nodded in understanding, but didn't, I noticed, reassure me that I didn't need to be nervous. I took the water he offered me and Brody, then settled on one of the big couches in front of the fireplace, with Rafe facing me on the other. Brody sat on the far end of the couch I was on, and Rafe launched in.

"I don't know how much of this you know, if any, so I'm just going to start from the beginning."

I took a sip of water, hoping it would ease the tightness in my throat. "I hardly know anything, so that sounds good."

"Okay." Rafe took a deep breath and started. "Before I tell you what happened with your mom, you need to know something about me. Asher is the only other person I've ever told this, so I'm counting on both of you to keep it to yourselves." He waited for our nods of confirmation. "My great grandfather was involved in a research project with an organization called The Tennings Institute. Whether it was voluntary or not, I don't know. I do know he was paid a nice amount of money for participating. To keep it brief, he underwent a series of procedures in an attempt to alter his genes to produce full wolf shifters with superior strength, speed, and senses – to create so-called 'warrior wolves'. Eventually, he discovered that the researchers were motivated more by the quest for power than science. The project was a bust, but the genetic modifications have been handed down generation to generation, from my great-grandfather to my grandfather to my father to me. I'm the last of the line. This will all be relevant later."

My head was spinning, and we'd barely begun. I should have known this wouldn't be simple.

"So, your mom...you know your mom was 18 when she had you. She left home soon after when you were just a few months old. Maggie said she left because she was afraid her family would take you away from her. Whether that was real or not, I don't know. Given what happened later, I have my doubts, but don't know anything for sure."

"About two years later, you both ended up here. Maggie never would talk about that time, so I don't know where the two of you were for those two years. We met when you were moving into an apartment across the street from where I was working at the time. She was trying to carry things in from the car with you in a baby carrier strapped to her back. I got a couple of the other guys, and we went over and helped her. I doubt she would have let us, but you were fussy, and it let her get you settled. I stopped over the next day after work to check on both of you and the rest is history. I was hooked."

"A month after we moved you into that apartment, we moved you out and into my house with me. I had you both for a little more than two years. Then one day you were gone."

"What happened?"

"Things were good for a while. Maggie was always a little skittish, a little moody, but she seemed better the longer she was here. I'd decided to ask her to marry me."

"Then one day – while she was cleaning, she said – she found some papers that I'd shoved in the back of my closet. They were letters from The Tennings Institute, informing me they were resuming the research program and asking me to come in – demanding it – telling me it was my duty and offering me big sums of money to do it. I tried to explain it all to her, but it was obvious it unsettled her. In hindsight, I'm sure I made a mess of the explanation. There's no easy way to say, 'I'm the last of a line of genetically modified warrior wolves and researchers want to study me to see if they can clone me for reasons that may include world domination.' I know the truth – I've lived with it my whole life – and still some days it feels like bullshit made up by a crazy man. We might have gotten through that, maybe, but then Maggie saw me shift."

Rafe stood and crossed to the fireplace, gazing down at the flames for a moment before continuing.

"We were coming back from a pack gathering one night, just as it was starting to get dark. When we got home, your mom lifted you out of the car, set you on your feet, and just like that, you were off and into the yard, looking for a doll or toy or something you'd left outside earlier. I was coming around the car, watching you as your mom got her bag and other things she'd taken to the gathering out of the car. Out of the corner of my eye I saw three of the biggest coyotes I've ever seen dart out of the woods headed straight for you."

"I took off toward you, your mom screamed, and in an instant, I shifted. Fully and violently – one second I was a man, the next I was a wolf, my clothes hanging off me in shreds. I've never shifted that fast or that hard before then or since. Poor Maggie – she'd never seen me shift – not fully – and to see it happen like that...it must have been like her worst nightmare come to life right in front of her, a mother separated from her child by wild animals."

Tears threatened as I pictured my mom, terrified, knowing she couldn't get to me.

"After I shifted, I don't have clear memories of what happened next. All I know is I went into a frenzy, ripping the coyotes to shreds while you and your mother screamed and screamed. When it was over and the threat was gone, I came back to my senses and found you lying in the grass, unhurt, curled up into yourself, sobbing, and Maggie lying by the car, unconscious. I don't know if she fainted from fear, or...I just don't know."

"To this day, I can't believe you let me pick you up in the state I was in. I was breathing hard, covered in blood and God knows what else. After what you'd just witnessed..." Rafe swallowed hard, then cleared his throat. "I took you inside, then came back out and got Maggie. I got you settled down then tucked both of you into bed together in the main bedroom. I kept myself from crashing long enough to shower off the worst of the muck. I think I didn't want to take the chance of waking you up, so I dragged myself into the living room and passed out on the couch. By the time I came to almost ten hours later, you and your mom were gone."

"Maggie took all your things, every bit of cash we had in the house – which wasn't much – and the car. I was frantic. I looked for you both for years, hired a PI when I could afford to, the whole deal. But we had nothing to go on and I had no legal claim to you. Law enforcement couldn't help, even though the ones who knew me – knew *us* – were sympathetic. There's nothing illegal about a mom taking off with her daughter, even if it's sudden. As time went on, I wondered if you'd even want to see me if I did find you. Who knew if you'd even remember me?"

"I remembered," I whispered.

"I know that now. And I never forgot you. Even when I gave up hope of ever finding you, I never forgot you."

I thought back to the things my mom had said. "She told me you were dangerous, that you had people after you and they or you would hurt us if you found us."

Rafe came back and sat across from me again, his eyes dark with regret. "I know she was scared – she had every reason to be – but that never would have happened. I never would have hurt you or your mom. And the institute people...they're persistent and aggressive and have a strange vision of what our world should be, but they've never threatened me. If Maggie had just stayed and talked to me..."

He shook his head, and I knew he was thinking of all the wasted years.

"If only," I agreed. "You know how she was, though. She'd be fine, then the smallest thing would set her off, and she'd hide in our apartment for days."

"I'm sorry you had to live like that, Bex. That was too much for you to have to carry on your own."

I shrugged, hating the guilt and sadness I saw on his face. "It was what I knew. She was my mom, and she loved me in her way."

"She did love you," Rafe confirmed. "I wish I'd known more about her life before she showed up here. Maybe I could have anticipated that she'd run and done something to help. I've gone over and over it in my head over the years, wondering what I could have done differently."

"I don't think we'll ever know. She never talked about her past with me, not at all. The only clue I ever had was that she always had enough money for the things we needed – not extras, but food, rent, gas, the necessities. She never worked but when I asked her where the money came from, she told me not to worry about it. When she passed away, I got access to her bank account and noticed that there had been a regular deposit of a few thousand dollars every month since as far back as the statements went. Then the month after she died, there was no deposit. They just stopped."

"So, somebody was keeping tabs on you."

I looked over at Brody. He'd been so quiet while Rafe had told his story, but still I'd felt him there. "It seems so."

"And the money was meant for Maggie, not you. Otherwise, the payments wouldn't have stopped." Rafe pushed to his feet; his expression thoughtful as he crossed into the kitchen and pulled a soft drink from the fridge, closing it again when Brody and I shook our heads at his silent offer of one. He popped the top and took a sip as he ambled back to where we sat. "Maybe some kind of government benefit?"

"I was thinking family. Maybe Maggie's parent, or grandparent, or a sibling supported her, but didn't continue it for Bethany because they didn't consider her family." Brody turned to me, an apology in his eyes. "It's cold, but families can be brutal that way."

"It jives with her fear that her family would take Bex away." Rafe agreed. "Like you said though, Bex, we'll probably never know."

"That's okay. It doesn't matter now." Did I feel a twinge at the possibility of having family who knew about me, but didn't want me? Of course. Was I going to let it affect my life the least little bit? No, I wasn't.

Brody looked like he was still mulling something over. Did he think it *did* matter for some reason?

"Do you think it's something I should worry about, Brody?"

"No...," Brody responded slowly. "Not that, but..." he looked at Rafe... "the people at the institute, are they still contacting you? It sounded that way when you talked about them earlier."

"Not still, exactly, but again. The last letter came, I don't know, six months ago? I have it upstairs somewhere. I hadn't heard from them for years, then about a year ago, the letters started up again. It's like they focus on it for a while, set it aside for years, then start up again. The letters all come to me through the pack now because I keep my personal information well-hidden."

"I can vouch for that. When I searched for you, I found nothing. Even the investigator I hired didn't give me much." I wrinkled my nose at him, letting him know I wasn't mad about it.

"Sorry about that, honey. Like I've done in the past, I sent them one letter back telling them not so politely to go screw themselves and their crazy so-called 'research program' and leave me the hell alone. After that, I just ignored them."

Brody gave a quiet grunt of acknowledgement but said nothing and I wondered what he was thinking.

"That's it, Bex, the whole story, at least as much of it as I know."

I let it settle in, the peace of finally knowing, though there were admittedly still unanswered questions. "Thank you for telling me."

Rafe pinned me with a look, his expression serious. "Thank you for coming to find me. I never thought I'd see you again. Now you have to promise me you're going to stay. I don't want to lose you again, Bex."

"I'm not going anywhere." I'd been undecided, but not anymore. "I'm here to stay."

# Chapter 36

Bethany

The next two weeks were some of the happiest and the hardest in my life.

Happiest because of the time I got to spend with Rafe, catching up and learning who we each were now. He was so familiar, yet I learned new things about him – and myself – every day, like the fact that he could play most instruments, and that my love of spicy food apparently came from him. He admitted to being reclusive, though he didn't use that word, and that he didn't trust easily, which I couldn't help but think was a holdover from what had happened with my mom. Knowing that, my heart warmed at the easy way he'd welcomed me back into his life, seemingly trusting me – and I him – implicitly.

On the other side of that coin was Brody. We didn't speak, and he interacted with me as little as possible. When he couldn't avoid it completely, he was polite, and ended the interaction as quickly as possible. If it was payback for the days when I'd made him feel like he was my least favorite thing, it was coming back to me tenfold. Despite all that, I missed him so much it was painful and wanted to be with him. No matter how much my head said it wasn't going to happen, my heart and soul yearned for a different answer.

The one benefit I could see to my rift with Brody was that I'd had a little more time to spend with Andi when I wasn't at Rafe's. I even agreed to get up at the crack of dawn one Saturday to go to a huge artisan market that Andi couldn't stop talking about. I surprised myself by looking forward to it, despite the early start.

The day of the market, I met Andi in the hallway outside our apartments, still barely awake. She stood waiting for me, holding two reusable bottles filled with a concoction that was an odd shade of pink. Andi was a terrible cook, so I couldn't help but wonder what might be in it.

"Morning, Bethany." Andi practically shoved one of the bottles at me. I took it reflexively, looking down at it once I held it.

"It's a new smoothie mix I'm trying." Andi smiled but seemed jittery, nervous, no doubt because her past smoothie-making efforts had been nowhere close to successful. "I figured I owed you breakfast for dragging you with me so early."

"I appreciate that, thanks." I did, but that didn't make me any less wary of tasting whatever was in the bottle. "Should we get going?"

On the way to her car, Andi chattered about the market, going on about this artist or that. I listened with half an ear, making appropriate noises now and then.

We reached the car and buckled in, then Andi took a long drink of her smoothie before setting it in the cup holder.

"Try it," she insisted, nodding at mine. "This one's not bad, I promise. The mix is pre-made so it's harder to screw up."

Harder, but not impossible. Still, there was no getting out of it.

Andi watched me closely as I took a cautious sip, then another, surprised at the good flavor and texture. There was a slight chemical aftertaste, but I put that down the fact that it was a mix.

"I added some peaches; that's what made the color kind of weird. I'm not sure I can taste them, though. Can you?"

She watched me again as I took a few larger drinks, concentrating, trying to taste the peaches.

"I'm not sure I do. It's your best yet, though. You may have a keeper."

Seeming satisfied with that, Andi started the car, and we were on our way.

I drank my smoothie and checked out the passing scenery, unsure if I'd ever been in the part of the region that we were headed for. The sky had started out cloudy, but as we drove along, the clouds began to thin. I squinted at the glare, wishing for my sunglasses as a vague headache bloomed behind my eyes.

Andi continued to chatter about the place we were going – I'd forgotten the name already. I tried to listen, but with every passing minute it became more of a struggle.

Was this a migraine? I'd never had one, but I felt so strange...

I leaned my head back on the headrest, frowning as I fought to keep it there as my neck muscles seemed to turn to rubber. I gave up, closing my eyes and resting my head against the cool window instead.

Andi's chatter trailed off and I sensed her looking at me.

"Bethany?" I'd never heard her voice sound like it did, so quiet and worried.

I wanted to tell her I was sick, to ask her to turn around and take me home, but I couldn't form words. My limbs, my whole body felt weighed down.

Andi's despairing whisper slipped through the fog. "I'm sorry, Bethany. I'm so, so sorry. They made me. I didn't want to. I'm so sorry."

They made her? She was sorry? What had she done?

Those were my last conscious thoughts as the darkness closed around me.

# Chapter 37

Brody

Something was off. I couldn't put my finger on it. I felt restless, my mountain lion stirring, worried about I didn't know what. Although it was a Saturday, I was in the gym at work, the building quiet around me. I stopped, listening, letting my mountain lion closer to the surface, opening my senses. It was then that I felt it.

The uneasiness reached deep inside me. Whatever it was had to do with Bethany.

We'd been avoiding each other, hadn't spoken in days, but as soon as I realized that whatever this was had to do with her, my phone was in my hand. I tapped on her number, exhaling in frustration when it rang, then went to voicemail. I hung up, paced outside, thought about calling Rafe, then tried Bethany again. Then again.

It went to voicemail again, both times.

The second time I left a message telling her it was important and to please call me right away. I didn't want to scare her if nothing was wrong but given the growing agitation in the pit of my stomach, the odds of that seemed small.

I headed for my truck. I'd swing by Bethany's apartment, see if her car was in the lot, then decide what to do from there. On the way, I called Rafe.

He answered on the first ring. "Little early on a weekend, don't you think, Brody?"

I got straight to the point. "Have you talked to Bethany today? Or seen her?"

The urgency in Rafe's tone matched mine when he responded. "Not today. What's wrong?"

I squeezed the back of my neck, clamping down on a rising sense of panic. "I was hoping she stayed the night at your house and forgot her phone or something. She's not picking up."

"She was here last night, but she headed home right after dinner because she was meeting Andi early this morning to go to some big artisan market. She had her phone, because she messaged me when she got home. I'll ask you again, Brody. What's wrong?"

"I don't know. Maybe nothing. I just can't shake the feeling that something's not right. Like Bethany's hurt or needs help, or...something."

"Never ignore your gut. It sounds like you're calling from your truck. Are you on your way to her place?"

"Yeah, I'm about 15 minutes out."

"I'll meet you there."

Rafe was much farther out, and I knew he'd drive faster than he should, just like I was.

"Be careful coming down the mountain. She'll never forgive me if I get you in a wreck over nothing."

Rafe huffed out a humorless laugh. "She'd forgive us both eventually, but not without a lot of yelling. Let's hope this really is nothing and we get to listen to Bex give us both hell for being the overprotective assholes we both are."

"Let's hope," I agreed, even as the tension gripping my body told me that wasn't the way this was going to go.

• • • •

HER CAR WAS IN THE lot.

That was good. That confirmed that she'd made it home the night before and fit if she was out somewhere with Andi, assuming Andi had driven.

I headed into the building and up the stairs to Bethany's apartment. I stopped outside her door, stilling everything within me, listening. Nothing I heard or felt made me think Bethany was inside, but I knocked anyway. I wasn't surprised when there was no response.

Next, I tried Andi's apartment, with the same result. No response, and nothing that indicated anyone was there. I debated, then went back down to the ground floor to check the laundry room, then down to the basement to check the storage areas. I didn't expect to find anything, and I didn't.

As I was finishing up in the basement, Rafe messaged that he was there, and I headed back up to the ground floor to meet him.

"Anything?"

Rafe's calm acceptance as I shook my head told me he hadn't expected to find her any more than I had.

"I'm thinking about breaking into her apartment."

The fact that Rafe didn't immediately shoot me down spoke volumes. "How pissed do you think she'll be?"

I was already moving back toward the stairs, Rafe right next to me. "It's not like it's the first time," I mumbled. Rafe shot me a look but kept whatever thoughts he was having to himself.

As it had the first time, it took me only seconds to jimmy Bethany's lock. It didn't take much longer to confirm that nothing looked out of place. Her bag and phone were gone, which again, fit if she'd gone somewhere with Andi. When we looked at the papers scattered on her tiny table, though, we got a break – a note that said "Northern Market".

I held it up to show Rafe as adrenaline flared inside me. "Is this where they were going?"

I saw the hope in Rafe's eyes that I knew was echoed in mine. "It has to be. I don't think Bex told me the name, but she said it was some kind of market. That has to be it."

Once again, we were moving as we talked. "We can take my truck."

We locked Bethany's door as we left, then all but sprinted to the truck. Rafe found the Northern Market on his phone, plugged the address into my GPS, and we were on our way. While we drove, Rafe tried calling Bethany, leaving a voicemail of his own when she didn't pick up.

After the longest damn drive ever, we pulled into a huge gravel lot lined with a seemingly endless sea of vehicles. I eyed the giant warehouse-like building in front of us in frustration.

"We'll never find them in there. It's like looking for a needle in an entire hayfield."

Rafe nodded slowly in agreement. "Let me try Bex again. Maybe her phone was off before, or she had a shit signal. If that doesn't work, we'll split up, keep our eyes open, and keep trying to call her."

I leaned my head against the headrest as Rafe tapped Bethany's number, telling myself I had to calm down, only to bolt upright in my seat a second later when the call connected.

# Chapter 38

Bethany

I hated waking up with a headache. Not only that, but my mouth was as dry as the desert. Whatever illness had come over me in Andi's car, I was grateful she'd gotten me home. It was easing – I didn't feel nearly as bad as I had – but I still wasn't 100%.

I rolled over, then stopped, running my hand over the surface I was laying on, pressing my fingers into it to be sure.

I was on a bed, not my air mattress. Wherever I was, I wasn't at home.

I sat up quickly, paying the price as my head swam and throbbed. I held it in my hands, trying to breathe slowly as the pain gradually ebbed. Once it did, I raised my head and looked around the room.

There wasn't much to see, just the single bed I was sitting on, and a straight-backed wood chair. That was it. There were two windows with no window coverings letting in a grayish light that gave me no clue what time it was other than it was daytime. I ventured over to one on shaky legs and was treated to a view of the side of another building. From what I could tell, I was several stories up, near the top of the building based on the sliver of sky I could see when I looked up. I tried opening the windows, but they were either painted shut or I wasn't strong enough – either way, they didn't budge. Neither did the door when I tried to turn the knob.

I walked back over to the bed and sat on the edge, my energy spent, and tried to take stock of what else I knew. I was fully dressed in the same top, jeans, and running shoes I'd put on that morning – had it been that morning? – but there was no sign of my bag, or more importantly, my phone.

There was also no sign of Andi. Was she here somewhere, too? And where was "here"?

I had a vague impression of her apologizing, over and over. Had she been in on this?

As I had that thought, I heard the key in the door, and I tensed. The man who entered the room was someone I'd never seen before – I was certain of that – but based on his features he was from the same sounder as Andi.

"Good day, Ms. McKay. I'm glad you could join us."

I straightened my spine, not wanting the man to see how weak I felt.

"It's not like I had a choice."

I probably should have been afraid. Maybe if my head wasn't throbbing and I didn't feel like I was in the end stages of the flu, I would have been. As it was, I just wanted this man to tell me what he wanted from me so I could figure out how to get home.

The man chuckled.

"Yes, I suppose we could have invited you to come speak with us. This way seemed more efficient."

"Efficient? Having Andi drug me was 'efficient'?"

I was guessing, but he merely shrugged, neither confirming nor denying what I'd said.

"The important thing is that you're here. Now..."

I cut him off, rude maybe, but I had questions.

"Why am I here? Where is here, anyway? And where are my bag and phone?"

The man's eyes tightened a little, the only indication that he wasn't happy with me questioning him.

"All in due course. We'll explain everything."

I was about to ask him who "we" were when the door swung open behind him and another man, this one wearing a white lab coat, entered. The men exchanged a look, then the one in the lab coat came closer, peering at me as he walked.

"I'm Dr. Ulkos and this is Mr. Dolion. How are you feeling?"

"About as well as you'd expect."

Though I'd kept my answer purposely vague, the doctor nodded as if I'd been specific.

"Probably a bit of a headache, a little nausea, a little weakness." I kept my expression blank, not wanting to give anything away, as he turned to look at the first man. "I told you Andi wouldn't overdose her."

The nausea grew worse, and not from the drugs. I'd thought Andi was my friend, yet she'd drugged me and helped these people kidnap me? Was that what was going on?

"She knew I'd cut her off completely if she screwed up; I made that crystal clear. She's stupid, but not that stupid."

Cut her off? Was this man Andi's father? They didn't share a last name, but that didn't necessarily mean anything. I'd heard her say many times how much they hated each other, but she was dependent on him to survive. If the contempt that filled his voice when he talked about her was any indication, this was him.

I disliked him more by the second.

"Where is she? Andi."

Both men swung their heads to look at me.

"Irrelevant." The doctor pulled a small bottle of water from the pocket of his coat. He held it out to me, shaking his head as I eyed it suspiciously. "It's perfectly safe, I assure you. If you examine it, you'll see it's still sealed."

I took it cautiously, confirming that what he'd said was true. I opened it and sipped it as the two men watched me, hoping I wasn't making a grave error.

"Good. Now..." Andi's father rubbed his hands together briskly, "...we need to speak to you about your father."

"My father?" Of all the things he could have said, I would never have anticipated that would be it.

He saw my confusion but misunderstood it. He held up his hands as if conceding a point.

"Fair enough. The man you consider to be your father, who considers you his daughter. Rafe Logan."

"I don't understand." Maybe it was the aftereffects of whatever drug they'd given me, but this wasn't making sense. "How do you even know about my connection to him?"

"Ah." Mr. Dolion nodded sagely, as if I'd asked a deep question. "We have my sounder-mate, Will Wyland, to thank for that. He notified us as soon as you contacted him for assistance. He's been feeding you just enough information to keep you on the hook until we were ready to move. Of course, you spoiled that plan, but we were able to recover. Then we discovered Andi's involvement with you and here you are."

He sounded so proud. Did he expect me to congratulate him?

"What do you want with Rafe?"

Dr. Ulkos pulled the chair close to where I sat on the bed, seating himself and crossing his legs casually as if we were two friends chatting. I edged back, not wanting to give up ground, but wanting as much space as possible between us.

"We've been wanting to speak with him for quite some time. You may not realize it, Ms. McKay, but your father is a very special man."

Understanding began to dawn. If this was what I thought it was, the doctor in front of me - if he truly *was* a doctor – was creepy in the extreme.

"I know he is, and I know *why* he is, to me." I injected my voice with as much innocent naivete as I could muster. "Why is he special to you?"

The doctor leaned forward, elbows on his knees. "He's a very rare type of wolf shifter. He may not have told you."

I nodded agreeably, playing along. "Yes, a full shifter. The only one I've ever met."

Dr. Ulkos chuckled. "Full shifters are a dime a dozen compared to your father. His genetic..."

He broke off abruptly as the sound of a phone ringing filled the room. Not just any phone, *my* phone. Flustered, Andi's father pulled it from his pocket and rejected the call quickly with barely a glance at the screen. He shot a guilty look at the doctor who gave him an icy stare, leaving no doubt who outranked whom in this situation. The doctor turned back to me and straightened his cuffs as if brushing off the interruption.

I held my hand out to Mr. Dolion. "I'd like my phone back."

He ignored me as Dr. Ulkos answered briskly. "Not just yet. As I was saying, your father's genetic profile is extremely special and rare. So rare that we believe he's the only one who has it."

I narrowed my eyes as if I was thinking hard about what he'd said. "That's interesting, I suppose, but why do you want to talk to him about it?"

The doctor gave me a big smile that was probably supposed to be charming, but which I found exceedingly icky. I fought hard not to shudder in reaction.

"It would be a bit more than talking," he conceded. "Perhaps taking a few samples, doing some observation...."

My mind filled in the far less innocuous things Rafe had told me about that Dr. Ulkos conveniently left out – forced breeding, psychological experimentation, holding him for weeks at a time if not longer...

"If it's that simple, what's the problem?"

Something passed behind Dr. Ulkos' eyes, something dark and calculating. "Your father has been unwilling to speak with us."

From what Rafe had said, that was putting it mildly. "That doesn't surprise me. He's a private man."

Dr. Ulkos grimaced as if I'd said something distasteful. "Private, yes. Unreasonably so."

I shrugged, making no comment on that. "I understand you want to talk to him, and he's declined to do so. What I don't understand is what it has to do with me."

I was starting to, at least a small inkling, but a niggle at the back of my mind warned it may be far more serious than I'd let myself think about.

"We were hoping..."

As Dr. Ulkos started to answer, my phone began to ring again. Mr. Dolion yanked it out of his pocket again, frowning at it as Dr. Ulkos frowned furiously at him. When Mr. Dolion's eyes popped open wide, I knew who it must be.

"It's him," he whisper-yelled at Dr. Ulkos as if I wasn't sitting right there. "It's Logan."

Dr. Ulkos sat unmoving as the phone continued to ring. Knowing it was Rafe – that contact with him was *right there*, just out of reach – it was all I could do not to launch myself off the bed and make a grab for the phone.

Dr. Ulkos slid an assessing glance my way, then back at Mr. Dolion and finally spoke.

"Answer it. On speaker."

# Chapter 39

Brody

"Bex. Where the hell are you?"

There was no response to Rafe's question. Just the faint white noise that told us the line was open. We both stared at his phone like we might be able to see Bethany if we looked hard enough.

"Bex, are you there? Say something."

"Not 'Bex' I'm afraid, but she's here with me."

The male voice was a shock. I gripped the steering wheel until my knuckles turned white as the situation turned serious in an instant. Bethany missing along with her friend was one thing; her phone being answered by an unknown male she was "with" was another.

"Let me talk to my daughter," Rafe demanded.

There was a low murmur, then Bethany's voice, the sweetest sound I'd ever heard. "I'm here, Rafe. I'm okay."

She sounded tired, but calm, and a little distant, as if she wasn't right next to the phone.

"Give her the phone," Rafe insisted. "I want to talk to just her."

"Mmm..." The male made a considering noise, then "That doesn't seem advisable."

Eyes narrowed, Rafe growled, "Who the fuck is this?"

"We haven't had the pleasure of meeting in person yet, though you may recognize my name from correspondence we've sent. This is Dr. Ulkos with The Tennings Institute."

Rafe recognized the name alright. His hand gripped the phone so tightly I was surprised it didn't shatter.

"If you hurt her, if you so much as leave a scratch on her, I swear to you I will hunt you down and make every last minute of the rest of your life a worse hell than you could ever imagine."

A chuckle came through the phone as Rafe practically panted in anger. I tamped down my own rage and reached for Rafe, squeezing his shoulder both for support and in effort to ground him. He didn't acknowledge it, but he also didn't shrug my hand away.

"We have no intention of hurting anyone. We're an academic research institute, not some sort of disreputable gang."

"Research institute, my ass. You're a bunch of lunatics and freaks who think you can take over the world."

Dr. Ulkos, when he responded, wasn't quite as pleasant this time. "There's no need for name calling. Given your genetics, one might even call you the freak."

"I don't give one single fuck what anyone calls me. Let her go, Ulkos. Now."

Dr. Ulkos sighed. "I'm afraid I'm unable to do that. We'll be in touch soon."

"Goddam..." Rafe raged before cutting himself off. "I'll find you, Bex. I love you," he rushed out.

"I love you, R -."

Bethany's voice cut off, the sudden loss of connection like a punch to the sternum, stealing my breath. A second later, Rafe roared, rage and pain radiating from him as he smashed his phone into the dashboard again and again. Finally, heaving, his hand bloody and his phone obliterated, he stopped.

He dropped the pieces of his phone to the floor and sat staring out the windshield, although I felt sure he was seeing nothing.

"We'll find her, Rafe. We'll get her back." We had to. I refused to accept any other possibility.

"She was right. Maggie. She was right." The anguish in his voice, a twin to the emotion twisting my gut, was hard to listen to. "Bex never should have come back here. She should have stayed far away from me."

“You’re wrong. She wanted more than anything to find you and she’s been nothing but happy since she did.”

Rafe shook his head slowly, whether in denial of what I’d said or the thoughts running through his head, I didn’t know.

“If they hurt her…” He finally looked at me, cold intent I understood only too well filling his eyes.

If they hurt Bethany, Rafe would find the doctor and his cronies, and he’d make them pay.

And I’d be right by his side.

# Chapter 40

Bethany

"You could have let me say good-bye." I wrapped my arms around my irritation and anger and held them close, using them to shove down my tears.

I would not cry in front of these men; I would *not*. No matter how much my heart ached at the pain this was causing Rafe.

He'd sounded so furious. I had no idea how much time had passed since I'd been taken, but he'd sounded so worried when he'd first spoken. He'd felt so close, like I could almost reach out and touch him. It was probably wishful thinking, but somehow it had felt like Brody was there, too.

I didn't know why I thought that. Rafe hadn't said he was there, and Rafe was the only one who had spoken. But somewhere in the silence between everyone's words, I could have sworn I felt Brody.

Whether Dr. Ulkos or Mr. Dolion heard my comment or not, they chose not to respond. I had no idea what game they were playing, and I was tired of trying to figure it out.

"Tell me why I'm here," I demanded as both men looked at me with vague surprise. Had they thought I'd just give up if they didn't tell me the first time I asked? "All you've done is make Rafe angry. That can't help your cause."

"That's not for you to worry about," Dr. Ulkos sniffed dismissively. "As for your purpose, we'll discuss that with you soon. For now, Mr. Dolion and I have an important meeting to attend." The men moved toward the door. "Food is being prepared for you. I assure you it is not drugged in any way." *Like I believed that.* "I strongly suggest you eat it when it arrives and that you behave."

That last part made me pause. Other than being a little mouthy, I hadn't been disruptive. So, what was with the warning to behave?

"Am I your prisoner?" I blurted out, noting how both men jerked to a halt.

Dr. Ulkos turned slowly to face me as Mr. Dolion opened the door. "You're our guest," he corrected, inclining his head, then closing and locking the door behind him, leaving me to wonder what kind of "guest" you locked in.

# Chapter 41

Brody

Twenty-eight hours.

It had been twenty-eight hours since our last contact with Bethany, more than forty-three since Rafe had waved to her as she'd backed out of his driveway.

I was losing my mind, swinging from cold rage one minute to abject desperation the next, racking my brain for any possible way to find Bethany, swinging from iron certainty that we would, to mind-numbing fear that we wouldn't.

Rafe was in as bad a shape as I was, both of us clinging to sanity for the sole reason that Bethany needed us to. If we lost it, we could lose her, and we weren't about to let that happen.

It wasn't lost on me that Rafe had never, not once, questioned my involvement or challenged my emotional and mental tailspin. He and the others just seemed to accept that I belonged there, though I wouldn't have stepped back even if they'd demanded it. The need to protect Bethany was embedded deep within me, at my very core. It may not have been my right, or my responsibility, but it was my instinct. No matter what had happened between us, I didn't know how I could ever stop.

I paced along the windows that lined one side of the small conference room in the clan's headquarters building. We'd commandeered it as our command center and had been meeting for hours – me, Rafe, our alphas and betas, and the heads of both of our security teams. We'd talked ourselves hoarse, turned over every stone we could think of, and come up with nothing.

Every direction we went, every lead we followed, had ended in a dead end. We were taking a break now to regroup before going at it again.

Adding to our worries was the fact that Andi was missing, too. It couldn't be a coincidence. During our brief contact with Dr. Ulkos, he hadn't mentioned her name, and we hadn't heard her voice. Whether she was a participant in Bethany's abduction or another victim, we had no idea.

I turned and paced back the direction I'd just come, needing to *do* something, to take some kind of action, just fucking *move.* I wanted to run outside, let my mountain lion take control, and search for my mate. I could feel him just under the surface, prowling, waiting, ready for the hunt. If I'd had any clue where to look, even which direction to go, I would have done it.

But running in circles would do no one any good, least of all Bethany. At best, it would deplete our resources and at worst it would distract us from something that would lead us to her.

Sooner or later, we'd find a lead that didn't dead end, that got us one, or two, or ten steps closer. *Then*, I promised my mountain lion, *then I'd let him loose.*

# Chapter 42

Bethany

No one had hurt me, but I was in imminent danger of dying of boredom.

I shouldn't joke. It wasn't funny. I should be counting my blessings that I'd been left alone – and I was – but the lack of news, of interaction, of *anything*, was starting to mess with my mind.

Every so often, a young woman, her facial features giving away her status as a boar shifter, set a paper plate of finger food and a small bottle of water just inside the door, watched over by a huge, burly fully human man. Neither one spoke to me, just unlocked the door, set the food down, locked it again and left.

Then were the times the pair escorted me to a small bathroom next to the room I was in, the man holding me with a hand clamped on the back of my neck, even as I did my business, the young woman watching me vigilantly. It was mortifying, but what could I do?

And that was it. Those were the only people I saw. As hard as I listened, wishing desperately for mountain lion hearing, I heard nothing. No voices, no footsteps, no opening or closing doors, nothing.

Late afternoon on the third day the door opened. I frowned when I saw the huge man who brought my food and took me to the bathroom standing there alone. I'd never seen him before without the young woman and the change made me wary.

"Come on." It was the first time I'd heard him speak and it startled me. He waved me to the door, but I stayed where I was, not sure what was happening.

The man huffed impatiently. "Let's go."

I stood and walked slowly toward the door. "What's happening?"

"You're leaving."

"Leaving? I'm going home?" Hope streaked through me, just to die a quick death with his next words.

"No. Another location."

"I don't want to do that. I want to go home." I sounded petulant, whiny, but I didn't care.

"Not my call. Let's go," he repeated, this time grabbing me by the upper arm to make sure I complied.

He pulled me down the hall, down several flights of stairs, and out into a bare courtyard, his long strides forcing me to nearly jog to keep up. He led me to a nondescript black sedan that was idling with the driver's side door standing ajar, opened the back door, and pushed me inside.

He closed the door, engaged the locks, then slid into the driver's seat. A transparent divider separated the front seat from the back, allowing me to see the man but not touch him, like a limousine without any of the luxury.

I thought about asking him where he was taking me but knew that would get me nowhere. Grateful I hadn't been blindfolded, I watched as the miles went by, looking for anything that seemed familiar or signs that might tell me where I was.

We'd been driving for a while when I heard a soft but insistent binging sound. When the man looked down at the dashboard and cursed, then pulled into the next gas station, I realized the sound must have been the low fuel alert. I looked around as casually as I could, again searching for anything to tell me where we were.

There wasn't much to see. A few warehouse type buildings sat just past the gas station, but I couldn't see the business name. Across the road and down a little sat a long-shuttered diner with a sign so faded I couldn't read it. If there were homes nearby or other businesses, I couldn't see them from where I was.

It was while the man was pumping gas that my stomach growled loudly. I'd eaten a little that morning, but the food had been cold and stale, so I'd left most of it. I knocked on the window to get his attention. When he looked at me, I pointed to my stomach and mouthed "I'm hungry." He didn't look happy, but when he climbed back into the car, he pulled into a spot in front of the small store rather than driving off. He sat watching me in the rearview mirror, obviously debating whether to leave me in the car while he went in the store, or whether to take me with him. He must have decided taking me with him was the lesser of the two evils, because he climbed out and opened the back door.

As I slipped out, he clamped his hand around my upper arm again, squeezing just hard enough to hurt. He leaned down, trapping me between the car and his body as he spoke harshly in my ear.

"You give me any trouble in here, anything at all, I swear to God, I will make you regret it. Do you understand me?"

For the first time since I'd woken up in the locked room, I felt a spark of true fear. The man was twice the size I was and probably outweighed me by a hundred pounds. I didn't have a chance of defending myself against him if I had to.

I nodded, letting him know I'd heard and understood him. He stayed as he was for another few seconds, then moved back, transferring his iron grip from my arm to my waist, holding me close as if we were just some normal couple making a stop.

Once inside the store, I made my selections quickly – two packs of peanut butter crackers and a bottle of water. As I stood next to the man as he skimmed the display of protein bars, it occurred to me that I should use the bathroom while I could.

"I need to use the restroom."

The man pinned me with a glare. "You're a fucking pain in the ass. Just wait until I'm done."

I ignored him, looking around the small store. "I don't see a sign for them."

"Dammit. They're probably outside." He looked up to the front counter, then back at me, pulling me over a little so I'd be in clear view. "Stand right here where I can see you. You move, you'll pay for it."

I gave him a stiff nod, then watched as he walked to the counter, glancing my way every few seconds. I stayed motionless, not wanting to rile him. The clerk handed the man a key attached to a large plastic keychain, and he headed back toward me.

"Leave me your shoes."

I looked up at him, sure I couldn't have heard him right. I looked down at my shoes then back at him. "Leave you..."

"If you want to use the bathroom, you have to leave me your shoes."

"But..." I looked around, trying to make sense of what he was saying. "It's outside, and it's a public restroom. You want me to use a public gas station restroom with no shoes on?"

"You have socks on; you'll survive. Take it or leave it and hurry it up. We're running behind and it'll be my ass on the line if we're late."

I couldn't believe I was about to agree to this, but...

I reached out and took the key from him. I toed out of my shoes, then he grabbed my arm as I went to move away.

"You have three minutes. If you're not back in here by then, I'm coming after you." The look he gave me warned me I didn't want that to happen.

This time I gave no response, just pulled free and headed outside. Just before I opened the bathroom door, I noticed something I hadn't before – thick woods that lined the gas station's lot along one side, opposite the bathrooms.

I stood looking at the trees as a crazy idea formed in my head. What if...what if I ran? Nothing had happened for days, but who knew what might happen next? I was outside, alone, essentially free.

I looked down at my sock covered feet. I was shoeless, true, but...

Precious seconds were ticking away. I had to decide, had to act if I was going to.

In a burst of motion, I opened the bathroom door, locked it from the inside, tossed the key inside, pulled the door closed, and walked quickly to the other side of the building.

Was I really going to do this?

I looked around me and saw no one. It was now or never.

I turned toward the woods and ran.

• • • •

I RAN FOR AS LONG AS I could, until my lungs gave out, my legs were wobbly, and my hands, arms, and face were covered in scratches from the many twigs and small branches I'd pushed past.

And my feet. I tried not to focus on them too much. They felt bruised and battered, and I was sure I had more than one cut on them from sharp rocks and sticks. My socks were covered in mud and who knew what else, but I was grateful for even the little bit of protection they provided.

When I couldn't run anymore, I trudged, one foot in front of the other. I had no idea where I was, where I was going, or how much time had passed, but I told myself to just keep moving. When I heard the sounds of traffic, I made a snap decision, and headed toward it, hoping, as I had earlier, for signs or markers to tell me where I was.

I crept cautiously to the edge of the trees and peered out. I was at the edge of a two-lane road with cars rushing by in steady intervals. Off to my right sat three buildings – a gas station similar to the one I'd run from and two fast food places. The one facing me was named That Taco Place and I couldn't see the name of the other.

None of the businesses seemed busy, but I could see a few people moving around each. I debated, looking from one to the other, then looking down at myself. My shirt was torn, my jeans were dirty, and I had no shoes on. I'd been wearing the same clothes for days, and hadn't showered, or brushed my teeth, or combed my now-greasy hair in all that time. In short, I was a mess.

As I saw it, I had three choices: walk into one of the businesses, looking like I did, and ask for help; try to find a phone, call the clan's business number – which I by some miracle had memorized from all the marketing materials I'd reviewed and posts I'd done – and ask whoever answered to get a message to Brody, or Rafe, or even Rhyne that I was near a restaurant named That Taco Place; or I could keep moving.

My well-learned reticence about strangers swirled through my brain as I contemplated the first option. Anybody could be in those businesses – *anybody*. Walking in blind felt like the wrong decision, even if it was the simplest. It might turn out fine, but if it didn't...

I should probably go with option three and keep moving, put as much distance between the man, who was now sure to be murderously furious, and myself as possible. I wasn't sure how far I'd come, but I knew it probably wasn't far enough. But it would be night soon and traipsing through the woods in darkness was foolish at best. With a pang, I thought of the night Brody and I had spent together in the hut. Even without the rain, Brody hadn't been happy about the prospect of a night hike, and we'd had flashlights. I pushed the thought of Brody, and option three, away.

That left option two. I ran my eyes critically over the business closest to me, the fast-food place I couldn't see the name of. I was behind it, making it a better possibility than the other two. All I needed to do was sneak in, find a phone, make my call, then slip back out and hide until someone came to get me.

Piece of cake.

Right.

I blew out a slow breath as I scanned the back of the building. This wasn't a good idea, but it was the best one I had.

As I watched, a door in the back of the building popped open and an employee appeared, pushing a big, rolling trash bin. She pushed it next to one of the dumpsters, heaved bag after bag of what I assumed was garbage in the dumpster, then pushed the bin back inside, letting the door close behind her.

I straightened, looking at the door intently. It hadn't latched. I peered closer, straining my eyes to be 100% certain. I was right. The door hadn't closed all the way. It was sitting there, unlocked, vulnerable to anyone who might want to enter.

If I'd been waiting for a sign, this had to be it.

Not giving myself time to think about it, I dashed out of the woods, limp-running as quickly as I could toward the dumpsters. I hid behind them, realizing belatedly that the door may be ajar because the employee wasn't done bringing out trash. Cursing myself, I hunkered down, peeking around the side of the dumpster at the door every few seconds, my heart in my throat. When minutes passed and nothing happened, I drew in a deep breath, only to grimace at the stench that filled my lungs.

I stood, steadying my legs as much as I could, then walked briskly to the door, pulled it open a fraction and peeked inside. It was at the end of a hallway, near an opening on the right that looked like it led to the kitchen and one on the left that looked like...

An office! Just on the left inside the door, with the lights off and the door standing wide open. Jackpot!

The hallway was empty, so I took my opportunity. I slipped inside, let the door close quietly behind me, took a few quick steps, and I was in the office.

I nearly sagged in relief. I was over the first big hurdle. Now to find a phone.

I moved into the darkest corner, then looked around in the light that spilled through the doorway, scanning the desktop and tops of several short file cabinets. I saw papers, a closed laptop computer, even a plaque of some kind.

The one thing I didn't see was a phone. What kind of office didn't have a phone?

There had to be one. I scanned the space again, hoping against hope that I'd just missed it.

Out of nowhere, a woman's voice yelled, "I'll check," the overhead light flipped on, and a woman stepped into the office, while I stood frozen in the corner, staring at her like a deer in the headlights.

# Chapter 43

Bethany

"Holy...!" The woman slammed her hand over her chest as if her heart had nearly jumped out of it. She recovered quickly, glancing back out the door, then turning back to me.

"Look, there's nothing in here to steal. Even the laptop is an ancient piece of garbage. You'd get nothing for it. I can't give you any money, but if you're hungry, I'll give you food. We might even have a coat in our lost and found that would fit."

She thought I was homeless, likely an addict. With the way I probably looked, it was no wonder.

"No, I..."

My explanation was cut off by another shout down the hall.

"Abby, there's a man out here raising a fuss. Wants to know if we've seen some girl."

For the second time in as many minutes, my whole body seized in fear. Abby's eyes narrowed as she saw it flash across my face.

"Is he here for you?"

I nodded, unable to form words.

"Is he law enforcement?"

A shake of my head.

Abby gave a quick nod and pointed to the desk.

"Hide under there. Pull the chair in behind you as far as you can. Don't make a sound and don't come out until and unless I personally tell you to. Whatever you do, don't panic and run out the back. He might have somebody watching for you. Just stay put. Got it?"

"Got it," I whispered, all I could manage to force out.

Abby shut off the light and closed the door as I did as she'd instructed. I made myself as small as possible in the cramped space under the desk, hugging my knees to my chest, ignoring the pain of the chair base that dug into my hip. My heart jumped at the sound of a raised male voice that was far too close for comfort. *It might not be him*, I thought, trying to calm myself even though I knew better.

Endless time passed while I waited for her to return. *Please, please, please, please, please* ran on a loop through my head as I rested my forehead on my knees, eyes squeezed shut, the tension nearly unbearable.

When the door opened, I nearly came out of my skin. The light came on, the door closed again, and Abby said in a low voice, "It's me. Don't be scared."

She came around the desk and moved the chair out a little bit. "I'm pulling this out a little, so you'll have more room. He's gone but stay under there for now until we know for sure. I don't trust him."

That made two of us.

I'd apparently decided to trust Abby, though. I stayed where I was, fully aware this could be a trap of some kind, but knowing it wasn't. Her instant reaction when she'd seen my fear had told me everything I needed to know.

Whoever Abby was, she knew the feeling of being hunted.

Abby headed back out, leaving the light on this time, but once again closing and locking the door behind her. Minutes ticked by. I didn't hear any more raised voices, and no footsteps came near the office, so I took those as good signs.

After some time, I heard the key in the lock again, the door opening and closing, and Abby's voice. "Okay, I think it's safe."

The chair moved away. I crawled out, Abby helped me to my feet, and I got my first real look at her. I'd been too scared and shocked earlier to notice what she looked like.

In short, she was beautiful, a pure human with black hair, vibrant blue eyes, and a compact, athletic body. She stood a couple inches shorter than my own 5'7" and energy seemed to radiate off her.

She held out her hand. "I'm Abby."

"Bethany." I shook her hand and released it. "Thank you for before."

She leaned her hip against the edge of her desk, folding her arms across her chest as I perched awkwardly on the corner. "No problem. That guy was intense. Thank God he's human and not a shifter or he probably would have caught your scent." I hadn't even thought of that when I'd run, but she was right. Many shifters would have been able follow my scent directly to me. I shuddered at the thought. "You're obviously running from him, but are you in any other kind of trouble? Have you been living in the woods?"

I shook my head, wondering how to explain. "I haven't, I just ran through them trying to get away from the man who came in here after me. It's kind of a long story. I snuck in here looking for a phone so I can call someone to come get me."

Abby nodded, then looked over at the clock hanging on the wall and back at me. "Here's what I'm thinking. I could give you my phone to make a call, but I have a bad feeling the guy is still watching all three of the businesses that are right here. You're only a few miles from the gas station where you took off, so this is the logical place for you to be. Here or in the woods."

I slumped in defeat. A few miles?

"I can't believe I'm so close. I wasn't sure how far I'd gotten but I'd thought it was farther than that."

"The woods can be disorienting. You're going over and around things, and it's not always possible to go in a straight line. Regardless, you did a great job getting away from him and getting somewhere safe."

Safe? Was I really? I trusted Abby, but I still wasn't home.

"Like I was saying, this guy seems sneaky. If someone comes to pick you up here, you could be right back in the same hot water, and he'll definitely be right back on your tail. I was thinking of another alternative. I think we should dress you in a uniform so you look like every other employee here, then you should come home with me when we close. You can make your call from there, then we can figure out what's next."

I eyed her doubtfully. "That could put you in danger, though. What if he recognizes me and comes after us?"

Abby didn't seem worried.

"I doubt he will. With your hair up under the hat..." she tugged the bill of the baseball style cap she wore, "...and dressed in our ugly, boxy, uniform, you'll look identical to everybody else. I have extras right there in the box." She nodded toward the corner. "You can wear my regular shoes home while I wear these." She indicated the sturdy, black, nonslip shoes on her feet. "I usually change them when I leave so I don't track grease in my car or house, but tonight I can just wear them home. I may even have a pair of old readers around here you can wear. We can pull it off. People see what they expect to. With the hat, glasses, uniform, and walking with the boss, he won't even give you a second look. I wouldn't suggest it if I didn't think it would be safe."

I gave it a few seconds of thought, then agreed. The last thing I wanted to do was lead Rafe or Brody into danger.

Abby slipped me two hamburgers and a drink, pointed me toward the box of extra uniforms, then left me in the office again, promising to be back in an hour or so. Once I'd locked the door, I checked out my options from the box.

Abby hadn't been exaggerating when she'd said the unforms were ugly and boxy, consisting of brown slacks, a brick red shirt, and a matching hat with mustard yellow accents. I rooted through the box and luckily found pieces that fit me okay. I wasn't in danger of winning any best-dressed awards, but that wasn't the point. At least the uniform was clean, unlike the clothes I'd worn for days and run through the woods in. Working without a mirror, I did my best to bundle my hair up under the hat, then sat down in Abby's desk chair to wait.

The relative quiet and the ticking of the clock lulled me into a light doze, and I startled when Abby came back into the office. Glancing up at the clock, I was surprised to see that more than an hour had passed.

"Sorry to scare you. I would have knocked but a couple of the crew were still on their way out the door and I didn't want them to realize anyone was in here. We should give them a minute or two so we're sure they're gone and out of the lot, then we can get out of here."

She stood a minute, looking at me critically. "Not bad. Try these."

She pulled a pair of glasses from her pocket and tossed them to me. They were cheap, the kind you can buy in a three-pack at the drugstore, with round lenses and tortoise-shell frames. I slipped them on, and the world blurred.

"Oh yeah, those work. With your hair under the hat and those on, he'll never recognize you, if he's even out there."

"I hope your car isn't too far." I stood, a little unsteady on my feet. "I'm not sure how far I can walk with these glasses on."

"It's right out back," she reassured me. "Let me get you the shoes and a bag to put your clothes in and we should be good to go."

She unlocked her bottom desk drawer and pulled out her shoes and purse. I'd already removed my ruined socks and thrown them in the trash. Now I wedged my feet into her slightly too small shoes, grateful to have them, but also grateful we didn't have far to walk. She bundled my clothes into a bag, and we were ready.

We stood at the back door to the restaurant as I took a deep breath.

"You'll see my car as soon as we step out. It will be the only car in the lot. If we see any others, we step right back in here and this door will lock behind us, okay? No one can come in this door."

I had earlier, but I wasn't going to press the point.

"We have to look casual. Remember, don't look around or if you do, make it quick and subtle. Looking around for someone to be watching you is a dead-giveaway. As we walk, I'm going to talk to you so we're not just walking silently. That's another red flag. You can just nod or give a short answer. Don't talk much in case he's nearby and would recognize your voice. If I say 'run' I mean run for the car. It will unlock when we get close to it. Ready?"

Abby looked so calm, alert but not concerned. I couldn't help but comment on the rundown she'd given me.

"It sounds like you've done this once or twice."

Abby shrugged one shoulder casually. "You could say that. Here we go."

She opened the door, we walked out, and I immediately had to squash my instinct to search the darkness shrouding the area around us. Abby locked the door, did a subtle scan as she turned, then led the way down the short walkway to the parking lot.

"Don't get me wrong; I appreciate the enthusiasm and spirit behind the idea. It's just the logistics I worry about. Getting people to sign up for an employee softball team is the easy part. Organizing everything else is a lot harder."

For a split second I nearly paused, wondering why Abby had suddenly started spouting commentary about a softball team, then I remembered.

Look casual...have a conversation...like we were a normal boss and employee on our way out of work.

"Mm-hmm." I didn't think the man would recognize my voice, but I wasn't taking any chances.

"Anyway, we have a few months to decide. If it gets brought up again, we can talk more about it then, okay?"

I nodded in response as we came up to the back of Abby's car.

"Okay, great. Your door should be unlocked."

We climbed in, buckled up, and Abby pulled smoothly out of her spot as if there was no reason to worry that a huge, furious man or his friends may be watching or tailing us.

Abby released a slow breath as we pulled out onto the road, then looked at me with a smile.

"Well done, just like a pro."

I shook my head at her, wishing I could take the hat off but knowing it wasn't a good idea just yet. "You're the pro. All I did was follow along."

Abby checked her rearview and side mirrors as she drove. "I'll watch for a tail, but it didn't feel like anybody was watching us when we left. I didn't get the creepy sense of somebody's eyes being on us, did you?"

"No," I confirmed. "I know what you mean, but I didn't notice anything."

"Fortunately, both That Taco Place and the gas station are open a lot later than we are, so if he's still trying to keep an eye on all the businesses, they'll keep him busy for a while longer."

A few minutes later we pulled into the driveway of a nice two-story townhouse, then on into the garage.

"Let me shut the garage door before you get out," Abby cautioned.

We waited until the door was all the way down, then she turned off the car, and we climbed out. At the door into the house, she keyed in a code, I heard a distant beep, and she pushed the door open. We went down a short hallway that opened into the kitchen, then Abby set her bag on the counter and turned to look at me.

"I'm sure you want to shower, and I can find you something more comfortable to put on. Do you want to do that first or make your call?"

Embarrassment warred with the need to hear Brody or Rafe's voice. I had to stink – not that Abby had said that – and being clean would feel amazing, but the decision was easy.

"Call first, then shower, if that's okay with you?"

"Entirely up to you." Abby pulled her phone out of her bag, then unlocked it and handed it to me. "If you want some privacy, I can go in the other room."

"No, stay." The offer was nice of her, but... "I'll need to know your address and everything. The only number I know by memory is the main business line for the mountain lion clan I work for. It will go straight to an answering service at this hour, so I'll need to leave your number for a call back if that's okay?"

"Sure thing." Abby settled back against the counter as I dialed, nerves jumping in the pit of my stomach.

When the answering service employee picked up, tears sprang to my eyes. I had no idea why.

"I need to speak to Brody Klein urgently." It made no sense to ask for Rafe. There was no reason for the answering service to have his contact information. "Are you able to transfer me through to his personal cellphone?"

"No, I'm unable to do that," the employee responded pleasantly. "But I can contact him with an urgent message if you'd like me to."

"Yes, please tell him it's Bethany and I need him to call me right away at this phone number."

"Yes, ma'am." He confirmed the number. "I'll send that to him as soon as we hang up."

I thanked him and hung up, hoping Brody wasn't away from his phone or...

I nearly jumped a foot when the phone rang in my hand.

I tapped to answer the call, putting it on speaker, my tears spilling over as I heard Brody's voice.

"Bethany? Are you okay?"

"I'm okay," I croaked out, the tension and anxiety I heard in Brody's voice bringing on a fresh wave of tears. Abby patted my back softly, lending her support.

"You don't sound okay."

I took a breath, wiping the tears away. "I am. I'm okay. I'm safe."

"Where are you? What happened?" That was Rafe. I didn't even question that he and Brody were together.

"I got away. They were moving me, and I ran."

"Good girl. Where are you now?"

"I'm with Abby. It's a long story, but she helped me. We're at her house."

"Where is that?"

I looked at Abby.

"Near Lilydale, about 20 miles from the regional border."

My breath rushed out of me. I was nowhere near home.

"So, four, four and half hours away." I heard movement in the background. "We'll head out now. We should be there a little before two. Just send us the address and we'll..."

Abby broke in, and all motion on the other end of the line stopped. "That may not be the best plan."

A second of silence, then...

"Why?" Rafe's question was a little curt, but Abby showed no sign of noticing.

"We're still not sure that the man Bethany ran away from isn't watching us, either him or somebody he's working with. He came after her, and we were able to hide her, but he was livid. Who knows if he really gave up and went away. If he or someone did follow us and is watching the house, you showing up here in the middle of the night would telegraph loud and clear that Bethany's here."

Which would put Abby on the bad guys' radar, too. I didn't want that.

"I agree with Abby. I want to come home more than anything, but I don't want to put anyone in danger if we can help it."

Brody was less abrupt than Rafe, but he still sounded cautious. "What do you have in mind?"

"Let me bring Bethany to you tomorrow. We can meet you somewhere that's familiar ground to you. We'll watch for a tail on our way there, and if all looks good, we'll go ahead and meet. If anything looks off, either to you or to us, we'll reassess."

There was another pause.

"What did you say you do for a living, Abby?"

I couldn't blame Rafe for the question. Abby sounded like this type of situation was everyday life to her.

"I'm a manager at our local Burger World."

The dual grunts we heard in response made me smile a little. I knew what she said was true, but I had to believe there was far more to Abby than met the eye.

There was a low murmur, then Brody spoke again. "If you get Bethany to my clan's land, we'll take it from there. We'll figure out the optimal location tonight and send it to you in the morning."

"Works for me," Abby agreed.

"Okay," I hesitated, bracing myself to lose contact again with the two most important people in the world to me. "I'm not sure I can make myself hang up," I admitted.

"Just a few hours, Bex, and you'll be home. Not long now at all. I love you, honey. Try to get some rest and we'll see you tomorrow."

"I love you, too," I told him, my throat tight. "Goodnight, Rafe." Unable to disconnect without it, I whispered, "Goodnight, Brody."

"Bethany." Brody's voice was strained, husky. "I'm so proud of you." Warmth coursed through me at his words. "Just hang in there a little longer. You're almost home."

"I will. Night, Brody."

"Night, Bethany."

I forced myself to disconnect. I set the phone on the counter and looked up to find Abby watching me.

"Rafe sounds like he's your father."

I nodded. "Not biologically – he's a wolf shifter – but in every other way, yes."

"And Brody is?"

This one was harder.

"My co-worker," I tried.

"Oh, girl." Abby wasn't buying it. "That man is *not* just your co-worker. If there was any way he could have crawled through the phone line and snatched you up, he would have done it. Even more so than Rafe."

I cleared my throat, searching for words. "He...we were...involved for a few weeks." It had felt like so much more than mere weeks. "We're not anymore." It hurt to say it out loud.

Abby still looked doubtful. "If you say so. He sounded pretty 'involved' to me. Mountain lion shifter, right, since he mentioned his clan?"

I simply nodded. When I made no more comments, she picked up her phone and headed out of the kitchen.

"Ready for that shower?"

The thought of being clean again nearly made me whimper. "Ready," I agreed, following her out of the kitchen and up the steps, promising myself I'd never take the opportunity to shower for granted again.

# Chapter 44

Brody

It was the longest night of my life.

When my phone rang the night before and I'd gotten the message from Bethany, my mind had gone a hundred different directions. After days of complete, agonizing silence, it had seemed almost unreal.

I'd called the number, my heart in my throat, Rafe tense and silent next to me. When I'd heard Bethany's voice and she'd said she was unhurt, the tsunami of relief and gratitude that swamped me had nearly made me lose my grip on my phone. She'd sounded worn down but there was no question it was her.

I was so fucking proud of her. She'd kept her head, stayed strong, and gotten herself free, while me and Rafe and the others helping us had gotten nowhere. Rafe and I had started staying at the clan's headquarters building in two of the guest suites to make coordinating our efforts easier. We'd searched both Bethany and Andi's apartments and come up with nothing. There had been no sign of Andi or her car, though we'd staked out both her apartment and her workplace. We still didn't know if Andi had been part of the whole thing or if she'd been taken, too. All of Rhyne and Asher's attempts to contact her wild boar sounder's leadership through Council channels had gone unanswered.

It was as if Dr. Ulkos and the research institute had taken Bethany, talked to us the one time, then fallen off the face of the earth. The silence, the not knowing, had been torture.

That was over. We'd have her back today. And over my cold, dead body would anyone ever take her away again, whether we were together or not.

I was up before dawn. I ran then did a full workout, needing an outlet for the nervous energy riding me. I wanted to believe this would all be over by the end of the day, that we'd meet up with Bethany and Abby, pick up Bethany, and that would be it. But it seemed too easy, too good to be true.

By the time I met Rafe downstairs, I'd gotten myself mostly under control. Rafe climbed into my truck, looking like he hadn't slept any better than I had.

"Ready for this?"

"More than." I was quiet for a second as I pulled out into traffic, then decided to put my concerns out there. Rafe and I were partners in this. We each needed to know what the other was thinking. "This feels too easy. I don't trust it."

"I don't either." Rafe checked the mirrors, and I knew he was checking to be sure we weren't being followed. "None of this makes any kind of sense."

"It doesn't. I don't see how this could be a set-up, though." I rubbed my chin, trying to force my brain to think. "The only unknown is Abby, but she can't be involved. However it happened, it sounds like Bethany came across her randomly as she was running, and Abby helped. If anything, she could have just handed Bethany over to the guy who was after her. It makes no sense to take the risk of taking Bethany home with her if she's doing anything other than trying to help."

"She seemed straightforward enough on the phone last night," Rafe agreed. "I don't know. There was something about her..."

I glanced at Rafe, surprised. "You don't think we can trust her?"

"No, it's not that. I think she's solid. I don't even know what I mean. At the end of the day, she helped Bex, so I owe her more than I can ever repay."

"Same," I confirmed. "And like Rhyne and Asher said last night when we briefed them, Abby's got my clan and your pack behind her for life. Even if you or I can't personally do whatever she might need, she's covered. We need to make sure she knows that."

Conversation lapsed as Rafe and I each got lost in our thoughts. When we'd briefed Rhyne and Asher the night before, we'd all agreed that the clan's eastern search and rescue base was the best meeting spot. It was off the beaten path, but not hard to get to, and would be closest given the direction Bethany and Abby were coming from. It was also well within the boundaries of clan territory. Anyone, shifter or human, who knew even the basics of shifter culture, knew it would be a serious offense to attack us within my clan's territory. We were counting on that as an extra measure of safety, even as we realized that people willing to kidnap someone didn't necessarily play by the rules.

An hour or so later, we'd just turned off the main highway onto the mountain road that would take us all but the last mile to the search and rescue station when we got the mayday call from Bethany and Abby. We'd agreed on no contact except in an emergency, so even before we connected, we knew the situation was serious.

I tapped to accept the call and noise filled the cab of my truck. Breathing, the crash of footsteps through leaves, twigs snapping, and a whirlwind of other sounds rang in my ears.

"What's happening?" I demanded when no one spoke at first. "Bethany?"

"They found us." Her voice was uneven, like she was moving fast as she talked. "We don't know how. We were watching but....out of nowhere they were just there. They..." she broke off for an endless second... "they forced us off the road."

My knuckles were white as I gripped the steering wheel. Out of the corner of my eye, I saw Rafe pull out his phone.

"We're on foot, in the woods. We don't know if they're behind us. Abby tried to trick them, but..." another excruciating pause... "We can see the gravel road to the station."

"Good, that's good." I tried to keep my voice calm. I'd been confronted with an untold number of emergency situations working with our search and rescue team, but none had ever felt more dire than this. "Parallel it but keep your cover in the woods. Go in through the door we talked about it, then get to the equipment room and lock yourselves in. Barricade the door with whatever you can find. Rafe and I are almost there."

The last we heard was Bethany's breathless "okay" then the call disconnected.

"What the fuck?" Rafe spit out. "They had to have been followed, but why let them get all this way? Why force them off the road?"

"No clue. Like you said, these people are fucked in the head. Let's just hope Abby's 'trick', whatever it was, at least slowed them down."

I drove dangerously fast up the mountain road, reaching the station road in half the time it should have taken, skidding as I jerked my truck onto the gravel. I accelerated toward the building, not bothering to try to disguise our arrival. If someone was here waiting for us, they already knew we'd arrived. There was no point in trying to be subtle.

I slammed to a stop near the building and turned off the truck as Rafe and I sat and scanned the surrounding area.

I felt Bethany's presence nearly the second we stopped. "They made it. Bethany's here. I can feel her."

Rafe nodded, even as he frowned. "I feel somebody, too. It's not Bex, though." He shook his head like he was clearing it, then reached for the door handle. "Let's get out."

We both climbed out, leaving the doors open, and stood, scanning the area again. I let my senses widen, listening for anything I shouldn't hear and everything I should, while Rafe did the same, scenting the woods that surrounded us. Satisfied, as ready as we were going to be, Rafe and I locked eyes as he spoke.

"Let's go get our girl."

We made our way to the door we'd arranged to have left unlocked just in case. We entered the building cautiously, then made our way to the equipment room. I kept watch as Rafe knocked softly on the door.

"Bex, honey, it's us. Can you open the door?"

We heard the screech of something being moved away, then the click of the lock. Then the door opened and there she was.

Rafe pulled her into a hug, holding her tight as she clung to him. I watched them, my arms aching almost as much as my heart, wishing I could do the same. After a few seconds, Rafe set her back on her feet, and looked at the woman standing next to Bethany, eyeing us both cautiously.

"You must be Abby."

I glanced at Rafe, wondering at the hint of possessiveness in his voice. If Abby picked up on it, she didn't acknowledge it.

"And you must be Rafe." She looked past him to me. "And Brody."

I nodded in acknowledgement, then got down to business, not letting myself think about the fact that Bethany hadn't said so much as said hello to me.

"When we get outside, you'll see my truck. The doors are wide open. When I say 'move' your job is to sprint to the truck like your life depends on it – no hesitating, no looking back, no matter what. Just get inside, lock the doors, and do not get out."

"What do you think is going to happen?" Bethany asked in a near whisper, and my stomach twisted as her eyes finally met mine. The dark circles under them wrecked me and I had to force myself to focus.

"We don't know," I told her truthfully. We suspected, but we didn't know. "We'll be right behind you. Just focus on getting to the truck."

She looked at me a moment longer, then nodded silently.

We waited while Rafe went ahead of us, cracking the door open to check the outside briefly, joining him when he waved us forward. Rafe gave Bethany another quick hug, then went back in the direction we'd come.

"Give me thirty seconds, then go."

He disappeared around a corner, and I moved along with Bethany and Abby up to the threshold of the door, counting silently in my head. Just as I reached thirty, I felt Bethany's hand brush mine, sending sparks all the way to my shoulder.

She leaned a little closer and it was all I could do not to pull her to me and cover her lips with mine. Her whispered "please be careful" hit me center chest, and I pulled back, fighting not to show how her simple words had rocked me. I swallowed hard as I gave a short nod, then pushed the door open a fraction and took a quick look out.

"Ready?" Bethany and Abby gave me a thumbs up and I pushed the door wide. "Move!"

We were nearly to the truck when the world turned to chaos.

# Chapter 45

Bethany

There were people, animals – I didn't know which – running out of the woods straight for us. I stumbled, the surprise hitting me hard, and Brody grabbed me by my shirt, yanking me back to my feet. I wanted to spin around, to see what was behind me, but I remembered Brody's words and ran as if my life depended on it, realizing with shocking clarity that it very well might. So, I focused on Abby, racing across the gravel in front of me, diving in one side of the truck while she dove in the other.

We slammed and locked the doors, then panting, looked out through the windshield.

The scene playing out in front of us was like nothing I'd ever witnessed. The violence was stunning as we watched more than a dozen demi-shifters – mountain lion, wolf, and wild boar – fight as if they wanted to tear each other to pieces. And in amongst them, a huge, snarling, grey and brown wolf I knew to be Rafe.

I scanned the fray for Brody, desperate to find him, inhaling a quick breath of shock when I did. I'd seen Brody in his shifted state numerous times and thought I'd understood but this...this was something else altogether. He was shirtless, facing me, grappling with a boar shifter. The feline features; sleek, taut, muscular body; and light coat of fur I'd seen before were there; but so were long, gleaming fangs; sharp claws; and murderous intent in his eyes that I hadn't. This was Brody at his most primal, at the fullest extent of his shift. He was both terrifying and mesmerizing.

Next to me Abby shrieked, her hand flying to her mouth, as I tore my gaze from Brody. A wild boar shifter had broken away, tearing toward us with a large rock in his hand, his tusks protruding and red eyes gleaming. He was mere feet away, his hand raised to launch the rock through the window on Abby's side, when he pitched forward, slamming face down into the ground, Rafe on his back. I lost sight of them, the truck blocking my view, as Abby stared out the side window at whatever was happening. We both jumped and Abby gasped as a short scream right outside the truck cut off abruptly. Seconds later, I could see Rafe again, his eyes locked on Abby's as he slowly backed away – one step, two – before wheeling around and running back into the chaos.

I reached across the seat and grabbed Abby's hand. She grasped it tightly, her blue eyes unreadable as they met mine.

"We have to do something." How could we just sit here, watching?

Abby squeezed my hand as she shook her head. "There's nothing we can do. This is their world right now, not ours. We'd be nothing but a liability. The best thing we can do is stay out of the way."

So, we sat, holding hands, watching, our stomachs in knots, as the mountain lions and wolves gradually gained control.

# Chapter 46

Brody

I dropped the boar shifter I held, letting him fall to the ground unconscious as I turned to take on the next one.

Only to realize there wasn't a next one.

We'd gained the upper hand, and the fight was over. I snapped my head toward my truck, looking for confirmation of the one thing that mattered.

She was there. She was safe.

I stalked toward her, unable to stop myself, my need for her overriding everything else. She watched me come closer, her beautiful brown eyes tracking my every move. As I drew closer, she opened her door and my blood surged. Then her scent hit me, and I lost whatever control I still had.

I pulled her out of the truck, crushing her against me as my mouth crashed down on hers. I pushed my tongue into her mouth, a low growl erupting from me at her taste, as I ran my hands over her, aching at the feel of her.

Fisting my hand in her hair, I tugged her head back and slanted my head, taking the kiss deeper as I reveled in the feel of her body pressed against mine.

Too soon, I forced myself back. Making my hands let her go, I spun on my heel and walked away. I didn't look at her, couldn't, unable to bear what I feared I might see in her eyes.

I kept going until I got to the small locker room inside the search and rescue station. I sat on a bench, head in my hands, and just breathed.

Awhile later, I heard a noise and looked up to see Rhyne walking toward me.

"Any injuries we need to take care of?"

I looked down at myself, taking stock. I'd been so lost in my head; I hadn't even noticed. My torso and arms were covered in scratches – some deep, some shallow – and I had what looked like a bite on my left forearm. My side...I twisted, trying to see the cause of the burning pain I felt. Rhyne helped me out, leaning around to look.

"It looks like one of the boars gored you. Fucking tusks." He dragged his hand over his face. "What a cluster."

"No argument." We'd come out on top, but it hadn't been a sure thing. My brain swung back to my number one priority.

"Is she still out there?"

I didn't want it to touch her, didn't want her to see the aftermath. She shouldn't have to. That level of violence and carnage should never enter her world.

"Rafe took her and Abby home...to clan headquarters," he corrected. "They'll be in the other two suites in the guest wing, at least for tonight. Is that going to be a problem for you?"

My mountain lion was still keyed up, still prowling right under the surface. She'd be much too close, far too accessible, but she'd be safe.

"I won't let it be."

Rhyne accepted my response without comment. "Let's go then. You need to get a shower and let the doctor take a look at you."

I followed Rhyne to his SUV, pulling on the shirt he grabbed from the back seat and tossed at me. As he drove, I leaned my head back against the headrest, fighting to push my mountain lion back, to settle him down to a manageable level. It was a losing battle. The second my mind went back to Bethany – which it did about every third second – my mountain lion was clawing at me again, growling for his mate.

Rhyne pulled into a spot in the headquarters parking lot, turned the SUV off, and turned to look at me. "We'll do a full debrief tomorrow. Everybody's wiped out. You can go straight to your suite if you want. I'll send the doctor your way in a bit."

When I looked at Rhyne, I saw understanding and empathy. He knew what I was going through, how hard I was fighting my instinct to fully claim Bethany. He knew the torment of having your mate so close, yet just out of reach.

I walked in the building with Rhyne, splitting off to the guest wing when he went toward the residence where the others had gathered.

I walked into my room, flipped on the small light by the bed, and headed for the shower, stripping as I walked. I turned the shower to scalding, hissing as the water hit the gouges and scratches that covered my upper body, focusing on the pain to drive everything – every*one* – from my mind. Finally admitting defeat, I shut off the water, got out of the shower, and toweled off.

Walking into the bedroom, I crossed to the chest set against one wall, pulled on a pair of sweatpants, and began to pace.

# Chapter 47

Bethany

He didn't show up.

I'd been waiting, fidgety and nervous, wondering how Brody would look at me, what he would say, and he didn't show up.

Everything inside me just...deflated when Rhyne walked into his and Kyra's residence without him. Rafe noticed – the others probably did, too – though I did my best not to let my dejection show.

"Sorry to keep you all waiting." Rhyne looked around the group – me, Rafe, Abby, Athena, Asher, and Bryan, beta of Asher and Rafe's pack. "I think it's best if we hold the full debrief for tomorrow. The crew up at the station will still be working on clean-up for several hours yet, and they'll let me and Asher know if they come across anything useful. For now, let's just do a status check on injuries and anything needing immediate attention."

Athena spoke up. "No critical or serious injuries to any members of our clan or Asher's pack. All except Brody have checked in. I'm assuming since he rode here with you and apparently walked in under his own power that his injuries aren't life-threatening."

"Not life-threatening," Rhyne confirmed. I waited, hearing a *but*... "He's got a nasty gore wound in his side that I asked the doctor to check out, but he'll be fine."

A *gore* wound? How had I not noticed that? Maybe because I was having the breath and every bit of sense kissed out of me, but still...

Athena nodded without comment and went on. "The boars..." She paused and her voice softened, at least for her. "The boars lost one, and one has serious injuries. The others are in similar shape as our guys."

We all sat in silence, taking in the fact that a man had lost his life today. And I knew very well which man it was. I snuck a glance at

Rafe, only to find him and Abby staring at one another, seemingly oblivious of anyone else in the room. I looked away, suddenly feeling as if I was intruding on a private moment.

Asher's strong, quiet voice broke the silence. "I'll touch base with the sheriff. I know they're usually as hands-off as they can be with shifter conflicts, but with one deceased, they'll have to be notified."

"Agreed and thank you." Rhyne pushed a hand through his hair, looking as bone-weary as I'd ever seen him. "Anything else urgent for right now?"

Other than my urgent need to find Brody and see for myself that he was alright?

Rhyne looked at us each in turn. I shook my head when he got to me, knowing that wasn't the kind of thing he was talking about.

"Okay, let's meet tomorrow, here, at ten. We'll take whatever time we need to walk through everything and try to figure out what the hell just happened. Everybody try to relax and get some rest." He turned to me and Abby. "Bethany and Abby, if you need anything at all, don't hesitate to call me."

We both agreed, though I knew neither of us would do it. I was relatively sure Rhyne knew that, as well, though he seemed to take our response at face value.

After that, the group broke up. I said goodbye to the others, then headed to the guest wing alongside Rafe and Abby. We left Abby at her suite and continued on to mine right next door. When we got to the door, I hesitated, looking farther down along the hall to where I knew Brody's suite was.

"What's on your mind, Bex?"

I glanced up at Rafe, then back down the hall.

"I want to check on Brody. I'm not sure I can sleep if I don't. I just need to see with my own eyes how he is."

Rafe blew out a breath, folding his arms across his chest and dropping his head for a moment before raising it again to look at me.

"Honey..." he paused, running one hand across the back of his neck, nearly squirming in obvious discomfort. "I can't believe I'm about to say this to my own daughter."

My heart warmed at that, even as I frowned at him. What was making him so uncomfortable?

"Just say it, Rafe. Whatever it is."

"Okay, look." He stopped fidgeting and looked at me. "If you're not...damn it...if you don't want to be with Brody...I mean physically be with him...you need to leave him alone. He's right on the edge, Bex, fighting himself, and having you near him, it won't help."

"You think so?" My mind flashed back to our kiss.

"No, honey, I know so. With the adrenaline from the shift and the fact that you were threatened...trust me, Bex. His mountain lion is riding him hard right now. It's probably taking every bit of his control not to come after you. That's why he took off. Being near you without...uh...being more than just near you would be almost impossible."

The thought of Brody needing to exert all his willpower to keep himself away from me sent a shiver down my spine. Still, though...

"I don't know. I'm not sure I believe that."

"Believe it. You and Brody have a future if you want it. If you don't, the best thing you can do for him is leave him alone. Don't make it any worse for him than it already is."

With that bit of fatherly advice, Rafe turned and entered his own suite, leaving me alone in the hallway. I stood and waffled, thinking through everything Rafe had said. I looked down the hall toward Brody's suite and immediately felt the pull. Whether it was coming from me or from Brody or from us together, I didn't know, but decision made, I turned and closed the distance between me and Brody's suite.

# Chapter 48

Bethany

I knocked softly on Brody's door before I could lose my nerve. I heard nothing for a moment, then...

"Go away, Bethany. You don't need to be around me right now."

His voice was tight, coarse, whether from pain or just the after-effects of the battle he'd been part of, I didn't know. Either way, he hadn't said he didn't want me there, only that I didn't need to be there. I begged to differ. If there was anywhere I needed to be right then, it was with Brody.

Gathering my courage, I reached out and tried the doorknob, pushing the door open when I found it unlocked. If Brody had really wanted to keep me out, he would have made sure to lock the door. At least that was what I told myself.

If the look in his eyes when I closed the door behind me was any indication, I may have been wrong about that.

The blinds were closed, and the light was dim, only one small light on the bedside table providing any illumination. Brody's eyes appeared amber-gold, as they always did when they reflected light in the darkness, yet so different than I'd ever seen them. They were feverish, wild, and I suddenly had the sense of standing across the room from a powerful, dangerous animal. One who nearly snarled as he spoke.

"I told you to go away, not to come in."

His body looked tense, rigid, as if he was using every ounce of his control to keep himself together. He was shirtless and barefoot, wearing only sweatpants, and slashes and claw marks littered his arms and torso. Bandages on his side and arm, stark white against his tanned skin, caught my eye.

"You're hurt. Rhyne said you were gored."

"I'm fine. You have to go."

"You're not fine." I walked toward him, pausing, surprised, when he backed up several steps with a growl. I wasn't scared, just even more worried than before. "You were hurt helping me, defending me. I can't just act like that's okay."

"It doesn't matter." Brody clenched his fists at his sides, making the muscles in his arms and shoulders stand out in sharp relief, and my heart raced at the display of pure male strength. "You need to get away from me."

"I'm not afraid of you, Brody." I chanced a few more steps in his direction, watching his Adam's apple bob as he swallowed. "And it does matter. It matters to me."

"What matters is you're not safe with me right now," he ground out. "I'm at the edge of my control. I've been fighting back my mountain lion for hours and I can't do it anymore. Not if you're close to me. Not when I can hear your heartbeat and smell your scent. It's too much. You need to go...now."

If he could have let himself touch me to physically shove me out the door, I believed he would have. As it was, mere words weren't going to drive me away. If there was ever a time to stand my ground, this was it.

"You won't hurt me." Physically, I knew that was true. Emotionally...that was a worry for another day. "I'm not leaving. I need to be with you, Brody, as much as you need to be with me. I'm not afraid of you losing control."

I all but heard Brody's self-imposed restraints snap. With a growl, he was on me. He pulled me forward, slamming my body into his a second before he captured my mouth with his own, his tongue pushing past my lips to tangle with mine. He ran his hands over me, seeming nearly frantic, as I clung to him, mindful of the wound in his side but desperate to be close to him. He buried one hand in my hair, clamped his other arm around my waist, and crushed me to him. His hold was too tight, nearly painful, but I didn't care; I just held on while his mouth ravaged mine.

He pulled back, ripping my shirt off me as I gasped, then lifting me, setting me down on the bed and pushing me to my back. He loomed over me, tilting my head up, baring my neck for him to kiss, and lick, and nip across my neck and shoulder. I felt the sharp edge of his canines against my skin, and I realized he'd started to shift.

He slid down my body, sucking one nipple into his mouth, torturing it with his tongue as he rolled the other between his fingertips. I moaned, arching into him, holding his head to me while the sensation shot straight to my center. I rocked my hips into him restlessly, and he moved over me more fully, trapping me against the bed, holding me down and sending a wall of fire streaking through me.

"Brody, please." I sounded desperate and I was.

Brody levered himself up to his knees, pulling me to him and parting my legs, capturing my mouth with his again as he pushed inside me with one hard stroke. My breath hitched in my lungs, the feeling of him inside me, filling me so completely, it was nearly overwhelming.

Then he began to move. His cat-like eyes staring into mine, his beautiful feline features highlighted by the play of shadow and light on his face, he stroked into me, shallow at first, then longer, harder. He leaned forward, grasping my wrists and dragging them over my head, pinning them in place with one hand as he slammed into me again and again. I felt the tension spiral within me, pulling tighter and tighter, leaving me gasping with need, my hips rocking into Brody's, meeting his every stroke. Then he slipped his hand between our bodies, pressed down hard on my clit, and I was gone.

I cried out as the wave crashed over me, the pleasure so intense I could hardly breathe. Brody didn't slow. He released my hands, lifting one of my legs over his shoulder, opening me even more as he thrust into me over and over, deeper inside me than he'd ever been.

He gripped my hips tightly, holding me right where he wanted me, while I dug my nails into his forearms, needing something, anything, to ground me before I spun off into oblivion. I'd barely come down when I felt myself start to climb.

Too soon, I teetered on the edge, then fell apart as my heart slammed against my chest and colors swirled behind my eyelids.

As soon as I began to calm, Brody lifted my hips, tilting them just right, hitting that perfect spot inside me. It was too much, too good, and before long, I shattered again, saying Brody's name, shaking as the storm raged through me.

This time, Brody leaned into me, his chest on mine, his breath ragged and harsh in my ear. I felt the softness of his fur on my breasts and stomach and lifted my hands to stroke the sleek, taut muscles of his back. With a final thrust, he surged into me, holding himself there, burying his face against my neck as I felt him shudder with the force of his orgasm.

Brody stayed there a few moments, his hot breath billowing against my throat. Then he levered himself up, pulled out of me slowly, and moved to the side, flipping to lay on his back beside me. He didn't pull me to him, and I didn't curl into his side; we simply lay there, side-by-side, eyes on the ceiling as we both fought to catch our breath.

• • • •

I DOZED OFF, SURFACING sometime later when a faint noise woke me. I reached out my hand and ran it across the bed, feeling the emptiness next to me.

"Go back to sleep." The light by the bed had been turned off and Brody's voice came to me through the darkness. I looked toward the door and saw his faint outline.

That's when it hit me...he'd been leaving me, slipping out without a word while I slept.

I forced myself to speak through the pain twisting through me. "This is your room, Brody. I can leave."

"It doesn't matter. I won't sleep anyway." His voice was muffled now, like he'd turned away.

How had we gotten here? From spending nearly every possible moment together to him just leaving me here, sneaking away after what we'd just had together?

I knew it was my fault, that my lies had driven us apart, and it didn't seem I could ever undo it.

I shouldn't ask him, shouldn't back him into a corner, but I needed to know. I heard the door crack open and knew it was now or never.

"Do you think you can ever forgive me?" I whispered.

He paused and I waited, breathless, for his answer. "I already did. I just don't know if I can ever forget."

Relief warred with confusion. "Is that why you're still so angry with me?"

He ignored my question. "I don't know what you want from me, Bethany."

He didn't know? How could he not? "I want to go back to what we had."

Now he turned my way. "What did we have? We were never on the same page; hell, we were never even reading the same book. To me, we were forever. I have no idea what we were to you. Can you even answer that for yourself?"

What could I say? I'd known Brody was ahead of me, thinking about the future, but I'd never let myself acknowledge it. I'd just lived in – and loved – the moment. He knew how undecided I'd been about even staying in the area until I reunited with Rafe; I couldn't lie about this.

"I don't know." The silence between us filled with disappointment and regret at my admission.

There was no response from Brody. He simply left, pulling the door closed quietly behind him, leaving me to my own jumbled thoughts.

# Chapter 49

Brody

I forced myself to walk into Rhyne and Kyra's residence for the debrief, then forced myself not to look around the room for Bethany. I felt her there, like always, but I wasn't strong enough at the moment to do anything more than be near her.

I was still reeling from the night before. I'd had no control at all. I'd taken Bethany hard and fast, pushing both of us, driven to claim her in the most elemental way possible, like the way I needed my heart to keep beating. It had been necessary, vital, and when she'd come to me, offered herself to me, I hadn't been able to hold back.

Even though I should have. There had just been no way to do it and stay sane.

I did my best to force the thoughts away, to shove them out of my mind the same way I'd fought against thoughts of Bethany for weeks now. I needed to focus on the task at hand.

I said hello to Athena and Cason, nodded to Rafe and Bryan as they stood talking, then grabbed coffee, ignoring the food that had been set out on the large island separating the great room from the kitchen. I leaned back against it, knowing I'd be too restless to sit, just as Rhyne walked in.

"Alright, everyone. Let's get this sorted out."

He waited as everybody settled in. Out of the corner of my eye, I noticed Bethany and Abby sitting next to each other on a couch, and Asher near Abby in a chair.

"Bethany, why don't you start us off? Tell us everything you can remember about what happened. No detail is too small."

Bethany nodded as she took a deep breath. "Okay."

She was nervous. Not only could I hear it in her voice, I could feel it. I wanted to sit next to her, hold her hand, and help her through this but that wasn't possible. Besides that, she didn't need me. She was strong, courageous; if she could get through the experience – and she had – she could get through talking about it.

She launched in, telling us about the drugged smoothie Andi had given her and about the building where she'd been held. She told us about Dr. Ulkos and Mr. Dolion – who we were all assuming was Andi's father, although it hadn't been confirmed – and their connection to Will Wyland; and about the boar shifter woman who'd brought her food and the human man who'd first guarded her, then pursued her. The most surprising thing she told us was that she'd never been told why she was there; that she assumed it was to persuade Rafe to cooperate with the researchers, but she'd never been told that directly.

"They mentioned that I'd messed up their plan by finding Rafe sooner than they wanted me to, so maybe they were still scrambling and trying to figure out what to do."

Athena asked Bethany a couple questions, just clarifying a thing or two, then Rhyne turned to Abby.

"Abby, can you fill us in on what happened once you found Bethany in your office?"

"Sure." Where Bethany had been nervous, Abby sounded calm and confident. "Right after I found Bethany, the man who was after her came into the restaurant. He demanded to search the whole place, but I told him the only possible place she could be was the restroom. I convinced him that the crew would be in an uproar if some random woman came crashing through the kitchen or tried to get in the walk-in. I checked the ladies' room, then let him check himself so he could see it was empty. He checked the men's room, then slammed out of the store and was gone. At least we hoped so. We disguised Bethany in a uniform, and we made it home that night without issues. That's when Bethany called Brody."

Rhyne nodded; we'd already filled the others in about the call. "What happened yesterday before you got to the search and rescue station?"

Now Abby tensed a little. "Everything was fine. Both Bethany and I watched for a tail, even went a few miles out of our way at one point to be sure, and we saw nothing." Abby looked to Bethany, who nodded in agreement. "Then suddenly, just as we turned onto the mountain road, they were there. At least two of them, possibly three, in a brown van. They came right at us. Whether they were trying to scare us into stopping or run us off the road, I don't know, but the second happened on a switchback. Two of the tires blew, but I was able to keep control as we went down an embankment, and they flew past us. I got the car wedged in behind a thicket of brush, so it was harder for them to find, and we took off on foot. You know the rest."

So that was the "trick" Bethany had mentioned. It had been good thinking on Abby's part, disguising where they'd abandoned the car. She'd shown a lot of grace under fire, and I wondered again about her background.

"Did you recognize the van?"

"No." Abby and Bethany spoke in unison, answering Rafe's question. "It was like it appeared out of nowhere," Abby finished.

Cason stood, looking thoughtful. "I want to check on something. I'll be right back." He left as we turned our attention back to Rhyne.

"Was the man who'd come after Bethany in the van? Or were they demi-shifters?"

Abby and Bethany looked at each other. This time Bethany answered.

"I don't know. I couldn't see exactly who was inside."

"I couldn't either," Abby agreed. "I was just trying to stay on the road."

"So, we know who took Bethany, but we don't know where or exactly why, and we know they somehow found Bethany and Abby yesterday, but we're not sure how," Rhyne summed up.

"They also knew enough and had enough time to have boar shifters waiting for Rafe and me when we got to the station." All eyes swung my way. "It was no more than thirty minutes from the time we got Bethany's call to when we got there. At least some of the boar shifters had to have been in the van. Once they picked up Bethany and Abby's scent, they could have followed it straight to the station. The girls were barricaded inside by that point, but the boars had to know we'd be coming to get them. All they had to do was call for back-up and wait."

"They were there when we got there," Rafe agreed. "Brody heard them, and I scented them."

"When did they attack?" Bryan asked.

"The girls and Brody had almost made it to the truck," Rafe said, regret tingeing his voice. He and I had gambled and almost lost, something that would stay with both of us for a long time. "The plan was to send them out the side entrance to the station, while I shifted and went out the back with our guys who were staged in the vehicle bay."

Bethany and Abby looked at him in surprise. We hadn't told them that several members of my clan and Rafe's pack were waiting when they got to the station, ready to help if needed, just as a precaution. If all had gone as originally planned and we'd picked Bethany up without incident, they'd never have known the others were there.

"We'd hoped we could run interference, get between the boars and Brody and the girls, and give them enough time to get to the truck. Then Brody would get the girls to safety while the rest of us took care of the boars and kept them from giving chase. But there were more of them than we planned, and we didn't buy enough time."

Rafe looked at me and I picked up the story.

"I turned around to cover the girls until they got in the truck and got the doors locked. The only reason they made it is they moved fast and kept their heads."

I looked over at them, allowing my eyes to skim quickly over Bethany, then away. "And the rest you all know."

"I don't understand the connection between this research institute and the boars. They're obviously working together, but why?" Abby asked.

Rafe shook his head. "No clue. I've known of the Institute most of my life and I've never heard anything about a connection to a wild boar sounder, not to mention the sounder only appeared in this area about a year ago. It's possible the Institute has a wide reach and multiple research programs, but that's never been my impression. It's nearly impossible to find information on them, though, so anything could be possible."

Cason walked back into the room, holding something up.

"This may be how they found you." He stopped in the middle of the group and extended his hand, a small object resting in his palm. "It's a tracking device. Brody, it was on your truck."

I pushed away from the island, pacing away from the group, staring out the window as I fought back a string of curses. Running my hand across the back of my neck, I turned back to face them. "They didn't follow Abby and Bethany, they followed me."

"How would that work, though?" Asher asked. "You were coming from different directions."

"A surveillance drone, multiple vehicles covering the most likely routes, an educated guess based on knowledge of the clan's lands – it could be any combination of things." Cason responded, slipping the tracker in his pocket. "That and a little luck, and boom, you've located your target."

"That would explain why they didn't show up until we were so close, and how they seemingly just appeared out of nowhere."

"I'd say you're right, Bex." Rafe agreed. "It fits, so that's one mystery solved. Now how do we solve the others?"

Rhyne stood, looking every bit the alpha he was. "It all comes back to the boars. They drugged Bethany, held her, chased after her, and attacked us and our allies on our own territory to get her back. They've hidden their leadership successfully, but that ends now. It's time we paid them a visit, and not a friendly one."

# Chapter 50

Bethany

I waited anxiously for Rafe's call telling me the meeting with the boar sounder's leadership was over. Using the attack as justification, the Alliance Council had applied significant pressure on all known members of the sounder, demanding to know who their leadership was, even going so far as to threaten to shut down members' businesses as leverage. It had worked, and the sounder's alpha was finally identified.

Rhyne, Asher, Rafe, and Brody had gone to the meeting. Rafe had promised to call me the minute he could to let me know what had happened. I wanted to know, but more than that, I wanted to know they'd all made it out safely. It was getting late, and I was getting more and more nervous. The sounder had shown that they had no respect for long-held, universal, shifter traditions and rules. Who knew what they might do?

By the time the phone rang, I'd nearly worn a hole in the carpet. It would have been a shame – I was still staying in a lovely guest suite at the clan's headquarters until I could move into a new apartment – but I couldn't stop pacing.

I snatched up the phone, confirmed it was Rafe, and hit the button to connect.

"You can stop worrying, Bex. Everybody's safe and it went better than expected."

Rafe knew me too well.

"Good. Tell me what happened."

He exhaled a long breath. "In a nutshell, a young, inexperienced, ineffective alpha who lost control of his group. Some of the younger members are essentially running wild, though they've been laying low lately. A few of the older members apparently came across Dr. Ulkos several years ago and bought into the whole 'warrior wolf' thing, though their ultimate goal was a 'warrior boar.' They believed the research on me would lead to a way to transform demi-shifter genes to pure, powerful, full shifter genes. They were the catalyst behind moving the sounder to this area. I feel sorry for their alpha. He had no idea what was going on, and his beta is one of the ones involved."

"What will he do?"

"I don't know. With the backing of the Alliance Council, we made it clear the sounder is banned from this region. The members involved in your abduction and the attack were turned over to law enforcement by the alpha; other than those few, all other sounder members were given thirty days to vacate. It won't solve their problems, but it will solve ours."

"Did he know anything about Andi?"

"Sorry, Bex; he didn't."

Andi was still missing. Her apartment had been cleaned out and there had been no sign of her. I couldn't be angry at her for the part she played in kidnapping me. I knew she hadn't felt like she could refuse. I only hoped she was okay somewhere and someday got away from her father.

"It's okay." Finally, I asked the question I couldn't stop myself from asking. "How was he?"

Rafe knew I meant Brody. That much, at least, I didn't have to say.

"Tired. On edge. Miserable. Pretty much the same as he's been."

I sighed, feeling a weight settle on my chest. I'd known the answer, yet I'd hoped somehow it would be different.

"I wish I could fix it."

*Can't you though, Bethany?* my brain whispered to me. *Can't you try?*

"I know, sweetheart. It hasn't even been two weeks since you came home. A lot has happened, and you both need time. Don't give up."

"I don't know. Right now, it feels like things will never be okay."

"They will. Try to get some sleep tonight, okay? You're not taking care of yourself."

"I'll try. I love you, Rafe."

"I love you, too, Bex. Sweet dreams."

I disconnected, then sat looking around at the lovely, but impersonal, suite around me, wondering if things between Brody and me would ever again be as they'd been – wonderful, amazing, the closest thing possible to perfect – or if I'd spend the rest of my life wondering "what if."

# Chapter 51

Brody

I couldn't settle myself down.

It was a week since we'd forced the wild boars out of the region, longer since we'd gotten Bethany back, and I was still restless and distracted.

Rafe was moving Bethany to a new, secure apartment so that at least was one worry solved. I knew where it was because Rafe understood I couldn't stand *not* to and had driven past several times to check it out. Until the apartment was ready, she was still staying – and working – in one of the guest suites, where I could feel her presence every day, although I never saw her. If it made me feel a little better to see her car right in her parking spot where it should be, or a light in her window when I left work later at night than I should, that was just a bonus.

It didn't help with the restlessness though.

Finally, Rhyne had had enough. Mountain lions are pretty chill as a group and my constant state of agitation was rubbing off on my co-workers, making them uneasy. Rhyne kicked me out, sending me up to the mountain house he'd built for him and Kyra not far from where Lacey and Jackson lived to stay and work for a few days.

I loved the house and had high hopes that it could help me find my balance. But as I sat out on the upper deck my first night there, listening to the night sounds and the quiet, I felt none of the peace I usually did.

I heard the tires before I saw the headlights. I waited where I was, certain who was on their way to see me, listening as the vehicle came closer.

A door slammed, then...

"Brody, come help me. It's dark as, well, night out here. I can't see a thing."

I heard her, as she'd known I would. I stood, took the stairs down to the lower deck, then the yard, walking along the side of the house to the front. Lacey stood casually leaning against the side of her SUV, no sign of nerves though she was standing surrounded by ink black woods on a nearly moonless night.

"Where's your flashlight?" I called out, not wanting to startle her by coming out of the darkness at her.

She turned toward me, though I knew she could probably barely make out my outline. "I have the one on my phone." She shrugged. "It's just easier to make you come get me."

"You should have one in your car. Your phone's not going to help you for long if you get stranded." I stopped in front of her as she rolled her eyes at me.

"Yes, and I have a big, grumpy bear demi-shifter in my life if I need a lecture." She went on her tiptoes to kiss my cheek while I gave her a one-arm hug.

"I imagine he's pretty good at it."

She hummed in agreement. "He excels." She peered at the side yard, though I doubted she could see much.

"Can I get around to the back without breaking an ankle, or should we go through the house? I've never attempted it in the dark."

I cracked a smile for the first time in days. She knew me so well, knew that of everywhere in this spectacular house, the upper back deck was my favorite spot, especially at night.

"Let's go through. We can grab a couple drinks on the way."

A few minutes later, we were settled side-by-side in our Adirondack chairs, drinks sitting on the table between us, a small light on inside in deference of Lacey's human eyes. It was enough light for her to see a little, but not enough so that it messed with our view of the stars.

I rested my head back, trying again to get lost in the stars and let the night sky soothe me.

"I saw Bethany today."

"Mm-hm." My body tightened with familiar tension.

"She looks sad, Brody. She talked about how happy she is to have Rafe in her life again, but still she looked sad. She misses you."

I flipped my head toward Lacey. "She said that?"

"No." I hated the disappointment that flooded through me. What had I expected? "She didn't say it, but I could tell. She's sad and she misses you, just like you're sad and miss her."

I stared back up at the stars.

"I can't do anything about that. We'll both get over it soon enough."

Or maybe never, at least for me.

"You could give her another chance."

I blew out a breath. "I can't, Lace. She had me completely fooled. I had no clue what she was hiding. Say I do give her another chance. How do I go through life like that, knowing my mate could be lying to me and I'd have no idea?"

Lacey changed positions, angling herself to face me. "I know you can't feel a lie through the mate bond like some people think you can, but I think you'd have some sense of it if it was serious. More importantly, though, I don't think you need to worry about it."

"I don't know how you can say that. And whether I could feel it through the bond or not is irrelevant. We're not bonded."

"Not right now, but..."

I pushed out of my chair and stalked to the deck railing, glaring out at the darkness as I admitted what was really eating at me. "She's not staying here for me. She's staying here for Rafe. Before she found him again, she was ready to cut and run. She was never thinking long-term with me, not like I was with her. I was just a means to an end for her, somebody to help her feel less alone, maybe. It's not about me; it never was."

"But she feels the mate bond, doesn't she?"

I flipped around to face Lacey, walking back to sit again as I realized she'd barely be able to see me.

"That doesn't matter – you know that. If she doesn't accept it, the fact that she feels it doesn't mean jack. And she wouldn't – won't – accept it. When we were together, she never once talked about the future, not beyond the next week or two. That was all me. I don't know how long she'd have stayed here, trying to find Rafe based on that crap information her fake PI was feeding her, but if she hadn't found him, I know, 100%, that she would be gone."

"Maybe, maybe not – you don't know that. You love her, Brody, I know you do. She's your mate, and you know I understand in every way what that means. I'll bet you a dollar she's just as much in love with you as you are with her. It's a risk trusting her, I know it is, but sweetie, it's a risk trusting anyone."

I stared at Lacey, frustrated and a little hurt. "I can't believe you're taking her side."

"I can't believe you think I am," she shot back. "I'm 100% Team Brody, forever and ever amen. You know that. Your life won't be complete without Bethany; *you* won't be complete. When I think of the possibility of a life without Jackson, it's like there's a huge, gaping void in my soul. I know it's the same for you. You'll never be happy without her. I hate that for you. If I can do anything to prevent it, I'm going to do it, even if it makes you mad at me."

Dammit.

She'd just described exactly how I felt. Like the center of my world had been obliterated and I had no hope of repairing the damage. I'd survive, but my future? When I tried to picture it without Bethany, there was nothing.

I reached across the space between us and nudged Lacey's hand. "Does Jackson ever win an argument with you?"

"Never. Not once."

I exhaled slowly, thinking of everything Lacey had said. One thing stood out from all the rest, circling around and around in my brain.

"You think she's in love with me?"

"I know it. No question."

"You did bet a dollar on it, so..."

"See? Big bucks are riding on this. I wouldn't mess around."

It was a risk, like Lacey had said. But what were my choices? Die a little more inside every day, watching my mate live life without me? Or take a chance, bet it all that Bethany and I could make things work, and spin the wheel?

It was a risk, a big one. But I'd never backed down from a challenge, never given up on anything I truly wanted.

I wanted a life with Bethany more than I knew I was capable of ever wanting anything, despite the lies, despite how things had started. She hadn't planned on a future with me, but that didn't mean that couldn't change. If she didn't want it, or if she left me someday, I'd be devastated. But what if she did want it?

• • • •

A LITTLE WHILE LATER, after Lacey left, I picked up my phone. Strung tight with nerves, I tapped out the first message I'd sent to Bethany in weeks. I started, stopped, deleted what I'd written and started again. After the third time of repeating the cycle, I huffed in frustration and went with a simple, direct request.

*Me: Can I see you tonight?*

The dots popped up almost immediately. I stared at them as they danced, willing Bethany's response to appear, riding the knife's edge of tension as I waited.

*Bethany: Of course.*

My breath rushed out of my lungs in relief. After everything that had happened, I wouldn't have blamed her if she'd refused. Then another message popped up.

*Bethany: When and where?*

Maybe Lacey was right. Maybe Bethany did miss me the way I missed her.

*Me: I'll come to you. I can leave right now.*

*Bethany: Okay. I'll be waiting.*

I grabbed my keys and headed for my truck, well aware that the next couple of hours could be the most important ones of my life.

# Chapter 52

Brody

I found her on the terrace, in nearly the same spot she'd been the night of the reception. It seemed like a lifetime ago.

I wasn't surprised when she turned as I came closer, even though, like that night, I hadn't made a sound. I had no doubt she felt my presence just like I felt hers. I stopped a few feet from her, mesmerized by her beauty as I always was. The words I'd struggled to find on the drive over suddenly came easily.

"Do I remind you of someone you hate?"

Her pretty eyes softened, and I knew she was remembering that night along with me. It was our starting point in a way, the first time she'd given me a glimpse behind her walls.

"No," she said softly. "You don't remind of anyone I hate. In fact, you remind me of someone I very much *don't* hate, not at all."

My heart bumped, but I couldn't ask her what I wanted to...not yet. I had some things I needed to say to her first.

"I've been mad. You may have noticed." The tiny curve of her lips spurred me on. "I've been hurt that you didn't trust me, while not acknowledging that you had every reason not to. You didn't know me, didn't know any of us, and had no idea what you might be walking into. I've been blaming you for keeping yourself safe, when that's what I want for you. But most of all, I've been scared. I've been telling myself and anyone who will listen that I'm scared you'll lie to me again, but that's not it. I'm scared shitless that I'll have you, think I'm building a life with you, and lose you. That's the straight-out truth."

Bethany exhaled softly as she nodded, acknowledging my words, her hands clenched together so tightly they were white.

"I've been mad, too, not at you but at myself. For not confiding in you earlier, even once I knew you...not just the person you show to the world, but who you are inside. And I've been blaming myself, for lots of things, but mostly because I didn't let myself admit, even to myself, that you and what we had together was everything to me. Most of all, I've been scared...that I'll never get that chance again, that you won't trust me, and I'll never get you back."

Bethany's eyes shone with tears, and I closed the distance between us, unable to stop myself. "Don't cry, sweetheart. I can't take it."

She looked up at me, so beautiful in the moonlight.

"I'm sorry, Brody. So sorry I hurt you. I'd take it all back if I could. If I'd known..."

I had to touch her. It was impossible not to. I brushed my fingers over her soft cheek, swallowing hard when she leaned into my touch.

"I know, baby. It's okay. I'm sorry I hurt you, too."

"I know you'd be taking a huge leap of faith believing in me."

"Mountain lions are good at huge leaps. It's one of our best things."

She didn't smile like I hoped she would, but the tightness in her body eased a fraction. "You don't have to be scared of losing me. I want to be with you, more than anything."

Relief, joy, possessiveness swirled within me, but I told myself to wait. She didn't fully realize yet what this was, what she was saying.

"I need you to understand something, Bethany. You're my mate. No matter what, no matter where, there will never be anyone else for me. You're the other half of my soul."

"You're the other half of mine, too," she whispered, reaching for me. I took her hand and rested it over my heart, letting her feel it beat for her.

"I believe that. I'm your mate, too. That hum you feel inside? That sense of completeness when we're together?" She nodded, her eyes intent on mine. "That's our mate bond. When you described it to me a few weeks ago and I knew you felt it, too, I can't even describe what it did to me, even though I knew you didn't understand what you'd told me. That's what I'm talking about, us being mated, bonded."

"I want that." Her voice was quiet, but strong. "What do I need to do?"

"All you need to do is accept it." Did she feel the way my heart sped up when I said those words?

Bethany looked up at me, questioning. "It's that simple?"

"The action is simple, but the implications aren't," I cautioned her, needing to be sure, 100% certain, she knew what she'd be committing herself to. "It's kind of like getting married in your world, but more. Not saying you will but doing it. In some ways, it connects us forever."

"I want that," she said again. "Tell me what to do."

"If you accept our bond, then it's done. All you have to do is say it and mean it." My mountain lion stilled within me for the first time in weeks, silently waiting to hear the words.

"Have you accepted it?"

"Yes." It felt like the vow that it was. I brushed my fingers over her cheek again. "A while ago, even before I realized I'd done it."

"I do, too. I accept our mate bond."

Something clicked deep inside me, like a key had turned in a lock or the last piece of a puzzle had snapped into place. Bethany's eyes widened as her hand flew up to press over her heart.

"Did you feel that?"

I drew her into me, nearly groaning at the feel of her against me after so many weeks apart.

"I did. It's just me finding my spot inside you."

I dipped my head and fit my mouth to hers, slipping my tongue inside when she opened for me. Her arms came around me, holding me close, and all the tension from the past few weeks – the anger, the hurt, the worry – drained away. My mate was in my arms, our mate bond strong and secure between us.

Bethany pulled back a fraction, her teasing eyes shining up at me. "I love when you find your spot inside me."

Heat streaked through me as I let out a low growl. "I love it, too. I love all the ways." I nuzzled her neck, loving her scent, making her gasp as I bit down lightly on her neck. "Almost as much as I love you."

She took my face in her hands, raising up on her toes a little to give me a soft kiss. "I love you, too, Brody."

She squeaked as I swept her up bridal style, making me grin.

"What do you say we go try some of these ways?"

She leaned in, brushing her lips across my jaw as all my blood headed south.

"I'd say my mate read my mind."

# Epilogue

One week later...

Bethany

I looked around the terrace at the people gathered to celebrate my mating to Brody – Rafe, Abby, Rhyne and Kyra, Lacey and Jackson, even Asher – and could hardly believe this was my life. A year before I'd been alone, scared, searching for Rafe, not knowing if I'd ever find him, no idea what my future held. Now here I was, surrounded by love and friendship.

Brody and I would get legally married at some point; it would make things far easier when it came to the human world. But for now, I just wanted to celebrate the day with my mate.

Speaking of my mate...I looked for him and found him, standing talking with Rhyne, holding Lexi against his chest. She patted Brody's cheek with her little hand, and both men stopped, smiling down at her as she grinned her sweet baby grin, wiggling in happiness. I shook my head; if that didn't make my ovaries go into overdrive, nothing would.

Feeling my attention on him, Brody looked over at me, his turquoise eyes blazing with happiness. He handed Lexi off to her father, and had just started my way when he stopped, spinning to scan the wooded area across the estate's expansive lawn from where we stood. Conversation cut off abruptly as Rafe, Rhyne, Jackson, and Asher went on high alert, as well.

When a figure burst from the woods headed our way, they went into action. Rhyne and Brody raced down the terrace steps and across the lawn to intercept the intruder, while the others moved me, Abby, Lacey, and Kyra – now holding Lexi – farther back on the terrace, closer to the doors to inside. We watched as the intruder slowed, raising his hands in the universal sign of surrender as Brody and Rhyne drew near. They stopped in front of him, utterly dwarfing him as they seemed to interrogate him. They glanced at us standing on the terrace, then back at the man, and not for the first time I wished desperately for mountain lion hearing.

A minute or so later, Brody and Rhyne headed back towards us, with Brody gripping the man's upper arm securely. I frowned in concentration as they drew closer. There was something so famil...I gasped, and all eyes on the terrace swung my way.

"That's Andi." I didn't need to say any more. They all knew the role Andi had played in my abduction. "What on earth is she doing here?"

Rafe came to stand next to me, putting his arm around my shoulders as they started up the terrace steps. Andi looked disheveled and haggard, far older than her years, her pretty hair cropped so close to her head it appeared nearly shorn off.

They stopped in front of us, Brody still holding her arm firmly as Rhyne looked from her to us. "Andi says she has information we need to hear. Go ahead, Andi."

To my surprise, she didn't look at me, but at Rafe.

"What could you possibly have to tell me?" Rafe's voice was stone cold, his tone demanding. "How did you know I was here?"

Andi swallowed hard, seemingly still out of breath from her dash out of the woods. "That doesn't matter now." She looked over her shoulder toward the trees, then back at him. "I don't have time. I was searching my father's house, looking for money. I found this." Everyone tensed as she reached into her jeans pocket, then pulled out a folded piece of paper. She held it out to Rafe, but he didn't reach for it.

"Take it," Andi insisted. "You'll want it. It's all the proof you need."

"Proof of what?"

"You're not the last, Rafe. The line doesn't end with you."

I felt the jolt of shock that blasted through his body.

"Yes, it does," he gritted out. "There's no one else." His tone brooked no argument, yet Andi shook her head refuting what he'd said.

Then she dropped her next bombshell.

"You're wrong. You're the last male, that's true, but you're not the last of your line. You have a sister."

• • • •

The End

Look for Rafe and Abby's story in Fateful Touch, the final book in the Fated Moments series!

# Also by Kristyn DeMaster

**Brothers Pub**

All of Me

Believe in Me

Count on Me

Trust in Me

Stay with Me

**Fated Moments**

Fateful Choice: A Paranormal Shifter Romance

Fateful Path: A Paranormal Shifter Romance

Fateful Lies: A Paranormal Shifter Romance

Watch for more at https://linktr.ee/kristyndemaster.

# About the Author

Kristyn DeMaster is a contemporary romance author. She writes everyday heroes and heroines finding their way to once-in-a-lifetime love through all of life's up and downs. She's a true believer in happily-ever-after and is living hers with her very own romance hero and their fur babies in the American Midwest.

Read more at https://linktr.ee/kristyndemaster.